NOBLE DEED

ROBERT LOGSDON

PAGE PUBLISHING
Conneaut Lake, PA

First originally published by Page Publishing 2023

ISBN 979-8-88793-890-5 (pbk)
ISBN 979-8-88793-900-1 (digital)

Printed in the United States of America

THE OLD HIGHWAY WAS INTENDED TO BE a grand road to allow the Allied armies to march in case of a return of the first born. In recent years, it had become just an unmaintained stone path leading from the human capital to what was once going to be the great fortress city of Kamadur, now but a dying farming town. On the road, a cart rolled slowly along on its way back from one of the larger cities with its load of ale and salted meat. The dwarven driver brought the cart to a halt as several trees were suddenly felled on the road and men rushed from the tree line to surround the cart.

The leader of the group approached, in tattered leather armor and a rust-pitted sword held over his shoulder, saying, "Give us your goods, and we may spare your life, Dwarf!"

"Why would anyone do that?" A slight tremor of fear shook the dwarf's voice. "I know very well that you will still kill me anyway. I doubt you are going to just roll several barrels of ale and salted meat through the forest to your little camp."

"Well, are you not a clever one, Dwarf? And a joker as well. Funny, very funny, I bet you get them all laughing at your tavern." Kalgrin, the dwarf, laughed weakly.

The three archers had been standing together taking bets on what the dwarf would do. Two thought he would hand it over and the last said something about him trying to run, leaving his supplies behind. Now dead, the three would never see the end their friends were about to meet. Taking up one of the dropped bows, Zyid drew back and let an arrow fly.

The arrow flew through the air, planting itself into the wagon with a dull hollow thud. The bandit leader's sentence sputtered and stopped. His face taking on a look of surprise as everyone turned to look at the arrow.

Kalgrin in one smooth motion threw off his ratty travel cloak, grabbed for his weapon, and brought it round. Before his cloak even settled, the leader was on the ground, his neck having been snapped from the impact of Kalgrin's great hammer. The remaining bandits quickly realized they were not dealing with your average tavern owner. Kalgrin's dwarven mail shone in the sunlight as he smirked, ready for the next opponent.

The bandit's second-in-command was quick to fall under the crushing weight of Kalgrin's hammer. The last two turned to run. Zyid quickly intercepted one, cutting him down with a smooth stroke of his swords. The last man sped away but fell screaming as he was consumed by a jet of fire projected from Kalgrin's hand.

The two men looked at each other, polar opposites. Kalgrin was tall for a dwarf, standing proud in his dwarven mail with great hammer in one hand, the other playing with a small flame. His hardened red eyes glaring at Zyid. Zyid in contrast stood almost two-feet taller. His long black hair pulled back in a ponytail and his well-trimmed beard looked out of place with his well-worn armor and traveling cloak. Only his two swords looked to be of decent quality. The silence between them lasted but a moment when Kalgrin began to laugh and pulled the arrow from the cart. "Well, Zyid, Arlana will not be happy to see you still cannot aim for shit with a bow."

Zyid shrugged, wiping the blood from his blades, and began stripping the bodies. Before long, he was speaking again. "I will check for more of them and meet you back in town." Zyid tossed the gear he had gathered into the back of the wagon before heading off deeper into the forest.

"Whatever makes you happy, kid. Try not have too much fun out there." With that, Kalgrin turned back to the road. The flame in his hand shot out to eat away at the fallen trees in his path.

With the path cleared, he called the flame back before extinguishing it in his hand. He casually climbed back onto his cart and continued on his way as if nothing had happened.

CHAPTER 1

EMMA STOOD OUTSIDE OF THE TOWN HALL looking back along the road as smoke drifted slowly from the western road. She sighed as her long brown hair flowed in the gentle breeze. She pondered over the recent events. Either bandits had sacked another trader, or he had killed more of them in the woods. Hopefully, it was the latter.

She took one more look through the statues at the road and sighed. Rubbing her head in frustration, she entered the building. The sound of her heavy footsteps echoed through the hall as she stormed up to the mayor's office. Throwing the doors open, Emma stormed up to the large desk, slamming her hands down upon it. "I have more important things to be doing than being at your beck and call, Mayor."

"Of course you do, Captain. However, this is also important business. I have had several complaints of dead bandits strung up along the roadside. It is quite disturbing for the few merchants we do get."

Emma began laughing at this. "That is Zyid's doing. He has been doing his best to keep the western roads safe. An impossible task for one man. We keep seeing more and more bandits and fugitives.

1

They are coming from both the western kingdoms and even some from through the Eastern Gateway. My guards cannot do anything to stop them. We can barely keep the town secure with the few men I have. You know that!" Emma turned to walk away.

"Hold on!" said the mayor, throwing up his hands.

Emma turned back and scowled at the mayor.

"That is not all. One of the farmers came in here this morning. He was yelling about a large creature flying by Dragon's Perch. A dragon if he is to be believed."

Emma fell back into a chair in shock and raised an eyebrow. "Are you sure?" The stern look in the mayor's deep green eyes told her he was certain. "So you are sure." Emma paused, dissatisfied with being given so little information. "There is more to it, is there not?"

Laughing, the mayor nodded. "You are good at reading people, Emma, always have been. A man came through and bought food and water, enough to fill a wagon. He said he had traveled from the east. Now if that was not strange enough, he was well-armed. So yes, something is probably going on. I want Zyid to check on it." The mayor looked grim; his brow furrowed as he steeped his hands over his desk.

"So why are you talking to me?"

"Well, two reasons actually. For one, he never comes when I summon him. Secondly, he still does not listen to anything I have to say. I figure you were childhood friends, so he might be willing to look into it if you ask."

Emma chuckled at the thought. "It is true I knew him when we were kids, but he was also gone for over fifteen years. So I cannot say that things are like they used to be. But I will ask him." Emma turned to leave, muttering on the way out. "Not sure what he is supposed to do against something like a dragon though."

After searching the town for over an hour, Emma settled on waiting in front of the Trolls Heads tavern. Pacing under its worn sign and two troll heads hung above the front entrance. Soon Kalgrin arrived to find Emma pacing on the stoop of his tavern.

"So where is Zyid?" demanded Emma.

Laughing, Kalgrin climbed down and began unloading his cargo. "Not even a hello, my dear Emma? Might I say you are looking quite beautiful, if slightly annoyed? I assume the mayor is breathing down your neck again, my dear?" Gently, he set down the barrel he was removing from the cart. He indicated a thumb to the bandit's equipment. "I believe that should answer your question."

Emma let out a sigh, shaking her head. "I guess it does. Why did they attack you two? How stupid can people possibly be?"

"I would figure they thought my dear husband was alone. He is very good at playing the lone terrified traveler when he wants to. He has lots of practice at it after all." The tall figure had quietly stepped through the tavern entrance. She stood wiping a tankard clean with a rag. She spoke with a soothing melodic voice and stood gracefully as only an elf can. Her long blonde hair flowing down her back. "I would guess that he is cleaning up the camp. After which he will try and drag the whole camp back with him."

"I knew I married you for your brains," Kalgrin chuckled to himself and added, "and maybe just a little for your looks."

Emma let a smirk cross her face. "I am sure it was all for her smarts, Kalgrin." She chuckled.

"I would never lie to the guard captain, would I?" He let a pause hang in the air. "Best not to answer that one, Emma."

"Just send him over when he gets back if it is not too late. I know he would barge in at any hour just to annoy me."

"Who are you sending to bother Emma, Kalgrin?" Zyid pulled up driving a cart loaded down with all manner of items, cloaks, and clothes.

"What the hell happened to you? Are you hurt? Do you need help?" Emma rushed over and frantically started looking him over as he stepped down from the cart, covered in mud and blood.

Zyid held her shoulders firmly to stop her movements, then spoke slowly. "Yes. I am fine. None of the blood is mine, so you do not have to worry. You should not let people see you like this. You are the guard captain after all."

Emma jumped back, shook her head, and started again. "So what did you do to them? How many? Come on, man, all the facts."

3

Arlana and Kalgrin finished unloading the wagon and headed into the tavern. Noticing that Emma and Zyid had not followed, Kalgrin poked his head out of the bar. "If you are going to tell a story, Zyid, then come inside. It is cold outside, and I am sure you are in need of an ale, my boy. Well, come on." He motioned with his hands for them to hurry inside. They quickly followed him in.

Entering the tavern, it was mostly empty. Few townspeople stayed this late. Poor farmers could ill afford to waste away the night in a tavern. The fire in the hearth burned low but warm and cast a dim glow across the whole room. As Emma and Zyid moved to the bar, the few patrons acknowledged them with simple hellos or nods.

As they sat, Kalgrin set drinks down in front of them. "Now, Zyid, you may start your story, if Emma is sufficiently calm now," said Kalgrin as he wandered off with a beaming grin on his face. She nodded and sipped from her ale, motioning for Zyid to start his recount of the afternoon.

Zyid took a swig and began to regale the group with his tale. Following the paths through the forest ambushing the sentries. The slow process of picking them off. Dispatching one in his sleep. Men began scrambling as they started to find the bodies. Then finally killing the last few as they cowered at the edge of their camp, a satisfying job well done. "Then I filled up a cart they had stolen from some poor merchant or whoever. Then I brought it all back here. Easy as that." Zyid drank the last of his ale, slamming the tankard down and wiping the foam from his beard.

"So let me get this straight. You strolled around the camp, murdered them all, then loaded up a cart they stole from some poor other slob, and then just brought it back here. You are not even hurt?"

"Yes, that is what I am telling you." Zyid smothered a laugh with a snort. "The look on your face is priceless, Emma. I am a lot different from the little boy who left this place all those years ago. Also, why are you here anyway?"

"I was supposed to tell you to go investigate a sighting of a dragon flying about near Dragon's Perch. I would hazard a guess though that you do not want to do that. You must be exhausted after the day you have had."

4

"A what? That is an odd thing to spot here. How has this not happened before? There are not supposed to be any dragons living in the west anymore."

"Now who has a funny look on their face," Kalgrin bellowed from down the bar. Zyid waved him off. Zyid thought it over for a few minutes then nodded a yes to Emma.

Emma finished her ale and stood. "I am headed to bed now," she announced, quickly followed with a sigh. "Just try not to get yourself killed with this dragon business."

Zyid shrugged off the concern and bid her, "Rest well, Captain."

CHAPTER 2

WHAT IS NOW USED AS THE TOWN hall was originally intended to be the headquarters of the Allied Armies during the Dragon War. The building seemed overly large for its current purpose. Human, dwarven, and elven craftsmen had labored on it for years even after the war. The intent was to build it into a large fortress to ensure that the threats from the east would never return. The fortress was never built, and the town just took the building for their own purposes.

As it stands, the town hall consists of several offices adjoined to several meeting rooms, which are attached to a large barracks. The barracks seem almost barren these days with the town guards numbering so few. Below the meeting rooms was an undercroft filled with books and reports detailing the history of the area.

Zyid sat surrounded by dust and cobwebs in the undercroft. He was poring over old records from the war searching for something on this supposed dragon. Footsteps echoed with the soft jingle of mail armor and sword signaling Emma's approach.

"Have you been down here since last night? Did you even sleep? You may be tough, but you still need sleep you know."

Zyid continued flipping through a tome. "No, I did fall asleep at one point. I woke up with my head in this dusty book, but I will be fine. I shall be heading out soon."

"So little sleep, no food, and you are off to go find a dragon. Smartest thing I have heard you do yet," Emma sarcastically replied. "By the way, what did you do with that cart of stuff you had?"

Zyid pointed in the general direction of the armory. "Your smith has the weapons and armor. Got to get that thing full to bursting and the cart I gave to one of the shops or something, not sure. I did not care too much about the details," Zyid mumbled as he continued scanning the pages of the tome in his hands.

"Why do you do that? You go out, kill bandits trying to open the roads, and you get nothing out of it. Why? Why do you do that? You could do so much more with your skills. Any of the western kingdoms would kill to have you in their employ. You could clean up the whole mess over there."

Zyid got up and shrugged. "I am heading to the armory. Then I will head up to Dragon's Perch. Should be interesting to say the least."

Emma followed behind, passing several guards each giving her brief salutes as they walked to the armory. The ring of hammer and anvil filled the space as they entered. Zyid moved to the wall and selected his armor.

"First, you bring me things to fix. Then you come in and take it like you own the place." The smith had not even turned from his work. "Are your swords still sharp, or do they need honed before you head out?"

"No, they will do. They are quite well made after all." The smith nodded slightly and kept to his work.

"You know, Zyid, you could take some of the better armor, but you always pick the ratty mail instead of one of the nicer pieces."

"My dear Captain, this will be more than enough for what I am going to do. I will be back tomorrow with a full report. Now, time to leave before the old man stops me with more of his useless dribble."

"Before you go, there were men in fine armor buying supplies in town recently. Watch out for them." Zyid nodded and slipped out in the early morning light.

*****

Zyid moved quickly through the morning dew. The forest was alive with noise. Birds and other creatures could be heard in the trees overhead. Keeping a steady pace, he soon found what had been a camp at the base of the mountain. It had very recently been left very quickly. A fire still smoldered with discarded food scraps and clothing lay thrown all about. A flag planted near the largest tent told the tale, a red dragon skull pierced with a silver sword on a blue backing. "Must be the silver slayers. Then she is indeed still here. Need to hurry lest they get to her first," Zyid mumbled to himself as he ran toward Dragon's Perch. Before reaching the cave, he stopped behind a large rock. Several men in mail shone bright looking like silver stood at the mouth of the cave with weapons at the ready. More scanned around for outside threats. No noise came from inside the cave.

As Zyid watched on, one of the guards walked up to what was obviously the commander. Dressed in plate armor, he stood out from the rest.

"Are we certain it is in there?"

"Yes, sir, we chased it all over the mountain. Lost a few men and supplies to its attacks. We have been attacked by wolves as well. They almost seem to be in league with the creature."

"Good. Now go hunt it down and kill it." The commander waved him off, and some of the men guarding the cave rushed in.

"You have sent those men to their deaths, sir. But you already know that. I have met some of your kind before. Very stuck up and full of yourselves if memory serves." All spun to find Zyid casually walking toward them. They had confused expressions as if unsure if he was out of his mind, cocky, or stupid. The leader's face read the same, but he quickly changed to a knowing smile as he saw who stood before him.

"You know the king told us you may come once the dragon went out into the open, and here you are, almost like," his speech faltered as he searched for the right words, "like fate guided you. I would prefer to challenge you as is our custom, but I cannot take that risk." The commander sighed and motioned to his men.

"So this is how it is going to be. You know me and yet you are still going to fight! Fine, come throw your lives away. I have other matters to attend to."

The men howled like feral beasts, charging toward Zyid. His blades danced through the air with a speed and grace they could never hope to match. They died swiftly. Showers of gore and blood flew through the air, and in a flash, it was done. The captain was the last to hit the ground. Lying on the ground, he clutched at the heavily bleeding stump where his right arm had been removed.

"It is as they say. I can see why you won now." Color ran from his skin as the blood drained. "Why did you leave? You could have been more. Why? Why?" The commander's ramblings dropped off as he fell into his final slumber.

"I have to stop that madman, and I could not bring myself to leave all that ever mattered, that is why."

A roar echoed from the cave and the ground shook. Zyid turned back toward the cave. The noise grew louder. Then with one last roar, the dragon emerged. Mouth and talons slick with gore. Its own purple blood stood out against green scales as it oozed from a gash on its shoulder. It slowly panned back and forth with intense yellow eyes. Spotting Zyid, it seemed to be studying him. Gauging him perhaps?

The dragon's voice thundered out, "You there! Are you one of these creatures? Sent to hunt me. To keep me out of his plans," ending in a hissing growl.

Zyid yelled his reply, "No, I came to see if the stories were true. I have a question for you."

"You? A question for me?" she scoffed. The dragon tilted her head inquisitively. "Well, that is something different. I will indulge you. What is it?"

"Are you the dragon from the tales? The gold, is it still in your cave?"

The dragon looked shocked at the thought. It nodded its head in reply. "As far as I am aware, I am the only dragon that has occupied this cave for several centuries. So yes, I am probably the dragon you are referring to. As for the gold, it is indeed still there. For what reason do you ask of it?"

"Good, but now we must fight for it. I have need of your gold, and you will not let me just take it."

She started forward, a slow walk forward causing the ground to shake with her approach. "You are right, I will not give you my treasure. At least not without a test!"

A spout of green acid erupted from her mouth bathing the area. Zyid launched forward under the acid, dodging a swipe of her claw along the way. He ran up the leg and onto her back, slicing along trying to hinder her ability to fly.

A flap of her wings put an end to his plans. Zyid was hurled to the ground, landing in a rough heap. Zyid rose up with a cough. "Damn, you are faster that I thought you would be. Just as strong but much faster. Guess now you can fly away whenever you want to, huh?"

She turned to face him, scoffing, "Well, of course I could, but where would I go? You stand before my home. You could just wait for my return. Also, I said I would test you. I cannot test you if we do not fight." Closing the distance, she reared up to rain blows with her claws. It was not long before Zyid's swords fell from his hands as she pinned him under a talon.

She lowered her head close to Zyid's face and drew in a deep breath. "It is as I thought. You have dragons' blood in you, do you not? How did you come by this? It does explain why you have such power, but it is not enough. You have been found wanting."

Zyid let out a roar. Grunting as he lifted the talon from him. He threw it off and rolled away, retrieving his swords as he rolled. Panting, he huffed, "We are not done yet, dragon. This has only just begun."

Shaking her head, the dragon began to shift, shrinking down to a much more delicate human form. She was tall for a woman with long black hair that shone almost green as the light glinted off it. Standing dressed in simple pants and tunic, she held out a hand motioning for a sword. "No, we are not, but let us finish this with swords. It has been some time since I have used one. However, it should tell me all I need to know."

With a shrug, he tossed her a sword. "Fine, then let us begin." The battle raged through the day and into the evening. They moved with speed and grace one moment, then strength and rage the next. The smell of blood and sweat filled the air mixing with dust and grime.

They both slumped against the mouth of the cave bloody and exhausted. Between labored breaths, Zyid asked, "So now what? We cannot keep going like this. We have been fighting for hours. My armor is destroyed. I am covered in cuts, some of which are quite deep, and you are looking just as rough. Can this be done already?"

She started to laugh but had to grab her chest with a wince. "Yes, we are done now. I think you broke some of my ribs with your last punch. You are indeed quite strong. Come, I will use my magic to heal us both." Standing, she motioned him to follow.

Shrugging, he followed. "Why help me? I was just trying to kill you."

Her hands were aglow with magical energy. She hushed him and placed them upon his chest. "If we had continued, we would both be dead. Then all would be lost for this place. Someone wishes me dead for reasons which I cannot fathom. I have bothered no one until those men came several days past." She stood and turned, throwing her arms up in frustration. "For centuries, I have been here since the deal was struck with the first that came here so long ago. Now they come to kill me, or gods know what else. So, to answer your question, I helped you because you have helped me. What was it that human one said? The enemy of my friend is my enemy?"

"I believe what you are looking for is: The enemy of my enemy is my friend."

"Ah yes, that was it, enemy of my enemy, so I suppose"—she turned back facing him sitting on the floor—"that makes you a friend."

"We already knew that, well," Zyid paused, "sort of, I suppose. That was you on the road when I first came back, was it not? How could you not kill a troll on your own? Why did you need my help with that?"

"I did not, as I recall, need your help. You butted in after it ran on to the road. You did very well back then. You have only grown stronger since then. I am surprised you have gained so much from the blood."

A small smile crossed his face. "Very astute of you. Yes, I have taken dragon blood. It was my reward, but how did you know?"

She ran a finger down his nose. "Why, your smell of course. You seem to have not gained that particular benefit. Or have you just not realized it yet, I wonder?" She paused just long enough to make him wonder her thoughts. Jumping back, she moved farther into her lair. As she strode out of sight, she shouted over her shoulder, "Do not just stand there slack-jawed. Come, we must talk."

Composing himself, he hurriedly followed. He found her having returned to her dragon form mostly healed but still bearing the marks of the recent fight. She was coiled around a small pile of gold bars neatly stacked in the middle of the large chamber. Moonlight was directed in through unseen holes in the roof of the cave. "Cozy little place you have here. Any comfy seats to be had around here?"

She panned her head around the room. "I suppose that pile of very hard rocks would be the closest thing to a chair in a dragon's lair. Surprisingly enough, not many come for friendly chats with the ancient monsters out of the great tales. I am just a part of glorious dramas and tales sung of better times and heroes."

His slow clapping echoed softly through the chamber as he sat on his pile of rocks. "You should be a traveling bard, more fun than staying in here all the time. Also, these hard rocks are iron. Good stuff by the looks of it, but I would have to have Kalgrin take a look at it to be sure." He held a large chunk up. "This stuff could be worth far more than that one hundred pounds of gold." She tilted her head in the way of a curious dog.

"More on that later, little one. We have other more pressing matters to discuss. Such as who were those men? Why are they after me? And how do we stop them?"

"To the first, I know of them. They are a group born out of the Dragon War. The Silver Slayers, simply put, used to hunt dragons. They were some of the best from the kingdom to the east. Though they seem to have lost their edge in the years of peace. They were a small order in the first place, so that is probably the last you will hear from that group.

"Second, you are a dragon, and he wants you out of the way for his invasion. His words to me were to the effect of: my armies must conquer the squabbling kingdoms of men in the west so as to finish the Great War. Whatever he meant by that." He paused, brow furrowed in deep thought. Sighing and running his hand through his long black hair, he continued, "Well, the last one is kind of tricky. I suppose there are several answers to it. We could kill him, defeat his armies possibly, or this could be the last attempt on you. I cannot answer it with any certainty."

She shifted to her human form once again, a simple gown covering her frame. "How is it that you know so much about this?"

"Well, I did live in the east for fifteen years training with my master. With those years of arduous training, I was able to win the tournament after which the king took me into his confidence. I did not approve of his plans, so I left." Zyid heaved a great sigh. "And now I am back, and things are even worse than when I left. I have few options left to me to try and do something to get them ready for war."

Her sweet laugh filled the air. "War? You want to get a place like this ready for war?" She paused as she closed her eyes remembering. "It was ready once long ago when the armies of dwarves, men, and elves gathered in this valley to finish their long fight for freedom. But those times have long passed. So what was your grand plan for doing this?"

Zyid sat up, crossing his arms and stroking his beard. "Well, the first part is to get products to market. These lands could produce a huge surplus of food, but most of the land is not used since farmers cannot get it to market. The few merchants that used to come have stopped or were killed due to the recent surge in bandits and other scum. The kingdoms to the west have been pushing all of their unwanteds this way for a while."

Zyid stood and began pacing the cave. "So naturally the next idea. Murder bandits, take their ill-gotten goods, sell what I can, fill the armory in the town hall to the brim, and use the coin to try and get merchants to run up here again. Sadly, reward not worth the risk is all I hear, and I do not have friends in any guilds to grease any wheels to get something moving."

He pointed at the gold bars. "Here is where the legend of gold comes in. That was the real reason I accepted the mayor's request to come up here. I hoped it was true and it is." He chuckled. "Was not expecting to actually find a dragon to be living up here. So that kind of derails that plan. Unless you are okay with losing your precious treasure." Zyid peered up at her with a questioning look. "The plus side, depending on how much iron is in these hills, we could start a mine and make this amount back plus more. Any other valuable minerals jutting out of the walls in this huge labyrinth you have for a home?"

She spun slowly with her arms outstretched. "Little one, there are wonders aplenty in this great mountain. I am intrigued by your idea of making more money. I have watched these lands and seen it fall. I would love to see the live and bustling town I knew so long ago." She took a moment to think it over, then announced. "Boy, you will have your treasure!"

"This will take everything we can muster, but it is the best chance we have." Zyid took a deep breath and held out a hand. "One more thing, dragon. What is your name?"

She looked surprised. "Ah yes, almost overlooked that detail, did we not? It is Kasala." She laughed and clasped his hand for a firm shake. The deal was made. "And who is it I am doing business with?"

With a smile, he answered, "I am Zyid. Now come, we have much work to do!"

CHAPTER 3

"HE HAS BEEN AT THAT MOUNTAIN FOR two days, Kalgrin! What do you think happened? Should I go look? How can you two look so calm? Zyid might be dead and rotting up there you know!" Emma gestured emphatically, nearly spilling her ale as she spoke. Worry evident on her face.

Kalgrin, with his back to Emma cleaning dishes from the evening meal, calmly replied, "Yes, he could be, Captain. Your fretting like a mother hen will do him no good. Though, I am sure he will be fine."

"I wish I had your confidence," she mumbled into her mug.

"Listen to my dear husband, Emma. He is right. Zyid will be fine," Arlana yelled from the hearth.

"But what if he is not?"

"Then that is his fate, my dear Emma." Arlana began to hum as she cleaned the hearth slowly beginning to sing the lyrics. Her soothing voice filled the tavern with an ancient elven hymn. The few patrons that remained seemed entranced by the words as she sang and swayed in front of the fire.

As the song came to an end, Arlana made her way over to the bar where Emma sat. "He will be alright, my dear," she whispered into Emma's ear. "He may yet surprise you. He is not the same little boy he was when he left us so long ago."

"If only any of that made me feel any better." Emma sighed as she pushed her empty mug across the bar.

A patron wobbled as he pulled himself to his feet. His words were heavily slurred by drink. "Just you wait, Captain! Zyid will come bursting in here with that dragon's gold!"

Another patron yelled over the laughter of the crowd. "No doubt he will have rescued some fair maiden from its vile clutches." The patrons raised their glasses in toast as another cheer rose from the bar.

As the cheering died down, Kalgrin turned back to speak to Emma. "See, Emma dear, they have faith. Why not you?"

She smiled weakly at Kalgrin. "I am just tired, and this place cannot afford to lose him on some fool's errand in search of lost treasure. Though this place will go on with or without him, will not it?" She paused as she heaved herself to her feet. "Now if you will excuse me, I need to rest. I have a patrol early in the morning." Emma waved her goodbyes to her fellow patrons as she made her way to the door.

She stepped out into the cool evening air heading toward the town hall. The streets were empty except for a few stray animals roaming the streets on the prowl for food.

She arrived to find the large building quiet. The guard had changed smoothly. She paused briefly to speak with her lieutenants and then retired to her chambers. The small room was very spartan, the very basics of life. It was a place to keep her equipment stored and maintained. A few clothes for her off duty times, simple dresses, and skirts. Piles of reports and various other paperwork took all the remaining spaces.

She hated and loved it all in equal measure. Trying her best but knowing it was not enough to change where she saw the town she loved heading. She stoked the small fire in the wall hearth. She locked her chamber door, flopped onto her mattress, and fell into a fitful sleep wondering what the dawn would bring.

Emma awoke as first light made its way through the wooden shutters on the window. Readying for the day ahead, she wore her mail coat, which reached a bit past her waist and sleeves extended to her elbow. Her thick belt bloused her mail coat and held her sword, which was old but well cared. It had been passed down to her from her father and his father before him.

As she took the first few steps into the hall, she realized how strangely empty it was. Missing was the bustle of guards and scribes moving through the halls. The only noise was coming from the main barracks room where she heard a great commotion. She arrived at the room finding it full to bursting. A roar of cheers and applause came from the crowd as she made her way through to see what this was all about. In the center, she found Zyid, arms thrown up in the air as he finished his tale with flair. "Ah, Emma, dear Captain, you have just missed my tale of victory over the mighty dragon of these lands." His laugh carried across the crowd but was cut short by Emma's cold stare.

"All of you out now!" came a mighty bellow from the small captain. Everyone paused for a brief moment then quickly the room emptied save her and Zyid. She shut and blocked the doors before returning to face him. "You bastard! How long have you been back? Why did you not come directly to me? Or actually just me?" Emma did not give him pause to answer as she pulled in close, nose to nose with Zyid, as she continued her tirade. "Why? Why must you do things like this? You always just come and go as you please. Why will you not tell me things?" She pulled herself back from his face and took a deep breath to compose herself.

"I am sorry, Emma." He held his hands out in front of himself. "I had to not come straight to you. There were things that needed arranging first. I had to throw out a story to appease the masses and hide our true motives."

"True motives?" She whipped around from her pacing and narrowed her eyes at him. "What exactly is going on here? What the hell happened on that mountain?"

Zyid quickly recounted what had happened on the mountain and the brewing conflict from the east. "And so I have Kalgrin and the smiths looking over what I brought back."

"So you think he will come through these lands?" Her brow becoming furrowed deep in concern over the prospects.

"No. I know he is coming." The words hung in the air a moment before he continued. "Finally starting to listen to my crazing rantings, are you?"

"No, but will any of it work?"

"I do not know if any of it will work, but I cannot sit and do nothing when a hostile army will be coming through here. He must be stopped here, or he will simply conquer the fractured human dukes, kings, and petty warlords. Then from there gods only know what would happen." He stood, shrugged, and headed for the door. "Now, Emma, I believe you have your duties to attend to. Doing what you can to strengthen your guard force, increase its numbers, or whatever you can. They will be needed." With that, he unbarred the door and headed toward the center of town.

Finding Kalgrin was simple, he and the town's two smiths were hunched over a wagon looking at the ore Zyid had brought down from the mountain.

"Zyid! Finally showed up, huh? Interesting find up in those caves. Nice dog by the way, where did that come from?" The two smiths looked up briefly but were too engrossed in the ore, and muttering among themselves, to care what Kalgrin was talking about.

"She just came out of the woods. Is that not right, girl?" Zyid chuckled as he replied. The dog jumped down from the wagon and happily ran around the two of them barking and wagging her tail.

Kalgrin followed her with his eyes but only chuckled before speaking again. "Well, more importantly, this is some fine stuff you brought back here. A very special metal indeed, and if that is in the mountain, then who knows what else may be found." Kalgrin stroked his beard as he turned over a chunk of rock in his hand. "We should take this with us next time we travel into the dwarven lands. Speak to some people." He tossed the chunk back into the cart with a rough thud. "I bet we could find some interested parties."

Zyid nodded to himself. He stroked his own beard in thought. "Well, it seems that would be the best place to start looking for big buyers. But we will need more resources to start a true mine."

"True. Well, with this kind of ore, you should be able to strike a bargain for what we will need. I have never heard of a time this ore has been discovered without many riches with it." He laughed. "That alone should be enough to get some things moving."

"I am going to take this wagon in the morning, and we shall see about getting a little business going. We need to get some money flowing," Zyid announced with a smirk beaming across his face. The dog barked seemingly in agreement. He then looked toward the Trolls Heads. "We may need to build a bigger bar. All the miners will want to drink away their spare time. It will be glorious." He laughed before turning back to the smiths. "What do you two have to say about it? What are your professional opinions of this ore?"

The two looked up lips curled in deep thought as they each turned over a piece. The older one spoke first. "It appears to be as Kalgrin says. This appears to be very high quality ore. Sadly, I have only heard stories of it. So I cannot say much more than that." Setting the piece down, he struck at it several times with his hammer. They nodded to each other and he continued, "Let my son and I have a few pieces, and we will begin working it."

Zyid nodded in approval as he hopped into the driver's seat. "That sounds like a fine idea to me. Take it and see what you can make of it. We will see you later at home, Kalgrin." The smiths each quickly grabbed an armful and made their way back into the forge.

"Fine. I have to finish the shopping Arlana gave me or I will never hear the end of it." He laughed to himself and strolled off toward the market.

Zyid drove the cart off toward the inn grinning ear to ear.

"So what is your next move, clever boy?" the dog asked.

Zyid rubbed her head as he chuckled. "Well, dear little dragon pup, we will be heading west to spend your or rather my hard-earned horde money and get a mining operation rolling. We need to get this town on its feet." He paused looking back at the eastern mountains. "We need to get it ready for war."

"War?" the dog scoffed. "I must say that does not seem very likely in this political climate. The human lands are too busy either with internal strife or the nobles fighting over who should be the high ling. There has not been one since the Dragon War, and they are all chomping at the bit." Flopping her head into his lap, she continued, "Along with that, the dwarves and elves are both dealing with their own issues. So I do not see them getting involved. Unless, of course, it will directly affect them. Why would anyone care about this out of the way little place?"

He continued rubbing her head as they arrived outside the inn. "Well, little one, are you not up to date on current events for someone who lives in a cave out in the middle of a valley! But let us just say that a storm is coming from the east, and we must stop it here if it is to be stopped at all."

CHAPTER 4

THE MORNING WAS COOL AND DAMP, THE smell of rain heavy in the air, as Zyid loaded the last of his supplies for the journey west into the wagon. Kalgrin and Arlana stood leaning on each other just outside the inn.

"Ready to be off to the big city now, huh, my boy?" Kalgrin and Zyid both laughed until Arlana glared at them.

"I heard you two talking all last night. I do not approve of this idea at all. This place needs you now more than ever, Zyid, and you know it. What will happen while you are gone for a year or more? Did that ever cross your mind?" Her voice had remained steady, but the look in her eyes betrayed her inner turmoil. "What if you do not make it back? What then?" Kalgrin began gently stroking her arm.

"My dear, he will be alright. Besides that, he could die in his sleep tomorrow. This is the best thing we can do for this place right now. If we get trade started, it will not make everything better overnight but in time it will make things better. This place needs some hope and a lot of help. We will stay here and do what we can in his absence. This town was here long before he was alive and will hopefully be around long after we are all gone. Zyid will be back as soon as he can? Right, boy?"

Zyid heaved himself into the driver's seat. "Of course I will. Going to have to keep my new venture profitable if I want to help my home improve." Zyid threw up his hood, took hold of the reins, and spurred the horse on as he and his new dog set off down the western road out of town.

The two of them stood until he had faded far into the distance. "Well, Arlana, we have got a lot of work to do while that boy is off in the big city to help his home. We managed just fine the last time he was gone. This time we might even have some excitement!"

She laughed. "Well, hopefully it will not be fifteen years this time." Kalgrin shook his head as they started to move inside.

"Wait!" Emma yelled as she was running toward the inn, looking quite disheveled. She had slid to a stop panting, propping herself up with the railing.

"Dammit! Did that asshole leave before I could get here? That is just like him to leave without telling me. Just like before, running off to God knows where chasing his foolish dreams. Why did you two let him leave like that?"

Arlana smiled, helping her inside the inn.

"Come inside, dear, the captain of the guard cannot be seen looking like this." Emma merely nodded as they entered the inn and sat at the table nearest the fire to fight the early morning chill.

"He left without telling me again. Why does he keep doing that?" Kalgrin set two mugs of warm ale on the table.

"Well, dear Emma, he left last time to follow that woman. She had quite the effect on him after she saved you two out in the forest." They both sipped in silence for a short while before he continued. "This time he wants to do something to help his home. The tales he read as a child drive him to action."

Emma took up her mug again, sipping lightly and savoring the warmth. "He sure has changed a lot in the time he was gone. He was always getting picked on by the other boys. Now he could kill them all with such ease." She stopped mid thought as if thinking about it for the first time. "It is pretty scary when you really think about it." She scoffed as she gently swirled the ale in her mug.

Arlana smiled at the memories. "Well, dear, he may be stronger, but he is still just as gentle as before. He is not a monster chained to his strength. The children bug him constantly when they get the chance." They all laughed.

Kalgrin stopped himself first to speak. "Be that as it may, he has a solid plan, and you need to do your part, Emma. You need to keep training your men and recruiting everyone you can by squeezing that mayor for every silver he has since Zyid will not be around to help pick up the slack."

"That damn old man will never give us more funding," Emma said, dropping her fist on the table.

"Well, find a way to make him listen, or we may just have to go around him." Kalgrin stroked his beard as he spoke. "Maybe we can get coin directly from the people." Kalgrin began pacing in front of the fire continuing to stroke his beard. The other two looked at each other and shook their heads.

"I love you, Kalgrin but you are still as crazy as ever," Arlana teased.

"Well, you did marry me, so what does that say about you?" he retorted back. Arlana merely shrugged as she got up from her seat.

"Well, we all have our duties just as Zyid has his now. So let us be at them and be ready for his return whenever that may be." Both nodded in agreement and went off to their work caring for the inn.

*****

The cart creaked and groaned as it went down the broken, uneven road, jumping with each bump in the road. "Must you find all of the bumps in the road? I am attempting to sleep back here," said a feminine voice from the back of the cart. "What kind of driver are you anyway?"

"You know, for a dragon you sure do like to complain. Also, I never asked for you to come along. You invited yourself as I recall."

"I would have been bored waiting around for you to get back. Besides, I need to be sure you use our wealth to good ends. Not squander it in the bars and whorehouses on your first visit to a large city."

Zyid laughed. "I can understand your concern, but I have larger issues to deal with. I feel I have a big enough incentive to not waste my newfound wealth already."

She moved onto the seat next to him, staring sidelong at him for a short while. "Is there a girl you like?" She paused and watched him, waiting for a response. He shifted his gaze over slightly but said nothing. So she continued on, "That must be it. Why else would a young man not be trying to let loose in the big city?"

Zyid shook his head. "Well, this is not the first time that I have been to, as you put it, a big city so not a lot of new things for me to see and do. Besides, do you really think there is a girl that could put up with me long enough to love me?" His gaze drifted toward the clouds. "On top of that, we do not have the time for it. Maybe after winning or averting the coming conflict then I might have time to settle down." He heaved a tired sigh. "So let us handle one thing at a time."

She smiled to herself as she flopped her head into his lap as she continued. "So no one at all hmm…Well, that is very boring. Do you not have anything you do for fun?"

He glared down at her. "Are you going to spend the whole trip asking pointless questions?"

"Only most of it." She laughed, sitting up and moving back to lying down in the cart. "I will be going back to sleep now since you are obviously not going to be any fun." She snapped up, "But do not think that your interrogation is over." With that, she quickly flopped over and was asleep in the blink of an eye. He could not help but smile at her in spite of himself.

*****

"This has been the longest five days of my life, you know that?" she asked from his lap.

"I would never have guessed it was so by all the staring you did at the landscape. I think I liked you better as a dog. When you could not keep asking me questions about everything the whole trip."

"Well, you try living in a cave for most of your life and see if you wish to speak with people." She reached up and ran a finger down his nose. "Besides, it is fun to see you squirm under pressure." She frowned as his expression did not change. "You just need to accept and come to terms with the fact that you are a decent-looking man and that almost every girl back home is fighting for your attention."

Zyid laughed as the city came into view. Stout walls and gates greeting them in the distance. "Are they now?" He struggled not to laugh as he spoke. "Boy, are they ever going to be disappointed when they all learn how boring and one-sided I can be."

"You are more interesting than you give yourself credit for, but we can argue about that later." She sat up, eyes focused on the walls ahead. "So what is our first step in getting things rolling with your grand scheme? You must explain to me again why we are going through all the effort of bringing trade and prosperity to your little hometown?"

He sighed, speaking slowly and deliberately. "Well, trade brings money. Money brings people who bring more money. With money, one can build walls, hire mercenaries, and those kinds of things. To do that, we need some experienced miners and basic supplies and equipment to get a mine started. Getting it all set up is going to take time." He reached behind, pulling a piece of ore from the pile—turning it over in front of himself. "But once it's set up, with what is in that mountain, I think it will grow rather quickly. Our first step is stopping at the inn and getting a room and giving our weapons to the innkeeper. Then it is off to the banking district."

"So this is going to take a while then?" She flopped back onto him after they had been allowed through the gates with a brief inspection. "You know, this place already has everything you just mentioned. Walls, people, soldiers. Why not just come here?"

Zyid shook his head. "No, it cannot be here." He sighed heavily. "Do you think these people will believe me? That they will prepare for a war from a place they have never even heard of before? No. I

25

have to do what I can with what we have. I can only hope they will believe me before it is too late. But enough of that, let us get to work."

*****

"Two weeks we have been at it. Damn, why are they so tight-fisted? Can they not see a perfect opportunity when they see one?"

Zyid lightly patted her shoulder. "Yes, they can. However, a guild is not going to just throw in with every man with a half-formed idea. Yes, they see it is a good deal or else they would have said no already. But they want to be sure. That is why they are testing the material we brought so they do not get taken advantage of. They will come around to it with starting capital and a rare ore on the line though." He snickered slightly. "I wonder if too many people are vying for the job? Might explain why it is taking so long. For a job and the potential profit, it will just take time to get the contract drawn up and finalized, people hired, and equipment assembled."

"Zyid, how are you so patient?"

"How are you not able to hold your drink at all?"

She smiled over her mug, running her finger along the rim. "Well to be honest, I have never drank anything like this. It is so flavorful, the taste of honey is overwhelming, and…and…" She tapered off mumbling to herself. "I just do not have the words for it."

Zyid shook his head. "You are not what anyone would expect. We should get you to try wine. You would probably enjoy it more."

"What are you doing over there anyway? You have been writing letters all morning."

Zyid peered down at his parchment. "I am sending a letter to my brother. He is a merchant in Brala just northwest of here. I am hoping he will be interested in this little venture and can help us get the trade flowing faster."

"You sure are on top of this. Most people would think you are just some dumb sword for hire. Yet you are here contracting with guilds and arranging merchant agreements."

He laughed. "I could play that part pretty well if I do say so myself, but I was not just trained in the arts of battle. I studied a wide variety of subjects—history, administration, strategy. Exhaustive study would be an understatement."

"So you did not have much fun after you left home, huh?" He shrugged, sipping from his mug before continuing to write. "So what did you do for fun while you were away?"

"Same thing I did for fun before I left. I read a lot of books," he remarked, never glancing up from the page he was working on.

She laughed overly loud, causing a few heads to turn. "Is that really all you did—read, study, and train? No misspent nights with some lovely maiden? You are a good-looking man after all. I am sure you could woo all the ladies with your martial skills."

Zyid laughed as he finished his letter, sealing it with wax. "You are never going to stop asking that, are you?" She grinned at him as she took another sip of her drink. "Since you will not stop…I once had a one-sided love. She told me very plainly it would not come to pass, but I cannot seem to let it go. And that is about as far as it went. I was young. So no, to answer your question, no steamy romances to sate your womanly curiosity."

"Well, what about your—" Kasala started but was interrupted midsentence as a young man walked up.

Zyid turned at a tap on his shoulder. "Excuse me, but your presence has been requested at the guildhall for a meeting. If you would please come with me?" The young man stood tapping his foot anxiously. Obviously ready to be off. His tunic and breeches were simple and clean, clearly displaying the merchant guilds markings.

Zyid stood, his chair dragging on the floor as he did. "Shall we go, Kasala? Things might be going faster than expected." He turned to the young man. "Young man, take this silver if you would please see this to the post and get it on its way. Then we will go to your meeting. You may keep the change from the coin." The man paused, unsure, so Zyid reassured him. "We can find our way to the meeting without you." The man fidgeted for a moment before nodding and rushing out of the door letter and coin safely tucked away.

The walk to the guildhall was not a long one. Zyid had purposefully chosen an inn close to the guilds. Upon arrival, they were greeted by guards who inquired of their purpose. Zyid quickly introduced them and explained they had been summoned for a meeting.

As they entered the hall, light poured in from the large windows around the room, distorting as they passed through the heavy smoke filling the room. Representatives from both the mining guild and the merchant guild were already gathered as Zyid and Kasala approached. The man sitting at the head of the table motioned them to their seats as he stood to welcome them in. "Thank you both for coming so quickly. We are all eager to get moving ahead with this business."

"I was getting bored of waiting. I hope it is all good news you have to share." The woman across from him chuckled softly, waving for the man at the head of the table to begin.

The four sat down at the large table with documents cluttered over a map. The mining guild representative, a shrewd-looking older man, sat at the table head chewing on his pipe. The scars on his face flexed and twisted as he spoke. "It is indeed good news. We have both received news from the people we sent ahead, and we are certain of the ore's quality." He paused to drink deeply from a mug before continuing. "Our smiths have studied the samples you brought, and I have word from our men that the ore appears as it should. However, they need more time to investigate the mountain. We will need to build infrastructure, but that can be done with local labor, which will allow my efforts to be focused on the mine." As he finished, he looked toward the woman on his left.

She nodded, clearing her throat before she spoke in a soft but firm voice. "Our people have also looked at the samples and agree with your findings. The market could easily accommodate this ore in any quantities as the constant warring among the various kingdoms and people of means ensure a steady market." She paused briefly, waving some smoke away from her face. "Add to that the dwarves reducing output then a tidy profit could be made by all parties." The two nodded at one another.

"Now that we are all in agreement, the proper charters can be drawn up. It has been some time since a vein has been found. I must ask, how it is you came across it?" She centered her gaze on Zyid as she had asked.

Zyid stood and moved papers to reveal the map. "I found it searching for treasure in the caves. I found ore instead, so I was successful in one sense." The guild masters both politely chuckled.

"Wish I had found stuff like this in my youth. It would have been a much easier life in those early years."

"The answer to your second question is of course all I can get out of it, money can move mountains, and I wish to move some mountains as it were. Get all I can out of our venture and use my wealth for more wealth. I am sure you can agree with me on that." The merchant nodded her head.

"Also, you have been sending some letters out. To whom are you speaking?"

Zyid shook his head. "I should have known you would be on top of that. My brother, as he is a merchant in Brala. I am sure he would know a few names of interested parties. I would say to get people looking to buy, but that is never an issue I am sure." The merchant nodded again, scratching her chin with a polite nod.

"We, of course, have done the same. Let us hope we can meet the demand."

"Let us hope that is our only issue."

"Sadly, it will not be but let us hope indeed," the mining guild representative said as he cleaned out his pipe and began repacking it.

The merchant nodded and stood up.

"If there is nothing else, I will begin arranging for merchants to get shipments moved and stored for delivery to our soon-to-be eager customers. A fine day to you all. I will contact you when things are in place." With that, she bowed and left the room.

The miner scratched some notes on a parchment. "Always more work to do, but I will send more material and begin hiring locals to help with construction and mining efforts. Food may be an issue as well if we send too many people without proper infrastructure."

Zyid nodded. "Fortunately, we will have the food problem pretty well sorted out."

He nodded back. "Well, that is fortunate for us. Good that at least there is a fine inn in town already up there so the men will have a good place to rest when not on the mountain. But without further ado, I will go and also begin arranging men and equipment. I need you to find some sort of guards for this little venture of yours, as the guild has none to spare for something of this size."

"I have been looking into it, but with you both on board, then I will begin my search in earnest."

"Very good. Carry on and keep me informed. Also, let me know if there is any way I can be of assistance. It might be hard to scrounge up men willing to travel."

Zyid was still staring at the map "I think I will be able to get men for our purposes." He nodded and left the room, wading into the many scouting people outside the room.

"So, Zyid, everything going according to plan? I am wondering how you will magically appear food and people for your grand endeavor."

Zyid sighed while still poring over the map. "Honestly, I am starting to run out of ideas, but I am open to ideas if you have any. It is generally hard to get people to move. Farmers and guards are even more so not big on moving once they are settled. But to answer your question, yes, actually things are going much better than I had expected. Even if we take one step forward and two steps back."

Kasala started pacing the room. "So you need people and food, huh?"

Zyid shook his head. "No, we just need people. My brother who I wrote a letter to will be starting to deliver food within a month or so. Add to that the unfarmed land that I own, it was easy to scoop up land when prices have been so low and families were leaving."

"So you swindled people out of their land? I might have to rethink my opinion of you now."

"I swindled, as you say, no one out of their land. People were leaving, and I paid them above value for them."

"Also how did you pay for it all?"

"Well, I made a fair bit of coin while I was gone, but that is a minor detail. At this point, let us focus on getting people to work."

CHAPTER 5

"CAPTAIN! CAPTAIN!"

Emma awoke with a start. "Yes!" she groggily answered.

"You ordered me to bring all messages to you immediately. Also, the mayor wishes to speak to you. At your earliest convenience were his exact words."

"Leave them there. I will get them in a moment. Thank you, Lieutenant."

"Very good, Captain." There was a scrape and a shuffle before she heard the door shut. Followed by muffled footsteps as he headed back down the hall. Heaving herself out of her bed, she cracked open her door. Emma looked up and down the hall as she grabbed the letters and slammed the door behind her. She threw the missives on her desk, settling down to begin poring over them. Patrol reports made up most of them. "Patrols are encountering fewer problems on the roads so that took a lot less time than I thought it would." She sighed heavily. "Rowdy miners drinking and causing minor issues. No worries there." There was another rap at the door. Emma flopped down the paper and hollered over her shoulder. "What is it now?"

Arlana answered from the other side. "Sorry, dear, might I come in for a minute?"

Emma quickly took the couple of steps to the door before opening the door and ushering her in. "Sorry, everyone has been bothering me this morning, and I have had nearly no sleep the last few days with all the people running about."

Arlana smiled gently. "I understand your frustration, dear, but sadly things are only going to get more hectic from here. The envoys have sent letters that both the mining and merchant guilds will be moving forward with this venture. They will be sending more men and equipment to start the mining operation in earnest."

Emma's head slumped to her desk with a thud. "I do not have the manpower for that kind of operation. We are stretched thin as it is patrolling the roads. I have scraped together every spare person and enlisted them into the guard. I have no one left."

"There, there, Emma. We will find people or hire more. Zyid is already working on it." Arlana rubbed Emma's head gently. "When there is a will, there is a way." Her soft voice soothing as it had always been. "So do not give up hope. Just do what you can and rely on your friends to help you along the way, alright?"

Emma was silent for a moment. "I wish I had your optimism." She sat up and turned to open the window shutters. "I guess that will have to do. When he gets back here, I am going to give him a piece of my mind."

Arlana chuckled. "Where did that come from, dear? He is not causing you trouble on purpose. Or is it something else maybe?"

"No, it is just." Emma rested her head in her hands, brow furrowed in thought. "It is just that I hope that someday we can move past this and just have it be simple like it used to be. I just do not want to be the captain forever." She sighed once again as they both stood. "But I suppose that will just have to wait now, will it not?"

Arlana turned Emma around, nearly pushing her back into bed. "We will find a solution to this issue. Now go to sleep, dear. We have much work ahead. So enjoy the calm while you can." Arlana closed the shutters as Emma crawled under her blanket and fell straight asleep.

She awoke in a field near the edge of the forest. Laughter drifting from deep in the trees. She stood brushing the hair from her face, surveying the land. *This is Zyid's farm, I think?* Wheat stood tall in a small part of the field as there was little point in working the whole patch of land. A man walked the fence line inspecting the posts checking for rotten or split staves. He passed Emma without a glance.

A dream! I am in a dream, she realized. *Why does this feel so familiar? Wait, that was Zyid's father. Is this that day?* She ran off toward the sound of laughter in the woods and saw what she thought she would, a young Zyid and herself bounding through the woods, a familiar dog in tow.

"Come on, Zyid, you are too slow. I thought you were a man." Hearing her younger self filled her with regret and sorrow at how she had treated him back then. It is no wonder why he was in such a hurry to leave this place behind and run off with her. She watched the three of them romp farther off into the woods, laughter and barking drifting deep into the woods. She followed lazily behind, smiling with fondness as she watched their innocent play. She froze in her tracks seeing the creature. It stalked them from the shadows, watching and waiting for its time to strike and take its meal. Rushing after it, she saw her memory play out before her eyes. They all watched as the creature leapt from shadow roaring its victory. She watched herself as her younger self's legs buckled with fear. She saw Zyid's legs tremble before he balled his fists, grabbing her younger self by the hand, running off into the woods with the dog close behind. She ran to follow, having forgotten how fast and far they had run. She spilled out from the trees into the familiar clearing. The rock wall hung looming over the clearing, casting its long shadow over them all. The three of them were pinned up against the rocks, the dog growling and barking in defiance to the predator. Terror filled expressions on their faces as the creature lunged forward, claws tearing up the ground, flinging rocks and dirt through the air.

Then a figure appeared as if by magic leaping down from the rocks behind them. She seemed to fly through the air, her feet so swift they never seemed to touch the ground. Her two swords were drawn in an instance, a flashing steel as she cut at the creature and dodged its blows with contemptuous ease. She moved like a dancer with long black hair flowing behind her as she moved, blood misting into the air. With a final roar, the creature slumped onto the ground into a pool of its own blood.

She turned and sheathed her swords, blood covering her armor and clothes from head to foot. Slowly, she approached the two children, stopping to let the dog sniff her hands before gently petting it as she approached. She stopped, kneeling down in front of them both and reaching out her hand. "Are you two alright?" She saw the awestruck looks on both of their faces. Emma could see once again that Zyid had that determined look on his face. "Come along now, you two, let us get you both home. I am sure both of your parents are quite worried about you both."

She blinked then found herself suddenly in the town square under the great statue. The sun peeking through an overcast sky as a steady drizzle came down. She knew exactly when she was. The day he had left for so long. She gripped her chest. Why this moment again? There the two of them stood—a boy with a driven but somehow terrified expression across his face and the women standing opposite two proud parents. "I am sorry for my son's selfish request. You do not have to take him with you if you would rather not have your travels hampered."

She shook her head. "No, it is quite alright. If he wants to be trained, then I will train him." She ruffled Zyid's scruffy hair as she spoke. "I will be glad to have an apprentice after so long."

Emma watched as his mother knelt down and spoke in a firm tone that seemed to carry through the whole square. "Remember, my son, to finish what you start no matter what. Do that and you will never bring shame upon yourself for that is a noble deed."

He nodded in understanding. "Yes, Mother. I will. I will get strong then come back and help the people of this place."

They both smiled. "Well, my son, we look forward to that day then. Thank you for taking him, and we hope he is not too much trouble for you." They both turned toward the town hall where Emma was trying to hide from view.

"Emma, are you not going to say goodbye?" his father called out.

She let out a huff and yelled, "I do not care what he does. I hope he never comes back!" She then quickly ran inside.

The woman looked down at Zyid and spoke soft but firmly. "Well then, we must go now." They both threw up the hoods on their cloaks and walked out to the west toward the gateway.

Emma shot up in her bed from her vivid dreams. Sweat ran down her back, and a tear trickled down her cheek. "Damn that man." She took a deep breath before muttering, "No, damn me for being so foolish." She lay back down but only tossed and turned. Unable to get back to sleep, Emma reached over to her sword and whetstone and sat hunched over. Sword in hand, she slowly and methodically ran the whetstone down the blade in rhythmic fashion. She stopped after a time and took a piece of parchment in hand and ran the blade gently down it, the paper cut as if it were wet. She smiled. Satisfied with her work, she sheathed her blade. "Well, guess it is about time I go and see what the old man wanted." She heaved herself to her feet and quickly readied herself and stepped out into the cool afternoon air.

*****

"What do you mean there are none? How is that even possible?" Zyid ran a frustrated hand through his hair. "I really do not even know if you can possibly be telling me the truth."

"Sadly, I must reiterate to you that I have no one I can recommend to you for your purposes. Most of the mercenary companies are already employed. Those that are not are in negotiations to finalize their contracts." The man was old and scarred from a chosen profession of war; he walked with a limp in his left leg as he hobbled around the table to throw open the window to look down across the bustling market center. He swept his arm out across the view. "I am sure you can tell that all of the nobles here are preparing for war." He leaned back from the window, shutting it to drown out the noise, as he shuffled back to his chair. "It is in their nature to war after all. They seem hell-bent on going to win glory and honor and so forth sacking and burning another one of the towns in the next province over. Though they seem more enthusiastic this season."

"What do you mean more enthusiastic?" Zyid tilted his head as he asked.

The old man blinked several as if just now realizing he had been talking out loud. "Well, never you mind, young one. The answer to your question is no, as there is nothing I can help you with here. Your only options are to either look in another city or perhaps the local villages. I wish I had men to give. It is rare to see both the mining and merchant guilds here moving with such zeal."

Zyid sighed as he heaved himself out of the chair. "Thank you for your time. I will take my leave then. A good day to you." Zyid stood, gave a curt nod, and left the room. Kasala joined him as he stepped out into the street.

"So how did it go? Is this part of your grand scheme going as planned?" He slowly shook his head as they began walking down the road toward the inn.

"No, it is going about as badly as is possible to be honest." They walked for a short while in silence. Zyid took in the world around him, seeing what the old man had been saying. All sorts men buying arms and armor, soldiers drilling out in the square, sword makers and smiths of all kinds making weapons. Kasala cut through his thoughts.

"What do you mean by badly exactly?"

"What? Oh, right. Badly, yes. There are no companies for hire. They are all already hired. Seems the nobles here are all getting ready for something big once the harvests are in."

"What does the harvest have to do with it?"

He shook his head at her. "It has everything to do with it. Once the harvests are in, every available person of age can be sent to the frontlines. Look around you, these people are buying the best weapons and armor they can lay their hands on. The fletchers are working round the clock. They are gearing up for something, and we are unable to get the extra people we need because of it." He stopped in his tracks, scratching his beard.

"What is it?"

"I just thought of something."

"Is it a useful something?"

"Only one way to find out," he said with a shrug. "But first we need to look at the last few years' records in the courthouse."

"How is that supposed to help?"

"Well, if all of the local nobility is buying up all the mercenary contracts, then that is that." He held a finger up to emphasize. "But with what we will be shipping in, we are liable to make a few friends. Perhaps in time we will be able to leverage that for more people. And that is the best I have right now." They both shrugged and continued onward.

The records building that adjoined the main court was full to bursting with scrolls and tomes. They had been allowed entry with little more than a glance over from the bored guard; he had seemed quite surprised anyone had come there intentionally and waved them through to be greeted by an equally puzzled clerk who pointed them toward the relevant items. The near silence of the place was deafening as scribes busied themselves by copying and recopying the many tomes and scrolls. Their furious writing was broken only occasionally by the tearing of parchment and what sounded like deep furious phrases in a language neither had heard before. With several stacks of material set before them, they began to pore over it in detail. The hours passed as they went through tomes line by line to tease out the needed information.

Kasala threw down a scroll in frustration. "These people write down every detail of everything. How are supposed to make sense of any of it?" A scribe briefly paused as he walked past to see nothing was damaged then continued on his way.

"Well, Kasala, while they do write most everything down, there is plenty we can gloss over, but here is what we are looking for here. A list of nobles captured and ransoms paid by the family. Now we just see where these people are from, and we know who the main enemies are here or at least who this city's nobles say is their enemy." Zyid set down the set of scrolls he was reading over and pointed as he spoke. "See, look at here. Barslin of Torm. Torm is to the northwest of here along the route to the dwarven kingdoms, and here Forlin of Garsen.

Garsen is to the west where the coast cuts in sharply. It is a major fishing port mostly from what little my father told me about it."

Zyid paused for a moment before continuing. "So what this is telling me is, one, they are looking to cut out the middleman in the trade with the dwarves. They must be tired of the extra costs of getting dwarven goods to them and not being able to sell their furs at a price they want. Not sure about Garsen though they fought them, but I do not see an obvious reason to do so." He shook the speculations away. "So if we are looking for more hired hands, as we are calling them, then we either need to look outside of those places to have any hope of finding people—quality people, that is."

Kasala flipped a book open to a map of the continent, thumping her finger on the dwarven lands. "If quality is what we are after, why do we not just hire dwarves or elves?"

Zyid blinked at her for a moment, his face blank as the idea slowly washed over him. "You know, to be honest, I never thought to even give that a try, but that very well may be the only real option. Elven mercenaries are generally too few in number to suit our purposes but dwarves…" Zyid began stroking his beard as he continued to think out loud. "Now the only real problem might be the price or gods knows what they might want as payment. It is a couple weeks' journey to reach the dwarven lands." He sighed. "I hope it will not be a waste of our time." They left the hall, stepping out into the rapidly approaching darkness. "So much to do, so much to do, Kasala. I hope this is not all for naught."

She put herself under his arm, snuggling herself up to him. "One thing at a time, Zyid. Worry only about what you can control for the rest will have to fend for itself," she said, jumping in front and spinning, pressing a finger to his nose. "We must make a plan, but first let us get food and drink. You have once again been trying to live on nothing but air. Now onward to drink and be merry." He shook his head but let her lead him to the inn with its now familiar faces.

The next morning came unseasonably warm and found them all around the large table in the guildhall. The merchant named Sorin drummed his fingers on the table, barely audible over the noise of the hall. He took a deep breath and spoke slowly, "So your great idea is to skip over everywhere and go straight to hiring dwarves? You cannot be serious, Zyid. The idea is just ludicrous. How will you ever convince them to go that far from their homes?" Zyid reached down and placed a lump of the ore gently on the table as if that answered his question. "What are you going to give them, ore as payment? That will never work. Surely you must know this?" His voice was calm and level, a teacher gently scolding one of his charges.

Zyid took the ore in hand and began turning it over in his hands. "Not at all. What I am saying is that this will bring them running. They will take gold in payment, that is the dwarven way." The miner Worstan jumped in with a sudden realization and rubbed his hand on his chin as he spoke.

"Yes, yes, I see the mountains they live in are lousy with ores of all kinds—iron, copper, tin, and yes of course, gold. But there is one thing they have precious little of." He reached across the table, snatching the rock from Zyid's hand, giving him a scorned look as he did so and held it up to the early morning light. "This!" Sorin sighed again.

"I see that you two are ever the optimists, but I fail to see how any of that will work. A few hired farmers would be quicker and cheaper than trying to hire dwarves for this work. It is just guarding a mine, not a hard task by any means." Silence fell and even the noise outside seemed to die down.

Worstan spoke slowly and softly. "Yes, for the moment that may be an option, but once people start realizing what is probably in that mountain, then things will quickly become more complicated. We can only keep people in the dark for so long before they figure it out then we will have everyone stumbling over themselves to get at it and for that to be a long as possible we may very well need dwarven guards. They are almost tailor-made for this kind of thing. Might be able to get some dwarven mining foremen to help us, for a small fee of course," he added dryly. Sorin stood and began slowly pacing around the room

"I am quite aware of this metal's value even if most would not." He snatched the ore from Worstan's hand as he walked past. "You came to us for discretion and to ensure a ready market and I can and will do that for you, but keeping your mine safe, well that is on you two after all. We merchants will ensure a market. You get it to us any way you can." He tossed the ore onto the table with a thump as it landed. "So you may do with this part as you please. If you get a supply of ingots, then I can feed us all a healthy sum of gold and that at the end of the day is what we are really looking for. Now, gentlemen, if you will excuse me, I have this and many other matters with which to attend, and I bid you both a good day." He strode through the doorway, quickly disappearing into the press of people in the hall.

"Pompous ass," Worstan huffed, "but he and his people are very good at what he does, which is why he has been running the merchants guild and is a very rich man after all." He picked up the lump of ore again, turning it over in his hands. "But he is right, and based on what you are telling me, this may be our best or possibly only real option. I had not realized it had gotten this crazy. Already people are really getting into the buildup this season. As if people will really be fooled, but in any case, you should hurry along with the lovely young woman and take just what you can carry on horseback, and you can get there in about five or six days."

Kasala turned to Zyid, gently smacking his shoulder. "Did you hear that, Zyid? He called me lovely. Why can you not be more like that?"

"Because he does not know you well, and he is just being nice."

Worstan gave an offended look on his face. "Only speaking the truth as I see it. But in any case, get your things and head straight out today. I will get horses prepared and be sure to bring ore samples with you. They will want to examine it in detail before they talk real business with you." Zyid nodded.

"Right you are. Kasala, let us get our things and be off before the markets open."

The rush had proved pointless as they sat waiting for the gates to be opened. The guards seemed to be moving extra slow as if waiting for something. "What is taking so long to open the gate? I have business to attend to!"

"Do not test our patience, trader. It will be opened at the appropriate time and no sooner." The sergeant stared intently at them both to make sure his point had been made.

"Right, right." Zyid waved him off. Minutes seemed to drag into hours then days, the sun slowly tracing its path across the sky.

A new figure came galloping past them, skidding his horse to a halt. "You need to open the gate this instant!" the new man shouted.

The sergeant squinted down at the new arrival. "This gate will open when it is the appointed time and no sooner. If you have an issue, you may take it up with the council."

Kasala leaned over, appearing to talk in what she thought was a whisper. "Did he really think that was going to get him anywhere?"

The man slowly twisted his head to look at them. "Do you know who I am? How dare you speak to me in such a manner." The man blustered out. "I should take your head for your insolence."

Zyid sighed as he leaned forward in his saddle. "I do not know who you are. Nor do I terribly care who you are." Zyid narrowed his eyes. "I am not one of your lackeys. I am not one of your serfs. If you wish to do something about the way I talk to you, be prepared for what it might cost you." The words hung in the air with an air of finality.

Anger flushed across the man's face. Kasala's laughter only increased it. "You are insolent, little worm! I will have your head for this lack of respect to your betters." The guards looked at each other and then to their sergeant.

"Gentleman, you will take this dispute outside and spill no blood on my streets or you can spend the night in a cell!" His harsh glare returned moving his gaze between the two parties. As a bell chimed in the distance, the sergeant gave a signal and the gate slowly swung open.

"Now if you want to take up the guard's offer, we will be outside soon enough." Zyid patted his swords hanging from the saddles.

The man's eyes burned with barely controlled fury. "No, I am above such things. I must be away as I surely have far more important business than showing you peasants the error of your ways." He spurred his horse into a trot, shouting behind himself. "This is not the last you have seen of me, peasant. You had best be careful out there."

Kasala struggled to hold in her laughter until the noble was out of earshot. "Did he seriously threaten us?" They rode for a short while before Kasala regained her composure to continue speaking. "If that child had any idea who and what he threatened. What was that all about anyway? Seemed very petty."

"Someone from a minor noble family by the looks of it. I am sure he will be someone we will have to deal with later."

"Will he not do something rash now that you have slighted him?"

Zyid nodded. "I would almost guarantee it. On the bright side, if he attacks us on the road and we kill him and whoever he brings with him, there are no repercussions on us and a minor family like his would be too weak to fight the charges even if they wanted to."

"Well, that is nice, I suppose." With that, they rode in silence until well into the night. They stopped at a small but well used area near the road edge. This was a common place to stop with a small stream running by and a well-used firepit already lit by one of the few other travelers that had stopped for the night. The two of them made their way out a little ways from the camp to make a resting place. The horses lazily grazed while they ate their trail rations near the fire's edge and spoke in low voices.

"So do you think we have been followed? It would be odd to not attack us soon, would it not?"

"Yes and yes. It will happen tonight or sometime tomorrow. If they wait any longer than that, we will be out of his family's influence area and that is too large a risk to take for small noble family." She slowly nodded in agreement.

"So does that mean we get no sleep tonight then?"

"Only if you do not want to sleep. I find it unlikely that we would be taken by surprise, but on the other hand, one never can truly know what will happen in the future. So we should get some rest, even if we do not really need it. Let us eat, check the horses, and we will get some sleep." An hour passed before they settled down to sleep under a tree away from the slowly dying fire.

"Can I ask you something?"

He looked over at her from his spot leaning on the tree. "Must you keep asking questions? I thought you were tired. But sure you can ask a couple since I know you will ask anyway."

She smiled and laughed softly to herself. "If this all works out, and you come out alive at the end of it all, what will you do then? If there is no more fighting to be done, then what?"

"Are you sure you are not asking for yourself?"

"No, I think I have done well enough sitting about in my time. Besides, I can fly as I please. Your kind does not have that same luxury."

He gave a shrug. "You dragons do have that on us, that is for sure. Though some people have figured out ways to have flight. But nothing like gliding for days on end."

"So what will you do after you have won?"

"Why do you want to know so badly anyway? *If* we win, it is still a long time off yet."

"I got my curiosity from my mother is all."

Zyid nodded slowly several times. "Yes, that explains everything. But what will I do?" He stopped and stared up at the sky for a time in the dim starlight. "*To* be honest, I am not sure. I am not a farmer. I never took anytime to learn. My father was maybe a little too hands-off in raising us." He chuckled. "But no matter how things turn out, there will always be those who fight, so at worst I go off and find another war to join." He paused, stroking his beard. "At best, I can just live out my days quietly. The Trolls Heads will always need plenty of firewood after all."

Kasala rolled over on her mat, turning away from him. "I suppose that is the best I am going to get out of you, is it not?" The chirping of the bugs was her answer. "Do try and come up with a better answer for next time. Okay?"

"Sure. Now go to sleep."

CHAPTER 6

"**G**ET OUT OF MY WAY, BENTIN. I have business with the mayor." Emma leered angrily at the old man with his faded but well-kept brown robes hiding his withered but defiant frame.

"You will not interrupt the mayor during his meeting, Captain." He glared defiantly from his position in front of the oak doors.

Emma briefly thought of slapping him upside of his head with her sword but quickly shook the thought away. "No! You will get out of my way. You hold no authority over me, you glorified secretary. Now out of the way." With a mighty step, she shoved him aside and stormed through the doors; the mayor and his guest quickly stopped short their discussions.

After a moment, the mayor cleared his throat. "Captain, while it is good to see you at last in my office, I believe you could have worked on your timing just a little bit." He folded his hands, setting them gently on the desk.

Emma smiled to herself as she pulled another chair in front of the desk. Gently and slowly settling herself down into it. "Well, dear Mayor, I was told to come to you at my convenience and this…" She adjusted herself before continuing. "And this is my convenience." The mayor let out a heavy sigh. "I suppose I should expect this of you. You are your father's daughter after all. But please next time could you not keep me waiting nearly a week?"

Emma shrugged. "I will do my best in the future, but I believe I will only be more busy going forward."

He rubbed his eyes and rearranged his robes. "I apologize for the interruption, good sir." He inclined his head toward his first guest. "But please allow me to formally introduce you to our very capable guard captain, Emma." He waved his hand at her for emphasis.

The man grinned and gave a curt nod. "The pleasure is all mine. I believe we have already met. She was quite helpful in breaking up some of my miners the other night." He briefly stood to give a simple bow. "Though I am afraid I must apologize for their terrible behavior and assure you that they have been punished for their excessive rowdiness this past evening." He turned back to more directly face the mayor as he sat down. "As I was telling the mayor, my name is Worstan, and I represent the mining guild from Grandulka. I have moved my offices here to help coordinate this new venture your friend Zyid has gotten us into."

The mayor stroked his chin. "So why has someone of your status in the guild come all the way out here to help run a small mine at the edge of the world, as many are so fond of calling our home."

Worstan laughed. "Well, several reasons to be honest. I have been looking to get out of the poisonous atmosphere of that city for years. This place seems nice enough." He laughed to himself again. "Also, I am betting, this little mine as you put it, will not be little for very long." He clapped his hands together. "I am bringing all of the resources I can get my hands on to get this up and running. When this succeeds, maybe, just maybe, I can become head of the mining guild instead of being stuck as a midlevel negotiator for the rest of my life."

Emma burst out laughing, throwing her head back and banging a fist on the desk. "You sound like Zyid already. What has that fool put into your head?"

He looked up scratching his head as he thought for a quick moment then said, "Nothing that was not already there to begin with." He shrugged. "He brought a compelling argument and a sound plan. Why, I would be foolish not to jump at this once-in-a-lifetime opportunity. There are few chances to stake new claims and open new mines. Times are getting harder for everyone after all, and when a fat goose is laid out before you, one would have to be crazy to not want to take a chance at it." Silence filled the room as they took all of it in, letting it settle in their minds.

The mayor coughed to break the silence in the room. "Well then, now that is all well and good, sir, and I hope you are successful in the endeavors that you choose to pursue in your life." The mayor narrowed his gaze. "What I want to know is that your miners will cease causing trouble for this town, as we do not have the resources to be dealing with this nightly. As I am sure the captain would tell you as well." His voice was smooth and calm as if he were explaining a complex idea to a child. Emma nodded her agreement.

Worstan held up his hands in defense. "I understand fully, Mayor, and again I have ensured that those responsible have been punished." He glanced over at Emma with a shrug. "Though no matter what, people will be rowdy."

She gave a nod with a sigh. "True, but if we keep it to about once a week or so, then it will be fine. Hopefully anyway."

He turned back to the mayor as he spoke. "But we will do our best to keep it to a minimum. After all, I am well aware of your guards' plight. And as we all would love more security for both the mine and the shipments. The guild is already working to increase the number of guards in our employ to relieve the strain on your own town's force. In the meantime, Mayor, I believe the agreement I have presented will help for the time being, and I am sure the captain will be quite happy with it."

Emma sat up straight in her chair now fully invested in the conversation. "What agreement are we talking about here?" The mayor shook his head as he slid a paper across his desk to Emma. Snatching it from the desk and scanning over the document, a smile slowly formed across her face as she finished and set it gently back down, drumming her knuckles on the desk. "So you wish to pay a small fee for our help until you can get more of your own guards, is it?"

Worstan nodded. "That is precisely what I am suggesting, my dear lady. Your men seem capable enough for the job, and the mayor was just telling me that you have been looking for more funds to recruit and train additional people for some time now."

She shot a disapproving look at the mayor. "While I do not approve of the mayor throwing my plight to the winds as it were, yes, I have been, and this contract seems very fair for what little we can offer you. You can certainly send the shipments with our regular patrols. Though they can only take you so far, but tis better than nothing, and we can possibly spare a few to watch over the mine once I can gather some more people with the promise of coin. Some men will probably do it on off-duty time for extra pay."

Worstan took a small purse and set it on the table. "If that concludes that, then here is the first small payment of twenty-five gold to get things started."

"Why yes, I believe it is," the mayor said as he reached to take the purse.

Emma quickly snatched it from him, waving a finger at him. "No, no, sir. I will be taking this to ensure that it goes to the guards. As things always seem to get lost in the mix of governance." She stood abruptly. "Now if you will excuse me, I have many pressing matters to attend to this day and little time in which to do them." She nearly ran out of the room, shoving open the doors and leaving. Nothing but the sounds of her mail armor slightly jingling in her wake.

Worstan let out a whistle as he chuckled. "Quite the fiery lady you have leading your guards here I see. I am sure they are well trained if possibly a little worried about your choice in leadership."

The mayor let out a hearty laugh. "Yes. Fiery is a fairly accurate description I suppose, but the guards here have always been more like soldiers than most guards. They were born from the founding of this place long ago, but she was the most capable one to take over when her father passed from the position. The guards practically begged for it after all. She is the best of them. Always working the hardest and training the hardest. She pushes them hard, but she is fair in her dealings. So yes, she was the best choice I think. That and no one else wanted the job."

Worstan nodded. "Well that is good then. That is very good."

*****

"So we made it all the way to Torm without incident. Wonder why that is?"

"Hmm?"

She narrowed her gaze at him "I know damn well you can hear me, Zyid!"

He laughed. "Why, yes I can. I am just getting you back for all the annoying questions I have had to endure in your company." Zyid ran his hands down the horse's neck. "But yes, I am rather surprised that nothing has happened. We should stay on our guard still, but we have other matters to deal with. While we will still have a ways to go yet, tonight we will be staying in a real building, even if it is outside of the city. So let us enjoy a hot meal, a bath hopefully, and a warm if most likely quite worn bed."

She let out a hardy laugh. "Is that why we have been riding so hard today? A chance for you to peek at me in the bath?" She moved her horse closer to slap him gently on the shoulder. "You may just be a man after all, Zyid. Come now we are getting close. Let us hurry. I could use a hot meal." She spurred her horse to a trot.

"As if I would peek at you! Not worth the trouble!" he yelled after her before spurring his horse after her.

*****

"Ahh...now that is what I was needing after all those days of hard riding." They sat on a covered porch looking out onto the walls of Torm. "Sadly, my hair will still be wet when we head out in the morning." She twirled her hair as Zyid shook his head as he sipped from his ale. "So how far away are we from our destination anyway?"

Zyid finished his ale, set his mug down gently, wiping the foam from his beard. "At our current pace, it should be another two days or so. Really it all depends on the road condition." He used the water on the small table to draw a crude map pointing as he spoke. "From here on out, the roads can be rather unkempt this time of the year. With the start of fall, it will likely rain more often, which could really slow us down." He nodded a thanks to the barmaid as she set down fresh ales. He took a swig of ale and peered through the window looking in on the inn. "Hopefully, there are not any holdups as this whole endeavor is going to take much longer now that we will have to get the dwarves involved." He sighed. "They like to talk and debate. It is just going to take time to work through the process." His head sunk at the thought. "Gods, this is going to be so much fun," he said with a groan.

She patted him on the head. "There, there, grumpy one. It will be alright. We will get them to look at it our way." He gave her a sideways glance.

"I damn well know we will. I am just dreading the whole process. We will probably have to drink lots and lots of cheap ale. The stuff is terrible. I do not understand how the dwarves drink it all the time."

"They drink terrible tasting ale? That seems rather odd."

"Well, they think that it tastes good or so Kalgrin explained to me the one time I went with him, but they practically feed it to you. They love to get visitors really drunk, and being a rowdy sort, they will start huge brawls, laugh, and go get more drunk after they are finished fighting. It can be very strange for newcomers."

"So you have been to the dwarven lands before then?"

He nodded his head slowly. Holding up a single finger for emphasis. "Once and Kalgrin has gone into or rather over every detail about it as we traveled on the road. Boy, can that dwarf talk and talk and talk. So I have a rough understanding of how it will go."

She laughed into her mug "You have spent a lot of time with him, have you not?"

He nodded slightly, staring up into the sky. "Yes, we have spent a lot of time together. He was like a second father to me. Taught me so many things before I left and never questioned me about it when I came back." He took another sip before continuing. "He just kinda nodded and put me back to work. Practically as soon as I had walked into the door."

"So that is how you feel about him, huh?" They both sat in silence for a time slowly sipping from their mugs looking out over the city. "So what do you know of this place, Torm?"

He finished his mug, ordering another from the passing maiden. "Not much really, the little bit I know for sure is that they trade food with the dwarves for metal and stonework. But that is about all I know. We did not stop here when last I came here." The maiden arrived with a fresh ale. He nodded to her as she quickly left again. "But all and all, this place is of little importance. The capital city is really the one place that is very rich and not dependent on other regions for something so the outlying places are just not very prosperous. But the dwarves like to get food from all around for some variety."

"So what makes you all think the dwarves will be interested in something so far from their homelands?" she asked over the brim of her mug.

"Well, they are not really that far away." He remade his water map. "If you look at a map, we are just on the other side of the mountains, and there was to be a road built through to the other side but it was never finished. Maybe if it becomes profitable they might even work on finishing it."

"That is all a part of your big plan too, huh?"

He leaned back and propped his feet up onto another table, resting his hands behind his head. "Maybe?" They both laughed. "Alright, it is getting late. We should head to sleep soon. We still have a hard ride to our destination." They both quickly finished their drinks and headed to their room.

It was small with two small beds and a tiny window at the far end of the room. The sounds of the crowd downstairs came muffled through the door as they both fell asleep nearly as soon as their heads touched the pillows.

The door creaked open slowly, letting a tiny sliver of light through. An eye appeared scanning into the room. Finding their two targets fast asleep, the man gently opened the door, allowing several men to slip through the opening. Their faces were covered by the long cloaks they wore. Stepping softly, they crept toward the beds, freezing stiff at the slightest movements or creaks of the floorboards.

After a few tense moments, they reached the bedsides. The first man looked between the group, giving a brisk nod and slowly drawing his blade followed by the rest of the group. He looked over once more and gave an affirmative nod to his men, raising up his blade and bringing it down toward his sleeping victim.

A man's screams pierced the silence, as one of the men fell stumbling backward as he took a foot to the chin, throwing him to the floor. Kasala rolled out of her bed, grabbing the man's dropped dagger, parrying the poorly aimed blow of the next man, and plunging the dagger into his face. The door burst open, allowing several more attackers in as she flung herself onto another assailant. Zyid had grabbed the man by his neck and flung him into the window. A mace came toward his head, which he sidestepped. Grabbing the man's arm by wrist and smashing a knee into the attacker's elbow with a sickening crack and a howl of pain. The two stood back-to-back as several more men entered the room. "Damn, how many of them are we going to have to fight tonight?" She laughed out.

"You are enjoying this, are you not?"

He felt her shrug as they came again. The room was now full to bursting and soon slicked with blood as the battle raged in the dimly lit room. After several minutes of furious fighting, the last two attackers, seeing the futility of their struggle, staggered backward and ran out of the room, nearly falling over their fallen compatriots. The pair stood still the night only broken by the moans of their attackers and the pair's heavy breathing. Kasala took one final steadying breath and moved to check the bodies tying up the one still living.

"Kasala, you talk to our friend. I will go and talk to our innkeeper to make sure he is not dead or tied up or something. You two have fun now." Zyid wiped some blood off his face and headed down to the common room, finding several patrons knocked unconscious and thrown behind the bar. The innkeeper was tied and gagged. Zyid undid his ropes. "Are you alright, sir?" The man let out a huge cough as he took Zyid's offered hand to haul him up.

"Yes, I am alright. Damn, what was that all about? One second I am asking for drink orders. Next thing I know I am getting clubbed over the head and tied up." The man scanned across the room. "They did not steal anything it looks like." He turned his gaze back to the bar, peering at his storage box below it. "Any idea what those men were after or who?"

Zyid had begun looking over his own minor wounds. "They were after me and my traveling companion. Not sure who they were exactly. My friend is talking to the one who did not die to find out who hired them." There was a thumping on the stairs as Kasala dragged the man down the stairs quite roughly. She then placed him in front of the bar. His hood was now down revealing a few cuts and bruises.

"Our mastermind is that noble from before. Hard to believe he followed us this far. He talked pretty quickly, believe it or not. Though I may have broken his nose though." The three of them shrugged at that. "So now what do we do about this mess?" she asked.

The innkeeper cleared his throat. "I will contact the guards once they open the gate in the morning and give this one over to them. I would like to thank you for dealing with them."

Zyid waved him off. "No, it is we that should be apologizing to you. This is our fault after all. Your place is a big mess now."

The man huffed at him. "One should not worry about what trouble other people cause, the fault lies with him not with you two."

"He did not take my words kindly, and now he failed at his petty revenge. Now he will face the consequences, but the ones who died, their belongings now belong to you. I hope that will recover some of your loss."

The man shrugged as he reached under the bar, grabbing several tankards and filling them. "It will, I suppose. The duchess will sort it out in the morning, but it should not take long to get you on your way, good guests."

Zyid nodded, grabbing one of the offered ales and moved to sit next to the fire with Kasala following suit.

"So will we really be able to be on our way? They are not going to detain us for causing trouble, are they?" She tilted her head to peer around him looking at the innkeeper.

Zyid shrugged. "No idea, but we are the victims so it probably will not be too much hassle. But we shall see in the morning." He took a long slow sip from his mug. "We will just have to see in the morning I guess."

*****

The morning was cool and bright as Zyid, Kasala, and the innkeeper were escorted to see the duchess by the city guard. Her hall was of fine construction but seemed entirely too small for all the people that were in attendance. The furnishings were equally well made, but the interior was sparse and plain in decoration. A theme that carried through the whole of the building, including the Duchess herself who wore clothing that many nobles would have found far too plain for their station.

The duchess gave a small nod to the three of them as the guards stepped away. After a few tense moments of silence, she pointed her fan down at the innkeeper. "Please be at ease and please recount to me what happened."

The innkeeper stepped forward, giving a polite bow and began to give his account of the prior night's events. As he was speaking, Zyid surveyed the room and its occupants. His gaze fell on to the duchess, a woman of advancing years an air of firm authority radiating from her. The innkeeper had finished his recount with a bow. She waved her fan at him with a smile. "Thank you for that. You are free to go now."

"Thank you, my lady. May your reign continue for many years to come." The man bowed once again and spun on his heels and left with a curt nod to the two of them.

"You two please approach," the duchess spoke softly, motioning with her fan for them to come closer. She got to her feet as they stepped closer. She began pacing slowly in front of them, looking the two of them over. She stopped midstride, snapping her fan in her free

53

hand, and she turned quickly to face them. She opened her mouth to speak again but stopped to adjust her dress. She curtsied to them. "I must apologize for the most rude welcome that you received last night. We will be posting guards at all the inns in my province." She slowly sat herself back into her chair. "Though I am aware that it is little solace to you since you and your companion have already been attacked. I am glad you appear to not be seriously injured. It seems your friends were not prepared for the two of you." She flicked open her fan, hiding her face as it curled into a small smile. "My guards went and took a look at your work, quite efficient. You both appear quite skilled." She snapped her fan closed for emphasis. "While this may be presumptuous of me to ask this of you, but I could use people like you in my employ. Conflicts are on the horizon, and I will need strong people like you." She stood stepped down from her chair and began walking around the pair.

Zyid followed her movement with his eyes, and she seemed intent on learning everything about them. The curiosity that flowed from her gaze seemed to fill the room.

The young woman standing next to the chair fidgeted as the duchess spoke again. "Well, you two? What do you think?"

Zyid cleared his throat before speaking, careful to choose his words. "While I am flattered by your gracious offer, we must respectfully decline as we are but simple merchants and—"

She cut him off again, snapping her fan into her free hand. "I do not believe that for one second. What you did to those men last night is beyond anything I have heard described in all my days. How can you just leave? Do you not care why it happened? Do you not want revenge?"

Zyid slowly shook his head as she passed in front of them again. "I do not wish revenge. I have much larger ambitions than worrying about the purpose of those simple men." The room buzzed with hushed whispers from those in attendance. He caught a coy smile on the duchess's lips.

"Oh, do you now? You say ambitions but it seems like you mean purpose." She flicked her fan open once again as she moved and fell into her chair. "I know much about you already. You have traveled by here once before. If my memory serves. A single boy and dwarf tend to stand out, and in the dead of winter no less. What a sight that must have been. A boy and a dwarf riding along through the heavy snow." She peered down at him over her fan.

Zyid shrugged. "What can I say, Kalgrin likes to serve dwarven ale in the inn. He is quite particular about it. Something about other stuff not being strong enough or some such nonsense. I think he just likes to take the trip for his own pleasure. He does not get out much after all."

She nodded slowly as if that had somehow answered some grand conundrum. She snapped her fan close again. "Well then, I suppose you must be on your way then. As I am sure you have business you must attend to." She waved her fan toward the door. "When you have more time to stay and chat, please do. I would enjoy talking to someone who is not afraid to speak his mind to me." She scanned the room, causing the discussions to stop as they caught her glare. "I hate how everyone walks on eggshells and will not speak their mind. You are quite refreshing, I must say. Perhaps I could interest you in my daughter's hand if you are a man of such ambition? You could do worse than becoming the leader of this province."

The young woman next to her chair gave her a harsh glare with an exasperated sigh. "Mother, if you would please stop trying to marry me off to every man who does not run screaming from your very presence. I would very much appreciate it." Her words held no venom, flat and cold like ice. Zyid stifled a chuckle. "What pray tell is so funny, sir?" Her gaze turned to him and her eyes met his; they were shades of green and orange. For one short moment, he saw a keen intellect behind those cold eyes.

"Just thinking that your words do not match your looks at all, but I would take a bet you are much more than the sum of your beauty." If she found anything in the compliment, she showed no sign.

Her mother laughed over the chatter around her. "Yes, my boy, you are welcome here anytime. Please stop by again when you have more time to stay, but you and your companion have important business I am sure, so please do not let me hold you any longer.

Zyid, was it?" He nodded. "Be sure to stop by soon." She smiled as they gave curt bows before marching out; hushed murmurs following them the whole way.

"Are you sure it is wise to let them leave after all the trouble that followed them, Mother? They seemed quite skilled in fighting, something we are always in need of. Times always benign as they are."

The duchess smiled and gave a flick of her fan. "No, I believe it is better to let them go. Souls with fire like that cannot be easily restrained. Their strength is quite self-evident, my dear, from what they did to their attackers last night." She raised her fan for emphasis. "But as I am sure you know I have no interest in conquering anything. Peace is what the people need most of all, it is what is best for them." She gave an exhausted sigh. "But I fear we will never see peace in our time, but maybe just maybe that may no longer be true. That man is a warrior at heart, but we shall see what course he wishes for himself and what that means for those around him. It should be interesting to hear from them again."

*****

A driving rain struck just as they rode out of the walls. It poured, limiting their view and soaking them to the bone. It followed them through the mountains driving them onward. They rode on stopping only to rest the horses before continuing on again. For three days, they rode and suffered through the rain and the mud. They stopped once they reached a hilltop overlooking the entrance to the city. "So this is the gateway to the dwarven empire, is it?" She shivered as she shouted over the rain. "Does not look like a very cheerful place."

Zyid shook his head. "No, it is meant to be a very strong message. It is a fortress within a fortress within another fortress. Not a welcome mat, but they are open to trade. They seem to import a lot of meat and wine since they have a hard time growing it underground."

Makes sense, I guess. Let us get in there so we can get out of this rain." He nodded and spurred the horse down off the hill toward the massive gates. The road outside was lined with statues of heroes; many were dwarves from ages past. Some were even elves and humans.

Stalls filled the spaces between them hawking their wares even in the pouring rain. The road split around the final statute just outside the main gate. The three generals from the Dragon War stared down at all those who wished to enter the city. Zyid stopped his horse, returning the stares of the three figures. "Is that statue everywhere? How is it so well maintained after all this time? It does not seem worn down like the others."

The rain ran down the Zyid's face as he contemplated his answers, letting out a deep breath a cloud of steam filling the air. "Well, it is maintained by the diligence of mages keeping it shielded from the elements. People are not as concerned with them as they once were. Kalgrin told me how people would leave things at the base of statues like this one. But it has been a very long time since the war after all, but people still will think back to the times when the people from all races and walks of life came together in the name of freedom for themselves and their descendants." He spurred his horse on again. "Let us hope they can be stirred to such action again. Come along now, we have much to do and little time in which to do it." They joined the line of people working their way into the city. The line moved slowly, the guards moving from cart to cart, person to person, ensuring all was correct levying the taxes, tithes, and bribes that were part of doing business in the dwarven lands. After several hours, they finally arrived under the awning of the gaping maw that was the entrance to Kalmontallin. The guard waved them forward.

"What is your business here today, lad?" His voice was gruff and tired; he was probably nearing the end of his shift. Zyid lowered the hood of his cloak laughing.

"Come now, Thalon, is that a way you greet a friend of your friends? How is the wife and those children of yours? I come here once, and Kalgrin will never cease talking about it." The dwarf tilted his head slightly to the side as if he was not quite sure he had heard the words quite right. A smile slowly crept onto his face as he recognized who he was speaking to.

"By the gods, Zyid, did not recognize you without the old man and his sad little mule. Boy, have you grown since the last time you visited here. How long as it been now?" They both laughed as Kasala looked between the two of them with a slightly confused look on her face. "Why the children and the wife are doing fine. She has them running through the streets hawking her newest creations. She is still quite a skilled smith. Still not sure to this day how I convinced her to marry me!" Laughter drifted down from the ramparts as the other guards laughed. He stepped closer as he spoke barely audible over the crowd. "So I must ask why you are here and he is not. Is Kalgrin not well?"

Zyid waved away the concern. "No, no, Thalon, I am merely here on business of my own." Reaching into his saddlebag, he removed the wrapped-up documents and ingot. "I believe this will explain it." Thalon took the folded parchment and scanned it thoroughly. "I had wanted to bring it to her anyway. Kalgrin holds her in high regard."

Upon finishing, he folded them carefully and handed them back. Zyid gently placed the ingot into his hands. "For you, my friend, if I could please bother your poor wife to check it for me. I am sure she will love it."

He turned it over in his hands before slipping it into a pouch on his belt. "Worried it may not be what you think it is, or just looking to spread a little gossip?" he said with a chuckle.

Zyid shrugged. "I have no idea what you could possibly mean by that. Shall we meet up after your shift for a nice tankard of ale at Kalgrin's favorite place?"

"I believe that would be grand. Until later then." Thalon quickly inspected the rest of their meager belongings and waved them through.

"Do you know everyone wherever we go, or is that just my imagination?" Kasala had moved closer to him and spoke in as low a voice as was possible in the bustling crowd. Zyid laughed heartily again

"While it would be nice to know everyone, I just learned or more so had it drilled into me that you make friends wherever and whenever you can it will only help you in the long run. Kalgrin was very insistent about that growing up."

They both fell silent for a time, as they rode slowly down the main road observing all the people hustling through their day.

Guards patrolled through the streets, eyes scanning for trouble in the crowds. The high ceilings allowing natural light in through intricate channels and vents through the mountain. Soon they arrived outside a large bustling tavern. Zyid dismounted, handing his reins to the groom and giving the young dwarf a few silver. "Make sure she is well tended to now." The boy nodded and waited patiently for Kasala to follow suit. She did so she had been nearly struck dumb by the number of people and all the many items for sale. "So what do we do now?"

"We do as we did before we go into the inn and hand in our weapons. You cannot carry them freely inside the city. It is common practice in almost every city across the land. You are not a fast learner, are you?" She glared at him fiercely. "Also, we need to arrange for our rooms and then we can begin our work in earnest though I am exhausted from our hard traveling, so we should take today and rest and begin in the morning sadly. So let us rest from our hard travels with a warm fire and hot food."

They walked up worn stone steps and through a large wooden doorway, faded engravings covering its entire surface. The tavern was near full to bursting with people of all sorts, dozens of tables, and hundreds of people of all kinds were sitting and drinking and smoking; a game of dice was being played as the smell of bread and ale floated through the air. Barmaids shuffled through the crowds with the many orders. They squeezed and muscled their way through the crowd to the bar. The man behind the counter took their weapons and laid out the prices with a quickness of tongue from years of practiced repetition. The man nodded his thanks, dunking two tankards into a partially opened cask and set them upon the counter. Zyid nodded his thanks and set off for an open table near one of the fires, setting down their drinks on the table. Kasala took a few small tentative sips. She smacked her lips then smiled and took down a huge gulp of the room temperature liquid.

"So we are here now. What do we do?" She had finished her tankard as their food arrived. She handed her tankards off to the poor lady, and she shuffled off to have it filled, a tired smile on her face.

Zyid slowly sipped from his drink, watching her as she cast her gaze across the room. He smiled at her look of wonderment.

"We just bide our time and rest like I said. Thalon will be here anytime now to join us and then we can have proper company after our long days in the rain." Their barmaid returned with Kasala's tankard full to the rim. She gingerly set it down, managing to not spill a drop. She smiled to herself and was gone just as quickly as she had appeared. They sat in silence for some time. Kasala rolled a pair of dice she acquired from one of the other patrons.

Thalon arrived as the streets began to dim and the streetlights ignited, his wife unsurprisingly in tow. They sat down quickly, ordering themselves food and ale. Thalon's wife was stone-faced, but her eyes betrayed her excitement.

Zyid stood. "Ah, Thalon my friend, you made it. I am most grateful that not only you have come but your lovely wife as well. A pleasure to see you again after all these years, Bellenta." She politely inclined her head as they all sat down, and silence settled over the table for a short while as drinks arrived, and they all slowly sipped from them. Zyid peered down into his tankard after he took a sip. "What did you all order? This is far too nice for the two of us to be drinking."

Thalon chuckled. "It is elven wine. Bell insisted we treat you." He nodded at Bellenta who returned his nod and deftly took the ingot from her blouse pocket and gently set it on the table. A house seal had been perfectly stamped into it.

"You are aware what this is, yes." Her voice was hushed and firm. Zyid nodded. "I am not surprised that you do. Why else would you be here with it? So what is it you are after? The tiny amount you have brought with you surely was not worth all the effort to bring it here." She smiled as she reached across the table to grab Zyid's cheek. "What is going on in that little head of yours? What has that old fool put you up to now?"

Zyid smiled. "Kalgrin did not put me up to anything. Actually, this is all our own venture." He indicated toward Kasala. "So is the metal to your liking then?" She nodded but motioned for him to continue. "I have come here to arrange for the services of guards for my mining venture." He let it hang in the air, but no one made any motion to speak so he continued. "As you have seen, I am in possession of one of the rarest metals in this entire world. With that, I am in the process of setting up to mine this ore for my own profit, but I find myself unable to source sufficient people to both operate the mine and give it adequate protection from the numerous brigands that infest my home lands."

Bellenta nodded while taking another sip of her wine. "I see, still have your heads in the clouds I see. You love that little town of yours, huh." She snickered to herself. "It was all you ever talked about when you were here as a little boy. Surrounded by all these new things." She shook her head again. "With this, I could make weapons and armor fit for kings. You let me have some of it so that word would spread, drum up interest, and have miners clamoring to be hired to work on it." She stopped to lower her voice to a whisper. "Even if the vein is small, it will be incredibly profitable. Add to that, it has never been found not surrounded by many other metals and even gems." A beaming grin crossed her face. "I will take this to my father, and we will see where it goes from there since that is what I assume you are really after. I would be insulted if it were anyone other than you, but Kalgrin has always had faith in you. That and it will not hurt my family to have some of this ore." They all smiled and drank the night away.

*****

Zyid awoke with a start. He wiped sweat from his brow and tried to sit up but found a sleeping Kasala draped across him, drool oozing from the corner of her mouth. He attempted to gently move her and was met with groans and mumbled threats. He finally got out from under her grasp, dressed, and went downstairs and sat down at the bar. The man from the night before was just opening and cleaning the bar one last time for the morning customers he scanned over.

Zyid chuckled while saying, "You are awake, good sir. I am quite surprised. You and your friends drank quite late and a fair amount between the four of you." Zyid nodded slightly as the bartender set

61

a large flask of water down in front of him with another laugh. "You helped sell a lot of ale last night with the ruckus you were raising. I am thankful, but you may not want to drink so much next time. Dwarven drinks are much stronger than the drinks you are probably used to." He walked away as Zyid nursed his water before returning to his room, sitting on Kasala's bed—looking at her sleeping form. Her long red hair was certainly eye-catching. She would have been a tall woman by human standards. A little over six feet tall with dark amber eyes. Zyid mumbled to himself. "It is a wonder she has not looked for a mate." A dragon mating with other races had once been almost common in centuries past but had fallen out of favor after the war. But many people still claimed dragon bloodlines and more than a few noble lines used that to leverage power in the court. His thoughts were interrupted as she finally stirred from her slumber. She sat up, flipping her hair off her face and rubbing the sleep from her eyes. She slowly surveyed the room with a slight look of confusion on her face. She stopped at Zyid and tilted her head like a dog, shrugged, and plopped back down onto the bed, burying her head under the pillow.

Zyid sat forward, resting his chin on his hands. "Kasala, if you could please sleep only in your bed, I would very much appreciate it."

She wiggled farther under the blanket. "But yours was so warm. How can I not crawl into it?" she mumbled from under the covers.

Zyid heaved himself up and headed for the door. "Well, if you get up, you can come enjoy a good hearty breakfast the best cure for a hangover of dwarven drinks but"—he slapped her leg—"if that is not enough to get you up, perhaps we can go look at the market for a few items." The inn was getting busy again. People were finishing their night labor and getting a drink before heading home and those getting ready to start the day with a nice heavy meal. He sat down at the bar, waiting patiently for the bartender to come over and take his order.

"Quite the night you had, Zyid. Never heard of you laughing and smiling so much." Zyid looked up as a fresh loaf of bread and a mug of milk were placed in front of him.

"So I am not allowed to have any fun, Brenda?"

She was shaking her head as she started washing some glasses. Her black hair swayed slightly as she moved revealing her lovely face. "That is not what I said. Once again putting words in my mouth, are we?" Zyid snickered before taking a swig of his drink. "Father just told me you were having a good time last night, and I thought that it was unusual that you made a ruckus. You were so reserved when you came with Kalgrin. Must be nice to see you smile every once and a while."

Zyid spoke around the bread in his mouth. "From what I remember, you also spent the time I was here ignoring me thinking I was very weird."

She blushed and turned back to the dishes. "I was not. You always had your nose in a book is all." She stopped cleaning. "It's just you always looked so...How do I put it? Sad really is not the word, more like distant but that really does not do it justice."

"I appreciate the thought, Brenda, but I am fine. Trust me."

"If you say so, not like I will get a better answer out of you." Zyid shook his head. "I thought my father said you had a woman with you. Who is she?"

Zyid answered with another mouthful of bread. "Business partner. She and I are going into the mining business. Should be fun and profitable." He gave a shrug. "Hopefully anyway. Should have some meetings today. Got to go shopping once she drags herself out of her drunken stupor. She is not used to dwarven drinks yet."

They both laughed. "They do take some getting used to. Lots of people lose bets that way. Though you seem to have an inhuman tolerance?"

He shrugged. "Just lucky I suppose." She smiled and went back to her work.

Kasala, after a time, plopped herself in the chair next to Zyid, setting her head on the bar top. "My head is still pounding. How did you drink so much and not be hungover?"

"Like I just told Brenda, I am just lucky, my friend. Dwarven ale is quite potent for those not used to it. But anyway, we need to go to the market for some new attire for our meetings." Zyid drained his mug as he rose from his seat.

Her eyes lit up. "So you are finally going to buy some nice things?"

"Only so we make a good impression on my business associate. For we are asking for a lot of things on the promise we will make a large profit, though with what we are offering, it would be hard not to make money. But come along, let us go, and please try and behave while we are in the market. We do not wish to draw too much attention. Keep our spots warm for us, Brenda."

"No promises. You two hurry back and I will try and have a warm mug for you when you get back." Zyid waved as they walked out the door.

"You should try and steal him if you want him, Brenda!" a patron shouted. The tavern erupted in laughter.

"That is not any of your business, and I would appreciate it if you would stay out of my personal matters. Besides, I hardly know him anyway."

"Do not let that stop you, lovely," another chimed in. The uproar continued as she went into the back.

Kasala scanned back and forth, analyzing every store and stall they passed. Running from shop to shop, her hangover seemingly lost to her excitement at all the vendors hawking their wares. Zyid walked slowly behind her as she jumped from person to person, inspecting everything she laid her eyes on. They came to an intersection where Zyid stopped and motioned for her to follow him into the shop on the corner. The building was large with a high ceiling, carved out of the rock walls like the other main building in the city. Its bright green paint making it stand out in the long row. "So this is the place we are looking to buy from then?"

Zyid nodded. "Indeed. It is Matilda's place. Bell said this is where we should go for what we need for our meetings with her father."

"I sorta remember hearing something about that." She nursed her head, suddenly remembering her hangover. They marched through the door. "Please do not let me drink that much ever again please."

Zyid laughed and walked past her looking for the proprietor. "Look around, but please do not cause anyone any trouble. We are just here for some clothes and then we need to get a gift, so please do not cause any trouble."

Kasala sighed and stalked off farther into the store, lost from sight behind overflowing racks and displays, as Zyid went toward the front counter. "Hello! Is there anyone here?" Pushing past an overflowing row, he arrived before a low set counter with one small section in the middle set at a roughly human height.

Behind it sat a dwarven lady, her hair in long gray-white braids. A pipe rested between her pursed lips, narrow brown eyes seeming to take him all in at a glance, nodding slightly to herself before taking a long draw of her pipe. Zyid leaned down on the counter meeting her at eye level. "Matilda?" She did not answer and was instead motioning for him to spin around. "Okay? So I guess that is a maybe then." He laughed but her expression did not change. She wrote with her other finger seemingly making notes in the air satisfied. She slowly stood up grabbing a cane that had been leaning behind the counter and slowly walked around, tugging him gently by the sleeve and leading him to a changing booth nearly shoving him into it. "Now what, damn well shoved me in here. Am I going to get an explanation or a word out of you, or am I just supposed to?"

She cut him off harshly with a soft tone. "If you would use your eyes, you would see there is already an outfit for you to try on, is there not?" A cloud of smoke snaked its way over the curtain. "Now hurry up and change, and we shall see how much more needs to be done to it."

"Oh, so you can talk. Are you always this chatty with your customers?"

"Only the annoying little brats who cannot seem to figure out how to change their own clothes quickly and quietly. Come, come let us see how they fit."

He stepped out looking himself over. "How did you get these measurements so spot on? I never ordered anything. I thought I would just be pulling something off the shelf."

She motioned for him to spin around again. "Bellenta gave me your measurements on her way home last night, and one of my seamstresses worked on it through the night. Her eyes are very keen after all, an armorer's vision must be very precise for high-quality work." She nodded her satisfaction with the work. "She was spot on it seems. A few minor alterations, and it will be ready for you to wear to your important meeting." Kasala's laugh came quietly from between the rows as she walked toward them and gave him a good look over.

"So you can clean up nice." He shrugged. "Maybe now I can see what some of your admirers see in you, maybe."

"I never will, but I suppose I will take your backhanded compliment in good faith." She curtsied.

"Why, thank you, dear sir. I would be nothing without your fine compliments and gentle words." He waved her off.

"Whatever suits you, but the dress does look quite nice on you." She smiled and spun around, her hair and the dress flowing out like waves on the shore.

"Did I take your breath away? Hmmm?"

The old lady had a harsh cough. "If you two are quite finished, we have more work to do, so go get changed and come back tomorrow, and they will be tailored and cleaned."

Zyid bowed. "Thank you for all of the work you do." She nodded and shooed them out of the door.

They exited back out into the now bustling midday crowd. "So what else do we require for this meeting of ours?

"We require a gift to present to our host, a fine wine would be a good choice since Bellenta told us her father loves the stuff. A solid gift will help with our talks."

"Do you really think that is going to work?"

He stroked his beard as they started to stroll down the street. "To be honest, I am not entirely sure. If it does not work, I do not really have a backup plan. Not a lot of other things we can do. Could just hope more people would flock to it looking for work, but that would be quite a dice roll." He stopped to scan the streets. "I have high hopes for this so let us focus on it and worry about what to do after that." She sighed and nodded.

They walked for a time before finding a wine merchant, finding a few bottles to purchase, and headed back toward the inn. "Shall we go and enjoy a good meal and drink? It's been a rather fun day. Did you enjoy our walk through the town?" Her beaming grin answered the question for him. "I will take that as a yes then." She nodded furiously.

*****

Emma stood on the back steps of the guard headquarters surveying her men training in the yard. A couple new additions were being put through drills to gauge their skill. The sun was just peeking over the tops of the great forest trees. "I see you are adding more guards every day it seems." She gave a sideways glance at the mayor, giving him a nod.

"Not quite every day, but as many and as often as I can afford to add." She leaned forward onto the railing. "It has only been a short time, and yet more people are moving back to this place. So we will need more men to keep the peace. Amazing what a couple weeks of moving metal will do I guess." She sighed. "I need to sock it to Zyid when he finally drags his ass back here. He has made my job so much harder."

The mayor laughed. "You are enjoying every second of this, and do not try and tell me otherwise. Your father is certainly very proud of you both. You are a fine captain and will lead these men well for many years to come. But just as you have more work, so do I sadly. This place is getting more lively by the day. I may yet live to see this place thrive." With that, he turned, shuffling back inside.

Emma started moving between the lines of guards, adjusting stances and giving some encouragement to her people.

"Captain Emma!" She turned to see a mounted patrol ride through the small gate.

"Ah, Sergeant Terence, good to see you have returned. Anything to report?" He dismounted as he spoke.

"Nothing at all, ma'am, quiet on the roads. We escorted them all the way there and back with no trouble. The mounted patrols are having a greater effect on them, and they might have moved on to easier picking."

Emma rubbed her chin. "Very good, Sergeant. Write up your report and get the men some rest after they have tended to their equipment." He saluted and went back to direct his men. *Finally*, she thought, shielding her eyes from the sun, *some good news*.

"Miss Emma! Miss Emma!"

Emma turned to see a young boy running toward her with a small parchment in his hands. He skidded to a halt at her feet, holding out the message. She took it, and before she had even opened it, he was gone again running to his next delivery. She laughed and read the message.

"So Worstan wishes to have a drink with me to thank me for all our hard work." She folded the missive, shoving it under her belt. "I hate having to play politics. Now I know why my father despised these things." Emma walked toward the Trolls Heads, smiling lightly to herself over how it seemed near full to bursting with patrons. Many a miner drinking his pay away and trying to woo the poor barmaids with their drunken exploits. Over all the bustle, she could faintly pick out Arlana's beautiful voice from her place behind the bar. Worstan was sitting near her at the bar seemingly lost in the beauty before his eyes. Emma quietly took the seat next to him. "I see even an old man like yourself cannot help but be entranced by her beauty?"

He slowly turned his head toward her, his eyes grew wide, and he nearly fell from his chair when he finally saw her. He straightened himself in his chair and cleared his throat. "I am quite sorry, dear, but it is quite easy to be swept away by such a beautiful voice. You are quite lovely in your own way you know." She snickered and both took a drink. "The lovely guard captain must have to beat the men off with a good strong stick." He laughed at his joke. "Or not I suppose, they probably are more afraid of you than anything." She slumped her head down on the bar.

"If you only knew the half of it, old man." He just laughed and drank his ale.

"I am sure that there are some who would like a strong beauty like you."

"Flattery will get you nowhere, old man." He just shrugged. "So why did you wish to buy me drinks? Do not tell me you are trying to woo me."

"While that would certainly appeal to a younger me, I am too old for that kind of thing, dear Captain. I was once a young impulsive miner just like most of them." He swept the room for emphasis. "But no, it was honestly to thank you and your men for doing such a fine job in keeping our shipments safe. This mine seems more profitable than we had hoped. Our backers will be very happy with our progress. Once Zyid returns, he will be quite happy to hear of it, but truly thanks be to you and all your men for the fine work that you do. To you, my dear, toast!" They raised their tankards and drained them.

"Thank you for the drink, sir, but now I must be off."

Arlana stopped singing and took their empty tankards. "Emma dear, that is exactly why the men avoid you. All business and no pleasure." Arlana had set down two fresh drinks. "Now sit, enjoy the food, drink, and be merry. Be a person. Even your father took breaks from work. People smiled with him, laughed with him, you must learn that or else morale will suffer, dear."

She slumped back into her chair. "Fine, I will stay then. Where is Kalgrin by the way?" She peered behind Arlana. "It is strange to not see him."

Arlana smiled, hooking her thumb toward the back. "He is out feeding his new dogs. He had to have some after seeing the one Zyid had with him." They both laughed.

"That does seem very much like him. Though he does not seem to be a man who enjoys all the work pets are."

"Oh, no, he has always loved animals for as long as I have known him. Though many animals are afraid of him since he is a mage. Many creatures can smell it on him and will go out of their way to avoid him. But he went out and bought a whole litter it seems." She laughed as she spoke. "He pulled up with the cart, and no sooner did he jump down did more than ten puppies come tumbling out after

69

him, with him trying to give me a look like he had no idea where they had come from. Quite funny really."

"You know I think I am starting to see why Zyid likes this place so much." Worstan gave a distant smile.

"And why is that, old man?" Emma asked with a point of her tankard.

"People care here. They help one another, going and helping the neighbors that kind of thing. It is no wonder he would like to see less suffering."

"Yes, I do believe you are right, sir. Now please enjoy your time here in my fine establishment." Arlana turned to walk away but Worstan stopped her.

"I will indeed, but I have noticed on your sign out front that your *S* is of much fresher paint than the rest, why is that?" Arlana and Emma both laughed. "Why is it so funny?"

Emma answered, still working through her laughter. "Well, this inn is called the Trolls Heads tavern but that has not always been so. When Zyid returned, he brought a freshly hewn troll head with him as a present as he put it, so Kalgrin cleaned it and hung it over the mantle." She indicated with her mug. "And so someone added two *S*s and the Troll Head tavern became the Trolls Heads tavern."

"He killed a troll?" He sat, mouth wide for a moment before speaking again. "That is incredible. He should be a mercenary captain with skill like that."

Emma chuckled. "That would suit him, but he has other ambitions I think than that." They nodded among themselves.

"Now back to drinking you two." Arlana waved at them as she walked down the bar.

CHAPTER 7

"THE OFFER BEFORE ME IS VERY INTERESTING. I would love to offer aid to expand both of our enterprises." He took a deep breath before continuing. "But I simply cannot." Bellenta's father sat behind a massive stone desk slowly shuffling through the parchment Zyid had handed him. He adjusted his spectacles before continuing. "We are currently experiencing a spider infestation within one of our major mines. To ensure they do not spread, I have been forced to send all the men that I have to keep them at bay."

Bellenta burst through the door, startling everyone "Father! Our positions are being overrun," she blurted out as she caught her breath. "I have already sent everyone we can down to the mines, but they may not be enough." If he was worried, it did not show on his face. He stood to go lean out the window behind his desk.

"Have any of the smiths who are willing to fight go as well." Bellenta nodded and hurried from the room "My apologies, Zyid, but it seems we will have to finish our talks later."

Zyid shook his head, slamming his hands down on the desk. "I will go and help you handle this spider problem for you. That should free up some men, will it not?" Zyid licked his lips. "Kasala, let us go."

"I cannot let you go running off into danger like this! Letting uninvolved parties get hurt is unthinkable." He slammed his hand on his desk.

Zyid cut him short "We are going to help whether you agree or not." They turned to leave. "If they get out, this will soon be every-one's problem. Come on, Kasala, we need to go get our weapons." They both turned and left running after Bellenta. "Why did you not tell me about this, Bell?" She cut him off.

"I did not want you to get involved in our matters is all. I had also hoped it would be solved quickly. It seems I was wrong."

"Could you two please stop this and just tell us where we need to go."

They slid to a stop before a large weapons store. "You two take what you need and go. You are much faster than we will be. Go on ahead and do what you can, at least drive them back." They moved through grabbing as they went, stopping at the door to give them-selves a once-over.

"A two-handed hammer, Kasala? Will that be enough for you?" She huffed at him.

"This from the man who cannot function without two swords. What kind of fool fights with a weapon in each hand? And a poleax, what good will that do against giant spiders?" He shrugged.

"I liked the way it looked is all. It has such fine etching I could not help but pick it up. Now come on, let us go. We have work to do." They nodded to each other and burst out into the streets. "We need to quickly get my swords. I have a feeling I might need them."

"Do we really have time for that?"

"Fortunately, the inn is on our way, so it will not take too much time." They rushed through the crowds dodging and weaving until nearly crashing through the inn's doorway. The gathered patrons stopped their conversations and gazed on the new arrivals. "Brenda! I need my swords now."

Her head poked over the crowd at the bar. "What in the heav-ens is this all about?"

Zyid shoved his way to the counter. "No time. I need them to go help in the mines." He set the poleax, leaning on the bar. "Please

I will explain it all later. I must have them. There are lives at stake here."

She hesitated for a moment before sighing and quickly retrieving them. "Here."

Zyid roughly snatched them as they came in reach. "Thank you, dear. I will tell you all the details later." He quickly strapped them on, grabbed the ax, and bolted out the door. Looks of confusion and worry spread across the crowd's faces.

"So what is the plan now, genius?" she yelled from behind him. She could hear the smile in his laugh.

"Same plan as it always should be. Kill all of the spiders, push them back to their main lair, kill the queen, and put an end to them forever. Save whoever we can along the way, but really it is about killing all of these damn spiders so we can accomplish our goals."

"Always a businessman, I see." They rounded the corner, running past as a guard stammeringly tried to stop them.

"Yes and no. I care for people and I will save everyone that I can, but the real objective is the queen. Kill her and we win. If we do not, she will breed more spiders and we will be worse off. Hurry, we are getting close. I hear fighting up ahead." Putting on a burst of speed, they came into a large barracks, broken barrels, and beds cluttered the floor around the feet of men, dwarves, and elves fighting for their lives. Thalon resolutely spurred his men on.

"Fight, men. Help is on the way! We have to hold them or they will reach our homes. We must fight! Fight to the last man! Fight!" Wading into the fray, dancers of death. The pair slashed, stabbed, and smashed their way through the room. What had seemed like an eternity had been mere moments and then as one fell near silent after the roar of battle had stopped. The pair stood over Thalon, spider blood and guts covering their clothes. Thalon, whose eyes were wide with shock and awe, dropped to the floor as his adrenaline left him. "By the gods, you two are amazing! Or monsters, I am not sure which!" Others in the room nodded weakly from their positions on the floor. Zyid tossed him the ax as he walked past and drew his two swords.

"Good work all. We are going in farther to finish this. Rest here. Bell is on her way with more help."

"What are you two going to do?" Thalon weakly asked as he regained his feet.

Zyid smiled. "Why, finish what these poor creatures started and kill their queen. If we find anyone else, we will try and help them as well but—" Thalon held up his hand to stop him.

"We know, just go. We will be along shortly." They nodded and continued on.

"How are they so powerful, sir?" One of the men asked.

Thalon shrugged and shook his head. "I have no idea, lad. I have never seen him fight before, but I hope those two can kill it. We may be doomed if they do not. But we have to go after them once we rest up some. Cannot be said we sat and let them protect our homes for us." A few weak laughs and nods came in response.

"Did you bring that just to give to him?"

"I figured his weapon would be broken, so I thought ahead. Bellenta made it so it will bolster his spirits. Morale is very important after all. There are fewer in the tunnels than I thought there would be. It would be likely they will ambush us in the next large chamber."

"That would be their best plan so they can use the numbers to their advantage."

"That would be my assessment as well. I see more light ahead. We seem to be reaching the mine face." The tunnel emptied into an enormous chamber. The walls and floor seemed to be moving from all the spiders crawling around. "They are on the far wall and see that hole we need to get through that to reach their lair."

Kasala smiled. "Right now, let us get going. A dragon will not be stopped by these pests." Her roar shook the ground, causing several spiders to fall to the floor with sickening crunches. Fully alerted, the spiders seemed to screech in unison and came climbing and skittering over one another for a chance to strike at fresh prey. The two stepped into the fray, a whirlwind around them. Blood and spider limbs soon littered the ground. No matter how many fell, more came; two killed, four replaced it. They soon were trapped in the center surrounded by a seemingly endless horde of the creatures.

"Seems we may have bitten off more than we could handle," she said through gritted teeth.

"If we had Kalgrin here, he could just burn them all. Hopefully, our friends will bring some mages and a lot of help so we can get to the lair because it is not that we cannot kill them in droves. We just may be overwhelmed at some point." He smiled at her. "We are not invincible after all. Even dragons have their limits."

She paused and tilted her head to the side. "I believe I hear footsteps. I think our friends will arrive soon. Also, did it get colder in here?" As she finished, a cold wind tore through the room as a blast of ice shot out from the tunnel entrance they had come from. "Good to know my ears are still sharp," she said with a grin.

"So it would seem." The ice was followed with a great war cry as people poured into the chamber, smashing the frozen spiders with furious abandon. Seeing more and more pouring in as they renewed their slaughter. As quickly as it had begun, the spiders retreated back into their lair. Zyid and Kasala hurried after them down their hole. The others could be heard following a ways back.

"So how hard will this queen be to kill?" They cut their way through the thick webbing, stopping at a fork.

"I do not know but only one way to find out. Any idea which way we should go?" She sniffed the air and shrugged and shook her head.

"I cannot smell anything. I will go right, you go left." They nodded and went down their chosen path. It was dark and musty skeletons mingled with fresh kills. Miners that had just been doing their job, adventures seeking glory and treasure, now just web-covered corpses. Zyid cut through the web, killing spiders and destroying eggs as he went, bodychecking the last spider and following slowly behind its corpse into another huge chamber. The whole of it was covered in a layer of webbing, but no other spiders seemed to be in the room. "Come out. Beast, I know you are here!" He stood over his last combatant thrusting a sword through its squirming frame. His words echoed in the chamber. "Your children are dead! Your brood of spawn has been put to the sword. You are all that remains! Once I kill you, the city and its people will live in peace, and we will use you for trade items! What else could I ask for? Now face your doom!" His booming voice filled the room and was answered by silence. "Do you fear your end? You will not run from here, for this is your lair, creatures always defend it to the end. Now come let us end this monster!"

The creature landed heavily behind Zyid, kicking up a cloud of dust and pebbles. It charged at him, swinging its front legs at him wildly.

Zyid deflected her legs and leapt over the creature's attempted bite. It spun round, smashing him with its thorax and sending him tumbling across the chamber floor. He recovered his footing just as the spider screeched and charged again, lunging with its fang-filled maw. Zyid sidestepped the bite, cutting his blades across the queen's face. He continued right to her front leg, severing it near the base and causing it to howl in pain. As he continued running, the spider followed keeping pace in front of him. Not wishing to give her the initiative, he stopped and lunged at the creature. The world seemed to slow as he ran in parrying her thrust, dodging a bite, and slashing her face as he jumped onto her back, slashing large gashes into her carapace as he moved. He continued until she violently shook him off. Zyid slammed into the ground. Before he could regain his footing, she thrust a leg down toward his chest. He dropped his blades trying to stop it. The leg slid through his hands, puncturing his chest. His scream reverberated off the chamber walls as blood oozed from the puncture.

The creature turned to bring its fangs to bare. They stared face-to-face; she slowly lowered her fangs toward him as he struggled to remove the limb pinning him. "If I thought you could smile, you would be beaming ear to ear would you not, spider?" It hissed its reply.

Zyid smiled back, wrapping his hands around the pinning leg, roaring definitely. "If I cannot throw you off, I will just take your leg off! Ahhhh!" The spider hissed as its exoskeleton began to crush. The tip of the leg snapped off just as Kasala crashed into the spider, clawing and biting. The pair wrestled. Kasala grabbed the queen in her jaws, tossing her across the chamber into the opposite wall. She roared and released a torrent of her acid breath at the queen who climbed out of the way, and the pair leapt at each other renewing their furious struggle. Zyid got on his knees yanking the leg piece from his chest and tossing it aside, blood flowing freely from the wound. Breathing heavily, he scanned around for his swords, which were thrown around the chamber.

"Looking for these?" a familiar voice called. Zyid's swords were placed in front of him.

"Thank you, Thalon. I will be needing those." Zyid grabbed the handles, rolling them over in his hands to fix his grip. He winced and gritted his teeth. "Damn this hurts."

"That will be the least of your worries if you keep moving around like that. Stay put. Let the dragon deal with it. You are in no condition to fight anymore."

Zyid spit out a wad of blood. "I have been more injured than this before. Besides, I will stop bleeding at some point." Thalon grabbed his shoulder but he shook it off. Taking slow deliberate steps toward the struggling pair, he uttered, "Kadan," the word dripped out of his mouth barely a whisper but somehow filling the whole room.

The sword hilts began glowing a sickly green, and he slammed the hilts together forming a great double-bladed sword. He broke into a sprint. The pair had split again having bloodied one another. Zyid jumped between them, and the world seemed to slow for him as he brought his blades to bare in a great spinning whirlwind of destruction and blood, his blades passing through limbs and body as if they were wet paper. He continued up and over the creature's body cutting chunks from its body. Zyid landed heavily off of its back covered in blood and venom sizzling were it all met "Valtalen." The words came out very weak, but the swords fell apart clattering to the ground as he roughly fell to the ground with a wet smacking sound.

"Get him to the healers now!" Thalon bellowed. "He must be saved!"

*****

The sound of drumming fingers filled the room only making the tension more apparent. "Bellenta, please make your report."

"Yes, Father." She cleared her throat. "The mines and forges have both been more productive in the two weeks following the incident. Also, there have been no major spider sightings since that time. We have continued scouting and have found no new nesting or spawning grounds, just a few eggs and young spiders that have been dealt with. We should be able to expand the mining operation for some time before having to worry about incursions, but we have increased the number of guards just to be safe." She paused, allowing for him to nod and continued. "Sales are up since the incident as well. People are buying more arms and armor in light of the attack as some slight paranoia has overcome many, but that will in all likelihood pass quickly."

He clapped his hands. "So some good news for once, but most importantly, how is Zyid's recovery coming along? He needs to be back on his feet. People are starting to worry for him. They want a live hero, not a dead one after all."

"Never one to let a good event go to waste. It is no wonder your family business has prospered for so long." Zyid had slipped in quietly, quickly crossing the room to stand before the desk and took a deep stiff bow. "I must offer my thanks for the care you have given to me, and I apologize for all the trouble." Bellenta looked back and forth between the men, a worried look on her face. "Do not worry, Belle. He is just a shrewd businessman." The two men smiled at one another. "I would do the same thing in his place. As what he is doing is harmful to no one least of all myself, and we both gain from it really. You get a nice public relations boost, and of course public interest in your products, and I gain good standing. So how can I possibly complain?" Zyid smiled, chuckling to himself. "What I am more interested in seeing is how fast we were summoned to the king's court. His messenger left in quite the hurry after I awoke, and he delivered her message."

Zyid waved the folded parchment, handing it to Bellenta who quickly passed it to her father who read through it carefully several times and nodding as he read. "So tomorrow we will be presenting ourselves before the king and the entire high council."

Zyid nodded. "It will be very interesting. I wonder what he will present to us for our service."

*****

The next morning came cool. The streets were lined with throngs of people filling the streets. There were no empty spaces in any windows or doors. Many stood on any ledge wide enough to support themselves. The roaring cheers from the crowds shook the air. A pounding noise drowning out the pounding steps of the marching soldiers. Armored feet thundered on the roads polished weapons and shields reflected near blinding light, songs of past glory and victories were chanted. In the center of it all, Thalon, Bellenta, Kasala, and Zyid walked along waving to the adoring crowds. The messenger girl from before walked before them holding Zyid's swords before her on a pillow of fine fabric.

"So is this a normal thing? Or is this a special event?" Zyid was nearly yelling to be heard above the roar around him.

Thalon shook his head, shouting in return. "No, this is fairly abnormal, but it is a great victory to clear out so many creatures from the tunnels in the mountains, and killing the queen ends that nest for good so it is a great victory indeed!"

Zyid nodded. "That only makes me wonder what we are going to encounter in the halls of the king. Also odd you are so quiet Kasala."

"I have never seen so many people in one place in my life. There must be little work being done today." They all laughed, and she looked slightly mad. "Now what is so funny?"

"Ah, my little girl," Bellenta answered. "There is no work getting done for now until later when everyone will drink themselves into a stupor. Little will be done for the next day or so." She nodded knowingly

"Indeed, lady, you are correct. It has been some time since something of this magnitude has taken place." A loud blast of many horns cut off further conversation. They had arrived at the foot of a great staircase leading to the king's hall. The soldiers parted, filing into the gaps left by their fellows holding back a great crowd of the lesser nobility vying for positions as high up along the steps as possible.

The mage from the battle in the tunnels stood at the foot of the steps, gave a great bow to them, then spun on his heels and flowed up the steps. The group followed behind swiftly reaching the top of the stairs. A massive ornate doorway greeted them; it swung open slowly and deliberately at his slightest touch revealing a chamber filled with the high nobility lining the sides and the king's elite guards arrayed down the center of the room. As they stepped inside, the door slowly and silently shut, leaving the room in near perfect silence. Time seemed to have slowed as the king's eyes surveyed them all one by one from his throne at the far end of the room, a knowing expression on his face. After what felt like an eternity, the mage bowed as did the young girl.

"Sire, may I present to you those who fought so bravely to protect the citizens of your realms!" His voice filled the chamber. The king made the slightest of gestures with his head and in unison the girl and mage started toward the throne the rest following after. As they started down the aisle, the guards began to pound their weapons on the stone floor. They sang in near perfect unison as the group made their way down the aisle. Everyone beat their hands and feet to the beat of the song. At the foot of the throne, they stood for what felt like an eternity before the king slammed his scepter against the ground and the chamber fell completely silent.

He motioned and the girl came forward presenting the sword before him with bowed head. Standing, he gently took hold of one of the swords offered to him deftly flicking it from its scabbard. He swung it a few times as if testing it. After he cut the air once again, he took up the other and looked at the hilts as if expecting some sort of mechanism to be present to stick them together. Finding nothing obvious, he made a gesture and the scabbards were presented, and he carefully returned them to them.

With a room-filling voice, the king boomed. "In times of great need, there will always be those that rise to the events around them!" He let the words hang for a moment in the air before continuing. "Today we stand before those who when adversity came to them.

When they heard of people in trouble, they jumped at the chance. To find those of such character has always been sadly rare." He hung his head for emphasis. "Today, we stand in the presence of just those foolish few who run toward danger when logic dictates they should run. Courage such as this is truly rare and must be encouraged and rewarded whenever it is found, so as to those people who will so often doubt that there is still the love of others left in this cruel and unforgiving world. And to add to that, it has been many centuries since one of the dragon kin has entered our fair halls."

The smallest hushed murmur drifted through the room, and he let it stop before he continued. "But even more astounding is the presence of a mortal man who has taken the blood and lived through the ordeal." The excitement could not be contained though no words were spoken from the assembled crowd.

The king had come down from his throne as he spoke. He stopped before Zyid, his crown barely brushing against Zyid's chest. Having placed the swords delicately on an arming belt of the finest tooled leather, its designs woven in gold thread. He placed the belt around Zyid's waist, placing it perfectly with a practiced hand. He stepped back, nodding in satisfaction with the fit. "The first reward are these." Stepping up a few steps toward his throne, he spread his arms wide. "Secondly, I hereby decree that you and your dragon friend may be armed at all times within my realm. As you have proven to be friends of the people of this land. Though I suppose your friend is always armed as she is both beautiful and a dragon. And no one has ever found a way to disarm that!" A roaring laughter filled the room, and he slapped a knee at his own joke. He waited for laughter to die down before he continued. He motioned and an ax was placed into his waiting hands. "Normally, we would present you with this, but it seems as if you will not be needing it. What pray tell should we do with it now?"

He stroked his beard looking over the four standing before him. He stopped in front of Thalon as he raised a finger as if an idea struck him. "Since our first pair of guests do not require it, then the next most fitting hero should have it then." The king held the weapon out before him.

Thalon hesitated for a moment before he reached out with shaking hands to gently pluck it from the king. "My liege, I am not worthy of such honor. I merely did what any other would have done in my place."

The king waved away his words. "No, while that is always said, it is very often not true. You and your men could have fallen back." He nodded as he ascended up toward his throne, softly setting himself into it. "But you sent word and held your ground. That is the kind of courage we require. But more importantly than a fine weapon. You and your house will be from this day forth recognized as a noble house." A buzz of murmurs flew about the room. The king scanned the room as he waited for any replies.

Thalon and Bellenta both fell to their knees. "Sire, we are forever grateful for this generosity. We will strive to live up to the faith you have placed in us."

"Indeed, I look forward to the stories your house will create. It is a fair reward for so many lives saved. Now that leaves you two." The king's gaze settled on Kasala first. "What does one give a dragon for reward? What is it you would like in return for the services you have rendered to my realm?"

Kasala pondered for a moment deep in thought. Turning her head side to side and looking admiring the banners hung around the hall. "I would like to request a troop of soldiers for our service. My business partner and I are bringing a mine up to speed. The ore I am sure you have already seen. As you well know it is extremely valuable." She let the phrase hang in the air. "We will require a more significant contingent of guards in order to secure our mine and our shipments of minerals. Some of these materials of course will be coming here so you have a vested interest in ensuring the safety of those shipments."

The king ran a hand slowly through his beard, his expression was stony, betraying nothing of what he was thinking. The moment of silence lasted but a moment before he slowly spoke. "You speak with care and knowledge though not a request I would have ever guessed. You are correct in all of this, but I fear I will not be able to offer the amount of support you will truly need," again the silence settled. "But we will see what can be done as merchants always seem to have a few friends." he let it hang a moment as he slowly scanned the room. "When he most needs them if he is good to others."

Kasala gave a fine curtsy with poise and a flowing of motion. A beaming smile on her face. "As you say, my lord, we will continue our chat with our friends later then." He nodded as she stood upright in another graceful motion.

The king half smiled at some of the looks he saw in the crowd. He turned his gaze to Zyid. "So now we come to you. You who rallied our people, saved uncountable lives. Families wake today to find them still whole and strong for all who are still present. You have slain a beast that surely would have rampaged through our homes." He had paused and stood up, sweeping his hand across the gathered crowd. Several nodded in agreement. He inhaled deeply before continuing. "We owe you a debt that cannot be repaid with words. It will take a great effort. So! What is it you would request from not only me but all of us?" He again swept the room before setting his gaze upon Zyid as he resettled once again onto his throne.

Zyid chuckled softly at the small smirk on the king's face, hidden from the rest of the room. Then cleared his throat and bowed gently before speaking. "My lord, I am honored by your words. I am merely glad that I was able to help your people in a time of need. I am but a simple merchant." A few grumbles could be heard in the room. "And as a merchant, we desire one thing above all others. But only wish for the profit I earn through my own trade. But asking for a huge pile of gold or preference trading terms seems to me to be in very poor taste. But a small amount of gold would certainly be welcome."

The queen snickered before she burst out laughing. "A great warrior goes and kills a spider queen." She stifled her laughter before continuing. "And instead of asking for a kingdom, you merely ask for a pile of gold? If only more merchants such as you roamed the land things would be far more interesting." Zyid could not help but smile at her words.

"It would most certainly make trade wars far more interesting." She regained her composure after a few moments.

"But for a man like you, that request is far too simple." The king nodded agreement as she rested her head on one hand.

"I see why you would think that, my lady, but I would like money of course to invest in my ventures. But I would also like to request that work on the Grand Highway be continued." The king and queen both tilted their heads slightly in unison.

"Is that more along what you were thinking, my darling?" the king asked. She simply nodded and motioned for Zyid to continue.

"If the road is finished, it benefits us all. Faster, safer trade and I am certain you can all see the benefits of such an arrangement." They were both nodding.

The king and queen both stood. The king then firmly addressed the gathered crowd. "While we will discuss details at a later date, we will find an amicable amount worthy of your deed. Now it is time for us to drink, sing, and be merry. Let the wine flow, eat your fill. After all, those are the things that make life worth living." A great cheer went up and the people all filled into an adjacent chamber set out with many tables filled with food. No chairs had been provided, just long tables each with one kind of dish on each, forcing people to move about and mingle. Very dwarven in arrangement. Beer and spirits flowed and the room was soon a jumble of conversations and arguments.

CHAPTER 8

THE PAGE STOOD OUTSIDE THE TRAINING AREA watching as the warriors spared with one another. The princess was close to the center facing off against two of her dragon-blooded guards. They circled slowly swords at the ready. She stood in between wooded halberd at the ready. In a flash, she struck the one in front with several sweeping blows breaking his guard and throwing him flat on his back. The second had charged in to assist his partner only to have his weapon removed from his hands with a sweep of the pole upward followed with his legs flying out from under with a swift kick. They both raised hands of defeat and the page ran forward. "My lady, your father wishes to speak with you in the keep." The small boy beamed with confidence and enthusiasm. Bowing lightly but failing to hide his grin.

She chuckled lightly and smiled back. "You may go and tell him I will be along presently after I have freshened up a bit." The boy bowed again and was off like an arrow. "The young ones will make fine warriors when their time comes."

"That they will, lady. Shall we not keep your father waiting long?" The guard captain Syrus stated matter-of-factly as he leaned on the fence, "And you two keep up the fine work! You did well.

There is much potential in you two yet." They both bowed and once again squared up against each other again and resumed their training.

A short time later, she stood before her father, halberd in hand, shoulder-length black hair neatly combed. She wore a simple dress—light blue, well-made, but simply decorated. Her light-brown skin unblemished save for the white scar that ran across her chest and down into her dress. "You wished to speak with me, Father?" She bowed her head lightly as she spoke.

"Yes, my dear, I have a task for you." He spoke slowly, deeply. He sat on a very plain chair mirroring the room around him. Only a great torn banner adorned the walls. Hung with pride. He wore plain clothing but still radiated the authority of a great leader. His black skin marred with many scars earned in battles.

"What is it you wish of me, Father?" Her curiosity radiated from her.

He laughed at her slightly before continuing. "Yes, I am holding another competition soon, and I require him to be here for it."

Her curiosity faded, and now she just looked slightly puzzled. "Father, if he comes here, he will know what we are doing." She sounded worried and slightly panicked. "Will he not see the progress we have made? He could warn them." His raised hand cut her off. A broad smile crossed his face.

"My dear, I have already considered all of those things. And him seeing my daughter is entirely the point. Those people have grown soft. And divided, they present no challenge to us in their current state. My warriors must be challenged in the fire of war. Not made to slaughter children playing at war. So go and tell him to come when the harvest is done. You need not remain there until he leaves. He will certainly come no matter." He waved his hand absently. "He knows of our plans already, my dear. That is why he left after all." A broad smile crossed his face as he set his head on a hand. "Remember, my daughter, he is still the champion. Afford him all that he has earned my daughter."

She nodded. "Yes, Father, I will do as you ask. When should I make ready to leave?"

"You should leave fairly soon. Take a few men with you as your guard, and I will have his official summons drawn up for when you leave. I imagine you will find his home very interesting. Be sure to cause no trouble while you are there. You are a princess and should act according to our customs and the laws of the land."

She knelt quickly. "Of course, Father! I would never shame you in any way."

He smiled. "I know, my daughter. But I am a father who worries just like all others."

She smiled. "If you say so." She turned to leave but stopped and turned her head to ask. "Father, where is Mother?"

"Oh yes, she is patrolling the border. She mentioned sensing something in the wind before taking off."

She nodded and stepped out into the open courtyard. She took a deep breath and slowly exhaled. "I wonder how he has been since he left?" she mused quietly as she moved off to make her preparations.

*****

"You mean to ask me for an army!" the king huffed as his mug hit the table with a resounding thud. His face was ruddy with the effect of ale. The attendants had brought more and those gathered around the table took them with gusto. Zyid sat at the opposite end downed his drink, slamming it down hard enough to break the handle free. He looked at it sideways for a second then tossed it away to the crowd's cheering.

"If I thought you would give it to me, then yes I would certainly have." He hiccupped, grabbing another mug from the table. "War is coming!" The room was silent for a short instant as all who heard stopped. "But why believe me? I have no proof. You cannot see what I have seen. So for now I ask for men to care for my mine and shipments. As payment for services rendered." He gulped the ale down again. "That and if I could convince anyone to finish the highway to my home that would certainly be a nice addition as well." They all laughed and drank more ale. "Sure would make it easier to get this ale back home!" A hearty cheer came from the assembled crowd.

The king took a large gulp of ale before speaking again. "All that notwithstanding, you have a dragon as a companion." He stammered out his words slightly slurred. "She is an army unto herself. What could stand against you two at this point? Speaking of her, where did she end up?" The king shielded his eyes as he scanned the room. One of the other nobles pointed weakly at a crowd. They followed his finger to the group in question.

"I believe she is arm wrestling any takers. She appears to be quite drunk indeed."

Zyid shook his head. "She has what, two? Three?" He shook his head again and hooked a drunken thumb at them. "She could not fight an army, she cannot fight off two ales." The group laughed once again. "But to be perfectly honest, I cannot stop them on my own. I can only ask that you keep an open eye. I will bring you proof some-how." He stood up raising his mug high shouting above the crowd. "But for now we drink and tell tales of glories won and friends lost!" He downed the mug to the roar of the crowd.

*****

Zyid winced as he awoke with the sun glaring at his face, head pounding from the previous night. He had fallen asleep on the top of a broken table, his swords embedded into it. He stood with a slight wobble throwing off the blanket that had been placed on him. He blinked several times as he freed his blades from the table top. As he slowly began picking his way across the room, stepping over other guests, as he moved toward the smell of breakfast at the other side of the room. The king and queen were sitting at a table in the corner eating their morning meal. Zyid knelt before the king. "Sire, I must apologize for my—"

The king waved away his sentence without a glance. "No need. Was a hell of a celebration, was it not?" He laughed. The queen was smiling but shaking her head. "Though perhaps next time, just try not to break too many more tables." He looked over at the small pile Zyid had been asleep on. "If we keep it up we will have an all-out craftsman war on our hands." He mused running a hand through his beard. "Though that might be a good thing, come to think of it?" He shrugged looking back at Zyid. "Also nice wrestling match. You put on a hell of a show. And may have bruised a few prides. Now stand up, find a chair, and eat your fill. We have more to discuss."

Zyid stood and nodded as he went in search of a chair with all its legs still attached. Weaving his way again through the crowd of mostly unconscious guests, he found one at length in a far corner. Only a few stumbles, scabbard whacks slowed his return. With that, he gingerly placed it, and no sooner and he sat that the area in front of him was filled with plates and cups. A fork had as if by magic been put in his hand.

"Well, are you going to eat it, or just sit there gawking at it?" Zyid's stomach answered for him with a loud grumble. The king laughed and continued his meal. With that, he began to eat.

"Where is Kasala anyway?" Zyid scanned the room while chewing on some pork.

The queen laughed and answered. "She seems to have had far too much of a good time, got sick all over a poor steward." She chuckled again. "Poor boy is still trying to wash it all off. The stench." She waved her hands in front of her nose for emphasis. "We took her upstairs. She will probably be asleep for quite a while."

Zyid had placed his head in his hands. "Well, that sure puts a damper on the mood of this celebration, does it not?" They both laughed and waved their hands across the mostly passed out gathering.

The king stood and walked down the table, running his hand gently along it. "My boy, this is how these things always go. Yesterday, they drank themselves stupid remembering all that could have been lost and those things that we did. Laughs were had, tears shed, and the stirring of questions asked." He stopped and took a deep breath. "Today, they will sit and debate. Talk of many things, what they have gained, what they stand to lose. You do not know my people well. But that is normal. It is hard to truly know people you do not live with day to day. But you have set many ideas into motion and the next weeks will see much debate on the council floor. You set many wheels into motion as we all do." He stopped again. "But this one event will shape the course of this city for some time." He nodded to himself. "Now let us finish our food, and we will hammer out the final details for what I can provide for you. Hopefully, some of the other noble houses will feel inclined to provide some troops as well." He moved back to his seat taking hold of a tankard, taking a slow swig from it. He held up a finger as if remembering something. "Before you leave, I would request that the two of you appear before the council in its chambers to drive home your point and to hear their lip service and all that. Politics—never easy or fun." He heaved another heavy sigh. "But one we all must suffer with for the good of many more."

The queen was smiling and gently laughed. "Not like you would have it any other way." He simply nodded.

Zyid stood and bowing deeply. "We shall do as you have asked and speak with them before we leave." They all nodded and continued with their meals.

CHAPTER 9

E MMA HAD ARRIVED AT THE MINE TO find it bustling with work. A palisade had been erected, slapped together buildings of all kinds lined the inside of the wall. People moved to and fro such she could make little sense of it as she and her men rode slowly through the mass.

Near the mine entrance, she found the main office. Dismounting, she motioned her men to dismount and rest. They tied the horses and stood relaxed outside as she went inside. The room was long and narrow, rough-cut planking making up the floors and walls. Sap could be seen oozing from a few spots on the walls, and the smell of fresh cut timber still hung heavy in the air. A few of the scribes and counters looked up and noted her entrance. A few nodded as they went about their tasks. At the back, Worstan's office door stood ajar. She stopped to knock, but he waved in as he saw her from the corner of his eyes. She stepped inside and waited for him to finish with the papers he was pouring over. At length, he put down his pen and sighed. "That boy comes and drags me out here, and what does he do? Go running off to do gods knows what out there in the other provinces. Probably laughing it up leaving old Worstan to do all the really hard work." Emma had sat and was laughing softly to herself. "My dear, what do you find so amusing?"

"If you think that man is out just wasting time and spending money with no plan or such, you are very mistaken. For as much as he is different now." She stopped trying to find the right words. "For all his strength, he is still very much the same as he was when he was young. But I have come to let you know that we returned successfully and without incident. Though I get the feeling someone is watching our movements." She rubbed her chin as she spoke. "But I do not have anything solid to back up that feeling."

Worstan nodded as they walked out of the door. The old man shielded his eyes from the bright light. Heaving a heavy sigh, he lamented, "That is to be expected. This mine is going to be one of the richest in the land. So I am sure that if we are not being watched, we will soon." Emma followed him and they walked in silence for a time. Worstan stopped several times to inspect lumps of ore or to inspect the palisade. Emma opened her mouth to speak, but he silently raised his hand, stopping her. "What we must do is watch posts. Actively patrolling the roads as you and your men have been doing. Perhaps a solid fence along the road and any repairs that can be done should be to speed travel. Perhaps those measures will be enough. I have sent requests for more support, but I do not think we will be getting much." He lowered himself down onto a pile of beams as he spoke. "Word of this place has already spread. I am sure you have seen it. Trouble is light now, but that will change in time. We need to make the route as secure as possible as quickly as possible. And unfortunately, I think that will have to fall mostly on your narrow shoulders, dear Captain."

She smiled, looking up into the sky. She fidgeted with her helmet with her hands for a moment looking around. Seeing they were alone, she threw her helmet to the ground. It hardly made a sound as it landed on the mud and recently moved dirt. She stared at it disappointingly for a moment and exhaled deeply before speaking.

"Dammit, so much for getting some frustration out." She picked it up, flicking off a few clinging pieces of dirt. "So once again we have to beg, borrow, and steal our way to what we need."

"That would appear to be the case. As I said, I am doing what I can. Still have a few favors I can call in…" He trailed off.

"But?" Emma finished.

"But as you put it, it may not matter much. They know that this mine will be profitable and that ore has always been found in the presence of all manner of valuables. So it is an essentially perfect gamble. But guilds always want more. So if it does not go so well, then they can offer more help for more profit. It is a sad fact of life the guild would love to have this for themselves." He stopped to wipe beads of sweat off his brow. "Think of what they could do with it. That mountain holds a key to many doors." He stabbed his thumb at the mountain peak. "So we should expect lots of trouble to come our way sooner rather than later."

Emma nodded, knowing how terribly correct he was. "What has that man gotten us into I wonder?"

Worstan laughed. "A great many things would be my guess." He rubbed his chin as he mused. "But how many burdens does he carry I wonder?"

"That is most likely the real question, sir." Emma nodded, placing her helmet on her head. "Well, I must be off. Many things to do and so little time to get them all done."

Worstan heaved himself up as he spoke. "Of course, Captain. I have duties as well."

They walked in silence back to the main building. Emma mounted her horse and rode away with the guards. They rode slowly in silence back to town. Emma surveying the road and its poor condition. After they arrived at headquarters, she stormed into her room, slamming the door in the face of several people attempting to get her attention. Falling into her chair, she quickly put quill to paper. With order written, she threw open the door, grabbing a passing page. "You get these where they need to go now." With that, she thrust the parchment into his hand before the confused boy could stammer a response. She stormed toward the mayor's office before stopping short. She quickly returned to her room, shutting the door softly this time. She slumped into her chair finally feeling the day catching up to her.

*****

Emma awoke with a start as a loud crash came from the hallway. From the seat of her desk, the tiniest sliver of light was peeking from under her door. Standing and rubbing her eyes, she slowly walked out into the hall, nearly tripping over a small stack of papers set in front of her door.

The hallway seemed more empty than usual, but picking up the papers, she went back into her room to place them on her desk for later. After changing out of her armor and washing her face in the courtyard well, she walked down the emptier than normal streets to the Trolls Heads. Stepping around the dogs sprawled around the porch, a couple raising their heads for pets, she stepped inside to be greeted by a larger than normal morning crowd. From across the room, she saw Arlana's beaming smile from behind the counter and worked her way through the crowd. Emma sat on an empty stool heavily. "How is it that you are always smiling and cheery?"

Arlana walked over, leaning on the counter, bringing herself eye level with Emma still smiling, tapping a finger on Emma's nose. "Practice, dear, lots of practice, and my smiles bring smiles to customers' faces and that is always good for us." She placed a plate down in front of Emma. "Now eat up, Captain. I am sure you will have another busy day today." She started to move away to another customer when she turned back saying "Oh, and Kalgrin is in the back talking with the mine foreman about the plans for the road. When you are done, just go speak to them." Emma weakly waved in reply and slowly munched on her food. She watched the crowd ebb and flow, many more people than usual stayed after they had finished their meals, as if waiting for something. Finishing a slice of bacon, she was looking over to flag down Arlana when the back door burst open and Worstan and Kalgrin strode out from the back room, several rolls of paper under both of their arms mugs in the other hands.

The pair moved to a grouping of tables that Emma had not noticed close to the fire.

Worstan set down his mug and rolled out one of the scrolls. The group of waiting men crowded around the table as he waved them over.

With a booming voice, he began. "Alright, boys, here is the final plan we got. Now remember this is all going to be extra work that you will be paid for, so if you got a few tabs racked up, you might want to get on board with it." The gathered crowd laughed with a few ribbings mixed in. Emma got up and wandered over with Kalgrin motioning her closer. Worstan's scroll was a full map of the roads from the mine to town and past through to where the guard escorted merchants to. "Cutting the woods back along the whole route one hundred feet, clearing all the brush and trees." The crowd let out a loud groan. "Ah, shut yer yap. You do not want good extra money then I will keep you here. Plenty others will do it." Emma surveyed the crowd, many unfamiliar faces were among the crowd with a few she knew scattered among them.

It seemed many townsfolk and miners were eager to join in on the project. Worstan had moved on. "Along with the fence along the whole stretch of the road, we will be having carpenters taking a portion of the best timber and erect guard posts at regular intervals along the road." He ran his finger down the map for emphasis. "One will be between the town and the mine." He dragged his finger to a point about halfway between the two on the map. "Somewhere about here." Then moving down to several circles at intervals along the road. "And of course many more through here. Maybe more depending on the amount of good lumber we can get." Standing himself straight after a vigorous shake of his head to focus in his inebriated state, Worstan then proclaimed, "Alright, you have been briefed. If you are interested in the work, it will be paid on a daily rate for work done just like the mines. Work will start tomorrow so be sure." He paused, blinking several times. "Now be sure to meet again here at dawn so we can get this started! Dismissed!"

The two stood just long enough for the last of the crowd to leave before they plopped down heavily and sloppily into their chairs, downing the last of their ale with satisfied grins on their faces. Emma shook her head with a chuckle to herself as she walked over to the table analyzing the map. She nodded at the map before staring at the two barely upright in their chairs.

"So just how much have the two had to drink while plotting all of this out?"

The two of them glanced at one another, and Kalgrin started to count it out on his fingers but kept having to start over. Worstan meanwhile rubbed his chin while starting into the bottom of his mug.

Kalgrin seemed to be the first to come up with an answer. "I do believe, my dear girl, that half a cask of ale was consumed between the two of us this very night." He had the grin of a child trying his best to wiggle out of a lie. Worstan held up a finger.

"Oh, oh, good dwarf, but I think you have forgotten that along with the half casks of ale, we may have also drunk what must have been at the very least three bottles of wine." He smiled quite satisfied with himself until Arlana shouted from the back room.

"It was four that you two drank. I will have you know, and you had better clean up this kitchen, dear husband." The two chuckled lightly and looked at each other before Kalgrin stood with a bounce.

"Right then, best I be off then." With a small bow, he wandered into the kitchen seemingly refreshed and unfazed by the night's drinking and his lack of sleep. Worstan rubbed his eyes then stared over the plans laid out before him. Emma dropped down onto Kalgrin's empty seat and began staring over the plans once again as well.

"So do you really think you can make this work?" He shrugged and sighed.

"Not sure how quickly, but it will get done at some point. Extra work and real money always gets people to go work. Add to that, people need lumber and the chance to get some good logs is hard to pass up." Emma nodded.

"I suppose that will have to do. We are stretched thin as it is." She gave a sigh. "We are going to need more guards. It is only a matter of time until trouble starts. Sadly, just the way of things." Worstan nodded in agreement.

"Shall I go over all the finer details with you, dear Captain?" Emma glared at him but gave a firm nod as he unrolled several more rolled up parchment papers and began the long process of explaining it all.

CHAPTER 10

T HE TRAINING HALL ECHOED WITH THE THUDS of wood hitting wood and grunts as staffs met flesh with a meaty sound. Kasala stood overlooking the training floor down below. Zyid, as he always seemed to, had found his way days prior and had seemingly made it his duty to come and train. She leaned on the railing, her boredom quite apparent. Zyid was fighting two dwarven guards who were by far taking the worst of it. Zyid's staff whirled, parrying and striking with fluid ease. The two quickly fell over exhausted, holding up a hand in defeat. Zyid slammed the end of the staff into the stone floor; the sound resounded off the walls. Zyid let out a slow deep breath. "Is that all?" He let the statement hang in the air. A deafening silence greeted him. "Yes, I am stronger, but do not lose heart or metal. If one of you cannot beat me, then bring more. Or better yet, fight me in a way that works against me."

All of the gathered guards had stopped and were staring. "If you encounter a foe who is strong at melee, then bury him in arrows. A foe with deadly aim, get in close to render his advantage irrelevant." Zyid paused and cupped his hand around his ear, turning his head as if listening to them all in silence. "Oh, but what is this, what do I know. A man as strong as you who has no weakness is unbeatable, right? I hear it all. A person at the top who is making fun of us all right now." He continued shaking his head. "No! Far from it. Here before you stands a man who almost died but a few days ago." Murmurs ran through the assembled guards. "And a man who most certainly has been soundly defeated in the recent past." Zyid stopped taking a slow deep breath before continuing in a dour tone. "A time will come when I will have to do battle with that man again. That is why every day I train to defeat him. That is why all of you should train every day to defeat him. For if I cannot—" He stopped leveling the staff and sweeping it across the room saying, "For if I cannot, it may fall to one of you to defeat him." With a sigh, he placed his staff back onto its rack and walked up to the balcony, taking a spot of railing next to Kasala.

"A bit harsh was it not, do you think?" She snickered at him softly.

"Probably a little bit, but it is what it is now." He slumped his head onto the stone railing. "Ah, this is nice and cool."

"So exactly how long have you been at this today?" She lowered her head to meet his gaze. He shrugged in reply. "Well, it is midday, so you might want to give it a rest."

Another familiar voice answered for Zyid. "Yes, he will be stopping as we have business to discuss." The pair tried to move to bow but were stopped by heavy hands on their shoulders. "Yes, his words were harsh, but the meaning I think may have made it through." He fixed his gaze on the room below. The training had resumed. "I think they may have heard what you were really trying to say. We shall see if they keep it up," he continued as he stood up while starting to wrap his beard ends around his fingers. "But that is a worry for other people soon. We will have a grand council meeting, and you two heroes of the people and honored guests of the king are invited to join in." He stopped and laughed. "Well, more properly said requested."

The king walking behind directed them through the seeming labyrinth number of halls. "And once you two have been cleaned up, we shall go to the council chambers. It should be a great deal of fun." He then wandered back to his chambers, his laughter carrying down the halls as he went.

Leaving the two of them between two sets of doors on opposite sides of the hall, two attendants stood and motioned them in after a brief moment. Zyid followed the attendant through and into a large and well-appointed changing room.

"Please take your time and soak in the bath as the meeting will be one hour after the closing of businesses in the city. So do not feel a great rush." Zyid nodded as the bowed attendant and left. He walked in to find Thalon already soaking in a small wooden tub on the marble floor. Thalon nodded as Zyid settled into a tub next to his, some of the steaming water poured over the lip of the tub spilling it onto the stone floor. Zyid heaved a heavy sigh, letting the warmth flow through him then turned his head toward Thalon.

"Cannot say I expected to see you here. Care to fill me in?" He laughed.

"Would you be mad if I said no?" Thalon answered with a laugh.

Zyid moved his chin back and forth thinking for a few moments before showing two fingers very close together. "Only about that much, but it would be awkward to sit here in silence the whole time." They both laughed. "So why are you here anyway? Hope it is not to just spy on me in the bath."

Thalon gave a side long grin. "In your dreams, Mr. Hero." He waved his hand in the air as if bowing. "Bellenta and I are to be your…" He trailed off as if not sure of what word to use. "I guess assistant is the best word to use for it." The main discussions will be in the traditional language but that stuff will not concern you two. But we are there to translate and help to keep the proceedings moving smoothly." He stopped splashing some of the hot water onto his face. "Honestly, all of us are there mostly as showpieces. But there will be some words at the very least relating to you. Many of the guilds are very interested in this project. The nobles are pretty divided on what to do, so we shall see what happens. A lot of yelling and all that should be fun and boring all at once."

Zyid nodded in understanding. "So what is the basic setup of this council meeting?"

"Well, the chamber is set up rather like a university. Much like a lecture hall. There is a speaking platform in the center. Everyone else sits raised above it in seats that are tiered upward encircling the whole room much like an amphitheater." Thalon drew with a finger in the air as he spoke.

"So how is someone heard from the speaking dais?"

Thalon raised his finger in an aha motion. "A powerful spell has been cast on the dais stone that amplifies the voice of whomever is standing on it. Making it so anyone can be clearly heard by the whole room. And so long as they do not shout it is in a perfect speaking tone."

Zyid laughed. "So no muttering under your breath on the stone, huh?"

Thalon shook his head and wagged a finger at Zyid. "No muttering the scribes must record it all down in detail. It is quite a feat to behold. But like I said for the most part, we will not be doing anything. The things relating to us will be at the end of the meeting."

Zyid nodded before looking up studying the ceiling. "So how many people are in these meetings?"

"Normally it would be a few dozen at most but…"

"But? Never good to hear."

Thalon laughed. "No, it is not. But not only has an extra track of tunnel been cleared. Two heroes are walking around, one of whom is a dragon no less. Add to that, I have brought word of a quantity of the world's most valuable metals to the very doorsteps of the merchants." Thalon slowly nodded his head satisfied with himself.

"You know you are pretty informed for a guard turned noble member."

A grin flashed across Thalon's face. "Yes, I can understand what you mean. Bellenta's father sat us both down at length and discussed it. Bell had been to a few of the smaller meetings, but this one is much larger, and therefore a far more important meeting."

Zyid nodded as he placed a cloth over his face. "But we can worry about that in a bit. Now time to relax and enjoy the bath." With that, they both drifted into the silence of their own thoughts.

*****

"So, Bel, how long have you two been together?" Kasala asked as she twirled in front of the floor-length mirror, taking the view of her dress in.

Bellenta stopped the brush midstroke thinking for a second. "Oh, about twenty years or so I think." She resumed brushing catching on a knot of hair. "Why do you ask?" She grunted, fighting the knot.

"Just wondering, that is all, never really knew anything about the dwarves." She pulled her hair into a long ponytail. "I have spent most of my life in a cave after all."

"Never thought to travel?" Bellenta stood, nodding at herself in the mirror satisfied with her look. "All ready to go?" Kasala nodded as she looked out into the now dimly lit streets, the faint chiming of the closing bells carried through the night. They stepped out into the hall. Zyid and Thalon were already waiting there for them.

"You ladies finally ready to go?" Thalon asked with a beaming grin.

Bellenta glared at him before answering. "Well, we are out here now, are we not?"

Zyid cut in first. "That does indeed appear so. Shall we go then?" He offered his arm to Kasala who took it with a small shrug.

"Walking out like that is going to start the rumors flowing my friend." Bellenta giggled out.

"My dear lady, you have probably already heard so many rumors at this point, and if you have not, a trip to the local taverns and I am sure they all have a few each." They all heartedly laughed as they stepped out into the evening air and the bustling crowds.

*****

Emma, having finished her work for the day, once again found herself staring up at the statue that dominated the courtyard out front the town hall. "Madam Captain!" The sudden shout startled her out of her thoughts. She turned on her heels to find Worstan shouting from atop his cart full of miners. "Fancy joining us for a drink?" A few of the miners whistled at the thought though a few groaned as well. She shook her head before shouting back.

"Not tonight, old man. I have other plans!" Worstan clapped his hand to his heart as though he had been struck. "You wound me, dear lady! But it is your loss at having a good evening, dear Captain." With that, he and his cart rolled off into the evening light. Emma grinned and chuckled to herself before she started her walk the short distance to her parents' home. She gingerly knocked on the door.

"Yes, just a minute." The door opened a sliver before quickly being thrown open. "Emma my dear, welcome home." Her mother embraced her tightly. "It is so good to see you. I know that your work keeps you busy, but be sure to not work too hard like your father," she said, casting a gaze inside.

"I will do what I can, Mother," she said with a tired smile.

Her mother heaved a sigh, shaking her head knowingly. "Now where have I heard that before? But enough of that, do come in. Dinner is almost ready, and we certainly have enough for you as well."

"Thank you, Mother, that sounds nice." Stepping inside, Emma found little had changed. Her mother stood over a stew pot to give it a stir on a small stove with its clay flu cracked and weathered from years of use. Through the small divide, her father sat close to the small fire nestled in the next room. The faint sound of a knife scraping on wood could be heard. The whitewashing of the walls was still chipped and peeling in places. Emma stepped into the room. "Father, you really should get someone to fix these walls." The knife stopped, and he slowly turned his head to reveal his milky eyes.

"Should I now? From what I can see, the walls look just like they did when I first had it done over twenty years ago." He laughed at his own joke as he slowly got up from his seat to embrace Emma. "My dear, I have heard nothing but good things about you, and that worries me slightly." They both laughed.

"They are just too afraid to say anything you might hear about and give them a good thrashing." The old man smiled and nodded in agreement.

"Well, from what I have heard, the guard have never had it so good, funding and recruits. A miracle if I have ever heard of one. But what has you so worried that you came to talk to me about it, dear?"

Emma opened then closed her mouth searching for the right words. Before starting in a low voice.

"To be honest, Father, I just have a bad feeling. Zyid has been sending regular messages to the mine, and they are doing all kinds of weird things in the name of their profits." Her father motioned for her to continue as she brought a chair close to his. "Clearing large swaths of trees saying they need all the timber. It seems excessive to say the least. And what kind of mine needs a palisade around it that is double-sided. I think they might be filling it with rubble from the mines. Worstan put forth a proposal to pave the road, and I swear he might be trying to put it in the townspeople's ears that we need a new stone wall around town." She rubbed her head. "It has me worried about what is going on in Zyid's mind. He seems to feel war is coming, but he will not say it to anyone."

He nodded while rubbing his chin, digesting what he was being told. "While some of that seems fairly normal, merchants are a scared lot after all. Someone is always out to get them even if it is only in their minds. They generally do not prepare for war so much as run from danger if they smell it in the wind." He chuckled. "Or prepare to raise the price on everything when war looms. Zyid seems to think war is in the air by the sounds of it. But unless he can bring proof, why try and convince people of it." He shrugged. "Much better to prepare for one in the meantime though." Emma slumped back into her chair.

"So where does that leave me? My guards are no army, too undertrained and far too few in number to make much difference one way or the other." The frustration in her tone was heavy in her words.

Her father smiled. "Well, if you feel you are not prepared, and you should be, then make it so. If, on the other hand, you think Zyid is crazy, then why worry? He is your childhood friend, but it has been many years you both have changed. You need to do the best you can in the way you feel best." Emma snorted under your breath.

"Some help you are, Father."

"I never said I had all of the answers." He turned and shouted toward the kitchen "Dear, is the stew ready yet?"

"Yes, dear, now you both come to eat before it gets cold." With that, Emma helped him to his feet, and they proceeded to the other room.

CHAPTER 11

Z YID SAT IMPATIENTLY ON HIS PART OF the bench, head resting on one hand as he slowly stroked his beard with the other. He scanned the room once again, noting the room was full to bursting yet somehow stone silent apart from the dwarf speaking, some guild leader or another, he had long since lost count. A large enclosed room much like an arena with seats terraced high above the speaking area just as Thalon had described. This area was a short drop surrounded by a worn stone railing. With two speaking dais. Thalon had mentioned something about them being enchanted, and he was a marvelous thing to see in action. Though now it was becoming a boring affair. Kasala leaned in and whispered into his ear, breaking his train of thought. "So are you following any of this?" He slowly shook his head in reply. "Good. Glad I am not the only one." Bellenta shot them both a harsh glance. But Zyid was already lost on thought again. The king, queen, and their closest advisers were seated at one end of the oval. Zyid and his party had been seated at the other. To his left sat the various guild leaders; there seemed no commonality between any of them though they all seemed to sit in a very precious order. The other side was the general public crowded into every available space. Most seemed to be gawking at him though it was hard to tell. Dwarves, elves, and humans all there to catch a glimpse of the hero though some seemed to hang on the words of every speaker. Perhaps work-related, Zyid wondered. His thoughts were once again broken this time by the speaker on the floor.

"Now with all of our normal business attended to, we must now turn our attention to the most recent matter to come to our attention." He waited till the silence had truly filled the room before continuing. "Recently, our city was saved from great peril by the intervention of two heroes. I have many questions of this incident. Our hero claims he is but a merchant yet…" He raised his finger to emphasize his words as he let the pause hang. "Yet he travels in the company of a dragon!" He thrust his finger at Zyid and Kasala. "They could have awakened the great spider by magic to swoop in to save us in our time of need. We must address this here and now before we move forward in more dealings with this pair." The gathered crowd murmured noisily among themselves.

A roar slowly began in the gathered crowd but was immediately silenced with the king's booming but calm voice. "This accusation will not be heard if there is no evidence to substantiate it." His seat seemed to have the same enchantment on it. "But our guest may speak for himself if he so chooses." He motioned a hand from Zyid to the empty speaking platform, a grin poking from his beard. Zyid stood straightening his clothes and giving a curt bow before slowly walking down to the center of the room. The deafening silence had once again taken over the room. Zyid jumped over the railing, catching his toes on it and nearly falling on his face. A few scattered snickers came from the crowd as he brushed himself off and stepped onto the platform. He cleared his throat while surveying the room.

"My good sir," he began in a low soft voice. "You were only partially correct with your statements." He paused before continuing, "First, I did not somehow cause the spider queen to attack," raising his fingers to count off as he went. "Second, I do indeed travel with a dragon. I do not believe this can be hidden at this point. And lastly, I am indeed a merchant, anyone who engages in the buying and selling of goods can hardly call themselves anything else. The fact that I am a well-trained warrior is merely a secondary thing."

"So you do not deny that magic could have been used to awaken it?" The dwarf fired off without missing a beat.

"Good sir, anything is possible, but as your mages will be able to attest, I personally have no magical ability. The only magical thing on me is my swords." He patted both hilts. "I did not awaken the creature. I came to trade. I need to strengthen my home. I am doing this the only way I can at this point. Wealth brings with it power. With power, I can save my home!" He cleared his throat and continued again in a low voice. "So I come seeking partners to help me grow. Take that for what you will." The crowd once again began murmuring among themselves. "You fear that I will take away from you, that I will rise to the top. In time maybe, but I am not interested in being the leader of your guilds or what have you. I am merely interested in coin." Zyid reached into his pocket to hold up a gold coin. "And with that coin gaining power. Like any good merchant."

The crowd's grumbling continued. The dwarf stroked his beard. Thoughtfully opening and closing his mouth several times unsure what to say. Before he could rebut Zyid's statements, he continued, "The last few days I have heard over and over that the debt you have can never be repaid." He paused before continuing and placed his hands on the railing of the dais. "But that, good people, is untrue. In time, I will be calling your fine nation to arms." This time the crowded and assembled guild leadership could be heard speaking in hushed tones. "As of now, I have no hard evidence to present to you. In time, that will change. Make no mistake, war is coming." The words came out cold and low. "With all its glory…and all its horror." A chill seemed to fill the air. "And on that day, I hope I can count on you all to aid me in my hour of need." Zyid hung his head and stood slouched for a moment before stepping down out of the dais and shuffling slowly back to his seat. He felt the eyes of those gathered followed him the whole way, but not a word was uttered. Even the king seemed stunned or at the very least pensive. The queen was the first to break the silence, her voice booming over the chamber.

"We shall await this proof of yours, and when that time comes, we honor our debts!" A few cheers came from the crowd that slowly turned to a great roar to fill the halls. Zyid stood and gave a deep bow, roaring to be heard above the crowd.

"I can ask for no more than that!" He let out a ragged cough from yelling. "And now I think a drink is required." The crowd howled in laughter and stomped out into the streets to start the festivities once again.

*****

Zyid awoke slowly, a pounding headache greeting him as he gingerly raised his head from the table a string of drool hanging from his mouth. The inn appeared near full to bursting with people passed out all around. The barmaid saw him stir and walked over.

"Are you going to finish that?" she asked, pointing to the pewter mug that sat before him. He slowly peered into it; the heavy smell of cinnamon and berries greeted him. He recoiled back, waving the smell from his face.

"You would have to tell me what it is first." She smiled, taking the tankard away.

"It is called dragon's blood brew. Strong stuff. You drank a fair bit of it but seems everyone might have had a bit too much fun." Her smile did not take away from her annoyed tone.

"Terribly sorry about that. I will be sure to pay what is owed." She waved a dismissing hand as she walked away.

"Already paid for heroes do not tend to buy drinks around here." Zyid stood and steadied himself with the table and began slowly weaving his way through the crowd and up to his room. The morning light was just coming through the crack in the shutter as he entered the room. Kasala sat on her bed, packing her few belongings.

"Finally awake I see. Drank a bit too much, did we?" Zyid flopped onto his bed arm over his eyes.

"That my dragon companion I certainly did. By the gods, how much did I drink last night anyway? My head is throbbing." She cocked her head slightly thinking it over.

"Well, everyone went out of the hall and basically followed us back to the inn. Then the drinks started flowing. Stories started flying around and then someone bought the dragon's blood stuff. A few people tried to drink a bunch, and you and they all ended up the same. Not much happened after that."

"I never want to drink anything again. This is a terrible feeling. But guess it is time we get going. Is everything ready?"

"Everyone who is coming along is waiting outside the main gate. No idea how many but a fair few seemed very interested." He slowly sat up.

"Guess that means I need to get ready too." He stood with a slight wobble and swiftly packed his things.

With a nod, they both marched down to the main room. It was beginning to empty as people awoke from the nights drinking and had begun shuffling out. But many stopped as the pair passed. Some bowed, some clapped them on the shoulder as they passed. Mounting their horses, they moved through the bustling streets. The crowd parted for them as they passed and guards paused in their patrols to offer salutes. Many people followed after them to the gateway and gave a great cheer as they passed through and into the chilly day outside.

Outside the gate, a line of carts and pack animals all loaded and ready to move awaited them. They rode to the front to find who was leading the wagon train. They found Thalon awaiting them in the head wagon. "So are you in charge of this mess?" Thalon turned, hopping down from the wagon.

With a beaming grin, he shot back, "It would seem you are quite stuck with me for the foreseeable future."

Zyid shrugged. "Or they just put you off on me to keep you out of the nobles' way."

Thalon nodded as he stroked his beard. "There is that too." He waved the idea away. "But anyway here is the inventory of our supplies and personnel. We have one hundred official guards, mostly mercenaries. Though there is closer to triple that since most of the houses and guilds sent a few along as well. They just are not officially part of the guards. Then of course family and hangers on and all that so this is going to be a long slow journey."

Zyid nodded as he looked over the list. "Well, let us hope not too slow. We do have to get things done eventually. Are they all ready to go?" Thalon nodded in reply and hopped back into the wagon. Zyid stood in the stirrups and bellowed as loud as he could manage. "Everyone, let us move out!" He watched them slowly lurch forward to great fanfare. After they all had passed, he took a place in the rear of the train slowly riding into the morning sun.

*****

"Kalgrin?" Arlana asked as she laid her head on his shoulder.

"Yes, my dear?" His eyes never left the road ahead as they slowly drove the cart down the road toward town.

"Why did we settle down? We used to travel all around the land."

He tilted his head slightly in thought, nodding after a few moments. He cleared his throat before answering. "If I am remembering correctly, it was because you got tired of riding around in a cart night and day. That and this place was really the best for us. Good to be away from it all as you said so long ago. And you cannot say you are not happy now."

He heard her smile as she spoke. "You know me so well, dear. I am very happy." She planted a kiss on his cheek. "Though there is much sadness coming again I fear."

He slowly nodded. "When Zyid came through that door, I knew something was wrong."

"So what do we do then?"

He shook his head. "Nothing we can do yet, but once we have something tangible, then we strike." She leaned back on the bench, reaching a hand back into the cart to run her fingers down the fuller of her sword. She gazed back at the long narrow blade with its winged-shaped guard.

"I had hoped war was gone from our lives. But it seems fate has other ideas. For we must do something, dear." He nodded in agreement. She breathed a heavy sigh. "I suppose we need to train the boy harder then."

Kalgrin snickered. "Do not break the poor boy. We need him after all. But he can handle it. I think he did duel a dragon and came out alright, so maybe he is not as bad off as we think." They both laughed.

As their laughter died off, Arlana whispered, "He is just like that one in many ways." They sat in silence for a moment then Kalgrin answered.

"Yes, yes, he is. If that is a good thing or a bad thing, only the gods know. But time will tell one way or the other."

CHAPTER 12

THE MORNING AIR WAS COOL AND CRISP. The sun was just peeking above the trees in the distance. Rashida stood in the shadow of the city gate, the entrance massive enough to allow a dragon passage. She exhaled slowly, her breath forming a fog in the air. "Is everything in order?" She turned to her guards.

They both were finishing looking over their horses, replying in near unison. "Yes, Princess." She nodded then mounted her horse. As she looked back, she saw her father and mother flying to meet them before they set out. They landed and walked over.

The queen spoke first. "Finally ready to head off, my dear. Please ensure Zyid comes, it would be no fun if he did not compete this time." They smiled at each other.

"Worry not, Mother, I will be sure that my brother comes here."

The king let out a laugh. "You two have nothing to worry about. He will come. He has to after all. If he does not, he cannot win the battle to come. But enough of this. Go forth, my daughter." He made a shooing motion with his hands. "And be sure to test that man for me. Ensure he has not been slacking. He needs to draw on more of his power. Or else I will not have any fun."

The queen swatted his arm. "Dear, this is not all about you. Well, we will stop holding you three up. Keep her safe, warriors."

"Of course, my queen!"

"Now off with you all. We shall look forward to your return, my daughter."

"I will be back before long, Father." He nodded and the three set off out the gate at a trot. The pair stood watching until the three had been obscured by the distant forest.

The queen sighed. "Are you sure he will come, dear? He left in quite the hurry after his last victory." They both turned and began slowly walking down the wide stone-paved streets arms linked.

"My dear, he has to come. He swore he would stop me. The easiest way to do that is to kill me." He laughed. "Failing that he will need solid proof that war is coming, those are his only options. He left in a hurry last time and did not think to take anything with him. But he is young and he will learn. He has to." He stopped and stared at the large peak looming far into the snowy wastes to the east and mumbled, "I just hope it is not too late."

*****

The rain came down in a fine mist as Zyid and Kasala sat by the fire, poking at it to keep it lit. "This was much faster with just the two of us." Zyid looked out from under his hood and stared blankly at her for a moment. "Fine, yes, I know of course it would take longer. But can we just hurry it up already? I want to get home."

Zyid poked at the fire throwing on another few pieces of wood. "Well, it just takes time. You could just fly back and be there in no time."

She laughed. "Quicker for sure, but I do not think a panic is what you need."

"Very true," Zyid replied softly. They sat silently for a moment before she broke the silence. "So what were you up to for all that time you were gone to the east?" He chuckled to himself softly.

"Now there is a story though one not as interesting as you are probably thinking. I spent most of my time training. It was hard but that woman was my goal so to speak. Days of harsh training. Reading texts in the evening. Long days for sure. But it was easy when you were driven." He paused, looking up, closing his eyes. "Good times. We would visit the court from time to time so some days training took place with them. The king had such strength." He stopped as she saw him shiver as a chill ran up his spine. "Terrifying is the only word I could put to it. That drove me on. And after many years I finished my training. I won the tournament and left soon after." He looked toward her. "See? Not nearly as interesting as you were hoping." She ran her hand through her hair, throwing back her hood.

"No, very interesting actually." She came in close to his face, making him pull back. "You loved her!" She trailed off before continuing. "It is just good to know that your heart is not hard, and no wonder you ignore that poor captain." He said nothing and continued tending the fire.

"Sun will be up soon, and it will be even slower going today with all of this rain." She shrugged.

"Guess I will just have to sleep most of the day then." He sighed heavily.

"That and food are your answers to everything, are they not?" She nodded excitedly, a smiling beaming on her face. He sighed again as the rays of sunlight began to pierce the trees. "Well, time for breakfast I suppose."

*****

The cart passed through the gate. Arlana huddling next to Kalgrin for warmth in the rain. "Nearly two weeks away from home sure feels longer than it used to." Kalgrin nodded, rain dripping from his beard.

"Shall we open up for the day? I am sure there will be quite the demand. The people love to see you wander around the place after all." He smiled at her and she returned a crass glance at him.

"You know people just love your cooking."

He shrugged. "Maybe it is both."

She smiled at that, closing her eyes. "I had hoped this peace could last forever." She sighed deeply. "But it seems that conflict is inescapable, but what will the future hold? We are getting too old for this, I think?"

Kalgrin pulled the cart around to the back of the tavern, hopping down, and handed the reins to the stable hand before he answered. "I think we are, but it is not like the last time. We do not have to shoulder all the burden. You would not stand by and watch anyway."

She smiled as she stepped down from the cart, resting her sword on her shoulder. She gave it a light pat. "You, my dear husband, know me too well." They entered, lighting the lanterns as they went. Kalgrin stoked the kitchen fire as Arlana stepped out front to change their sign to open a watchman appeared, leading three riders faces covered by cloaks toward the inn. The rain began coming down in sheets as they approached. The guard called out as they came close.

"Ah good, Arlana, it is most fortuitous that you are here." The man nearly had to shout over the rain. "These fine folks asked to come to your inn and none other. I even said you may be out, but they were having none of it. I will be on my way home then." They nodded at each other, and he continued on his way. She examined the strangers as they dismounted and hitched their horses. Their cloaks were simply but finely made and of rich colors deep blues and reds. Two fell in behind their leader who after dismounting had taken a halberd off her horse, bringing it before Arlana. Holding it outstretched, she spoke gently but with authority.

"The guard explained that it is customary that we turn in our weapons to our place of residences." She smiled as if very amused by her own words.

Arlana took it. It felt heavier than it really needed to be. Simple but well made, its blade engraved with a dragon spitting fire. Arlana bounced it in her hands a few times before answering and motioning them inside. "A fine weapon, young lady. Now you and your companions should come inside out of the cold." She nodded and followed her inside. "Kalgrin!" she bellowed as they walked in. "We have some new guests. Please get them something warm to ward off the cold." He nodded from behind the bar, retrieving three tankards and dipping each into a large bowl of liquid being warmed over a fire. The strangers had seated themselves at a table with the lady facing the bar. Her two companions facing the door.

Kalgrin set down the tankards. "This one is on the house seeing as how we just returned from a trip ourselves." The lady had removed her hood, shaking some lingering droplets from her hair.

She smiled warmly at the dwarf. "That is most kind of you, sir. You are just what I had expected."

Kalgrin lifted an eyebrow "Oh, so you have heard of me? Now that is most interesting. Where, pray tell, did you hear of me?" Kalgrin had moved down the bar and taken the ledger from below and set it on the bar top.

She chuckled to herself. "Why, Zyid seemed to speak of you and this place any chance he got. It was so easy to see he loved this place. It is no wonder he came back."

Kalgrin had produced a pair of spectacles and was thumbing through the book as he answered, "Oh, a friend of his, huh. That is good to hear. He never seems to take any time for himself."

"So then I see nothing has changed then." She laughed.

"A fine lady like yourself should not be after him anyway. He is not worth all the effort I am sure. A trek from the eastern lands through the mountains is never an easy trip. This is why so few venture it."

She nodded. "Difficult certainly but not so difficult as to make it not worth doing. My father commanded. So here I am. He wishes to speak with Zyid once again in person."

"Very well then I suppose. Will you be staying until he returns then? It could be a fair time till then."

"Indeed we shall. Though I hope it is not too long. I cannot shirk my other duties forever."

Kalgrin began writing in the ledger. "Well, I am sure he will return swiftly, but one never knows. But I am sure you will find ways to pass the time. A growing town is full of fun for the young and adventurous after all."

"That it is, sir, that it is."

Arlana had returned. "Your weapons are stored safely and will be returned once you are leaving the city. Now let one room or two?"

"One will suffice." She answered over her mug. "My attendants would not stand not being as close as possible. No need to have them blocking the hallway. Adulfas, please take our things to the room if you would." One of the robed figures nodded and marched out the door. "Are meals included with renting a room? Also, this drink is very weak but tasty. What is in it?" Kalgrin laughed as Adulfas reentered the inn carrying their few possessions. Arlana motioned for him to follow her to their room.

"You, young lady, must have a very keen sense of taste and smell. Only the morning meal is included with the room, but we serve three meals a day. It can be quite busy, and if you would like, there are seemingly more street vendors here by the day. And as to your other question, it is a mix of fruits that we ferment the juice similar to wine. It has a low alcohol content but will keep you going all day instead of making you drowsy. It is something I have enjoyed making over the years." He finished writing in the ledger, turning it around and setting down a quill and ink in front of her. "If I could bother you for your signature on the line if all is in order." She nodded, moving her mug to the side and scanned what he had written. The great scar across her chest almost glimmered in the candlelight as she wrote.

Kalgrin turned the book, adjusting his glasses and blowing on the ink. "Quite the scratch you have there." The remaining attendant's chair fell to the floor as he stood, hand floating over a nonexistent sword hilt. She raised her hand with narrowed eyes, and he slowly recovered his chair and resumed sitting.

She looked down at herself, running a finger along it. "It is indeed a wound earned in a mighty battle. It was quite painful, but it did show me that I had to try harder to catch him. But that is all I will say for now." Kalgrin shrugged in defeat as he finished the entry. "If all is in order, I feel a rest is in order." He nodded as she stood up. Adulfas had returned and the three of them marched off to their room. Kalgrin and Arlana exchanged glances, waiting for their guests to retire to the room.

Arlana broke the silence. "She seems very familiar, does she not?" She moved behind Kalgrin, leaning on his shoulders resting her head on top of his. "Things really are on the move, are they not?" She felt him nod but he said nothing. "I hope that boy gets back soon."

CHAPTER 13

Z YID COULD FEEL THE PEBBLES BENEATH HIS boots, the feel of liquid as it dripped down his face. He looked down to find his hands holding his swords slick with blood. He slowly raised his gaze to see a familiar sight, the body facedown in the road very dead. The gathered crowd was caught between gawking, cheering, and deathly silence. Running footsteps echoed in the distance. His eyes closed, and when he opened them again, there before the king he stood dirty and battered. The king looked down at the young man before him. He leaned forward, resting his hands on his knees. Zyid saw him slowly speak. "Boy! What you have done was fair by the rules of this land." His words echoed with finality. "My fool of a son should have known better." The world turned to mist and reshaped itself into the arena, the crunch of the sand under his boots familiar calming and terrifying all at once. He stood victorious but then he came. The king, striding out of the mist laughing with a grin beaming across his face. Zyid felt his arms flail at the monster before him. The king parried with his sword and shield absentmindedly as if swatting away insects. Soon Zyid felt the warm sand beneath him as the man slowly pushed his boots onto his throat. The world dimmed as Zyid heard. "You disappoint me, boy. I told you to do better." Zyid awoke as the boot crushed his throat. He tried to rise but found a bag of grain had fallen on his chest. Panicking, he threw it off. The driver turned back at the noise but shrugged and tipped his hat at Zyid before returning his gaze forward. Zyid forced his breathing to return to normal. He poked his head out the back of the wagon to get fresh air, the sun shone brightly over the train of wagons. Kasala saw him and strode over.

"How was your sleep, partner?"

Zyid hopped down, brushing himself off as they began walking. "I have slept better that is for sure."

She laughed "So even you have bad dreams."

"That I do. I am just a man after all." He rubbed his neck as he answered. "Will be nice to sleep in a real bed once we reach the city."

She nodded. "That it will though I imagine they will not be too happy with us all staying inside the walls."

He shrugged. "Well, a stack of hay is still better than a blanket over the ground."

She laughed again. "You humans and your need for such comfort. My pile of rocks was plenty comfortable. Someday it will be a pile of coin, Now that will be the day." He shook his head as she was lost in her daydream. He tried to forget his dream taking in the clear blue sky and focusing on the sound of wagons plodding along. His bliss only occasionally broken as he stumbled into a wagon track. "Careful there, hero, you cannot go looking like you are not perfect now." Zyid opened his mouth to reply but closed it again and mock bowed. She and some others laughed but the silence returned for a while. Broken only by the occasional change of scouts and creaking of wood.

"Will we be there soon, Mommy?" He heard a child ask.

"No. We still have a ways to go, yet but we will be stopping near another city soon." He smiled at the child's innocent laughter.

He looked over to see Kasala smiling at him. "What are you smiling at?"

"Oh, just you know. Ah, those were fun days back then."

"What days?"

"Hmm? Oh just many years back when I was younger running around the hills and forests. Why did you think I spent the last couple hundred years sleeping in the cave?" Zyid stared back with a blank look on his face. "Well, I did not." She huffed. "I even went into town sometimes. Was always fun to see the children running around and playing. Even you used to have fun if I remember correctly."

"I do not know how to have fun now?" He scoffed defensibly.

"Oh, you do? Well, could have fooled me. All you ever seem to want to do is read, write, and train. What happened to the boy who ran through fields laughing and smiling? Gone forever in the frozen lands to the east?"

Zyid gazed up at the sky and heaved a heavy sigh before answering. "I am not sure that little boy is gone so much as just unimportant. My father told me to go after what I wanted. So I followed her to her homeland. The training was harsh, even brutal at times." He paused, a smile crossing his face. "But through it all, I just kept trying to catch her to impress her. A little boy trying to win his first crush. His first love. But once I had learned everything from her. Reached the peak that she could bring out of me, she simply shooed me away telling me it could never be."

"But you still love her, that is quite obvious." She clapped a hand on his shoulder.

He nodded. "It is hard to forget your first love after all. And so I hold on to the hope I can still win her over."

"Well, good to know you are totally hopeless. That guard captain will be so sad to hear of this," she added under her breath.

"Hmm?"

"What?" she replied. He gave a sidelong glance but did not pry further.

The day passed quickly, and as evening came, the column gathered as they had previous nights. The dim light came through the trees, finding Zyid sitting under a tree when a scout came riding into the camp. Seeing him, he shuffled over after dismounting. The dwarf slowly sat down and unrolled a piece of parchment before he began to speak in a low hushed voice. "Sir, we have a small issue." He paused for a moment as Zyid motioned for him to continue. "It would seem that the city is under siege." Zyid stroked his beard as he listened and looked at the crude sketch before him. "From what we gathered, they have it surrounded though it is not a terribly tight siege. They seem only concerned with watching the gates." He looked up, ensuring he was moving too fast. "We spotted some ladders. And possibly a tower though they did not seem very enthused with building them. I would guess they are trying to look threatening without risking themselves too much."

Zyid sighed. "Seems this will make buying supplies slightly more difficult. Gather the rest of the group leaders, and we shall see what we want to do about it." He nodded and hurried away as Zyid continued studying the drawing.

They all arrived in short order and quickly drew a copy of the map into the dirt. Once completed, they all sat and looked at Zyid to begin. "Everyone, it seems we have a minor problem. That I am sure is easy to see, but the real question is what do we do about it? Thoughts?" Time seemed to slow to a crawl as they thought it out.

Before one piped up. "Well, it is not really our problem. We could just continue on our way after all." Zyid saw a few nods in agreement.

"But that does not feel right, and besides, helping could give us an advantage since they are already a trading partner. So would it not be in our best interest to help?" a second voice offered.

"Even if we would like to help, in what way do you suggest?" The first voice chimed in. "We are but a few hundred warriors and camp followers, even a surprise night raid would only lead to our slaughter. They have several thousand men at least."

A silence once again crept over them. "Well, maybe something more cunning than trying to kill everyone will be better than?"

Zyid finally added in. "A good fright might be what we really need. Our scouts report they do not seem very enthused about this siege. Most of these are farmers and would much rather be home in their own beds." Some murmurs came from the group. "So any ideas on how to shock them into leaving?" A short silence fell over the group once again.

"Could she just not fly around?" a third voice chimed in, hooking a thumb in Kasala's direction. She looked up mouth stuffed with bread. She cocked her head as she continued to stuff her face. Several people laughing.

Zyid shrugged and replied, "While dragons are certainly scary, not sure this one will do that job." They all started laughing now. He continued when it had died down. "That on its own probably will not do it. Maybe with something else to add a bigger threat to it." A silence once again fell over them. Kasala broke the silence this time as she slammed down an empty tankard. She got up walking over to the crudely drawn map taking a stick and spoke as she began drawing.

"While a dragon flying around might not do the trick on its own..." She finished her additions to the map. "But if we light many campfires within sight of their camp, they will probably start falling over themselves to get away. Also if the dragon is seen with a figure on top of it, they are sure to think something very odd is happening. So they will either pack up and leave or send troops to check it out. Maybe then we could set some terms since they will not be able to easily figure out what they are up against." Murmurs of agreement went through the group.

Zyid stood and looked at her scribbles. "Well, it seems that might be our best bet. But..."

"But what?" she asked, annoyed.

"What in heaven's name did you draw here?" They all leaned in closer to see the mess she had drawn. She just shrugged. "Well, let us get to work before it gets too dark. Merchants have to protect their markets after all, right?" They all roared in agreement and dispersed to start their work. After they had left, Kasala sat back down and began drawing idly in the dirt.

"Think it will work?"

Zyid shrugged. "It is the best chance without us flying in and just killing. We might be able to do it, but it would be costly. And I do not want to burn any possible bridges for allies later down the road."

"Always trying to think ahead, are we?"

"Of course I do need an army after all." He laughed. "Well, actually I will need as many armies as I can buy, borrow, or steal if we want to have a chance of winning."

"You sure are greedy, you know that?"

He thought for a second then nodded in agreement. "Yes, yes I am. Why should I be forced to settle for just surviving? I will aim for winning not just defending my home. I will invade his lands and burn them to ash. So he can never threaten my home again."

She smiled, speaking softly to herself. "You really have not changed at all."

Zyid could hardly believe his eyes as he walked, observing the preparations around camp. Hundreds of fires burned around the hillside. Women and children had made makeshift drums and chanted and howled at the top of their lungs. The noise was near deafening. Warriors stood armed and ready. Someone had taken all the spare horses, tied them all together, and fitted them with fake riders, bolstering their numbers. Thalon rode over to him as he neared the camp's edge. "We have done everything we can. Now what?"

Zyid ran a hand through his beard and shrugged. "I am not entirely sure to be honest. I was hoping you would know." They both laughed.

Thalon dismounted. "We will just have to wait for our scout to return. He should be along any time now." A short while passed in silence until a wolf crept out of the forest and returned to Kasala's human form. She took a moment to catch her breath before speaking.

"Well, they have seen us that is for sure," she proclaimed softly, arms outstretched. She waited a moment before she continued. "You two were supposed to laugh, you know?"

"To laugh at a joke, it has to be funny," Thalon retorted.

She huffed but continued, "They are preparing to meet the force, at least that is what it looked like from what I could see. They were falling over themselves trying to be ready."

"Good, good. That means they are on edge, right, Zyid?"

He nodded in reply. "It might be about time to get moving." He nodded at Kasala who spun on her heels. Taking a deep breath, she let out a mighty roar. The trees near them shook with the force of it. The pair took an unconscious half step back. Birds took to the sky in flight. The warriors in the woods were stunned into silence for a moment then let out a mighty cheer of their own. They yelled and banged their weapons on their shields, slamming polearms into the ground. She turned back to the two of them with a smile then turned into her true form. Her green scales glistened in the firelight casting a great shadow upon the hill.

She craned her neck backward, motioning at her back. "Come now, Zyid. We have some more fun to have." He nodded and climbed up onto her back a simple rope harness was slung over so he could stand on a somewhat stable footing.

Drawing his sword and thrusting it into the air, "Forward to victory!" she roared once again, a dribble of her breath escaping with it and took to the sky. The rest of them moved carefully forward, making as much noise as possible. From the air, Zyid could see it clearly. His forces marched slightly out of the trees far enough to be seen but not far enough to be counted. The enemy ranks stood down the hill. Several arrows arched into the air but could not hope to reach them. "Swoop down low in front of them and blast the ground if you can." If she replied, he could not hear it as she immediately dove toward the ground. Zyid was now holding on to her back spines for dear life. She soared down across the treetops, blasting the ground just before them with a jet of her acidic breath before swooping back into the air.

She gave a small satisfied grunt to herself before looking across her back. "Are you still on back there?" she called once they were back in the air.

"And people did this back during the great war? This is insanity." Zyid's words spilled out with a slight tremble.

"I will take that as a yes. Their lines seem to be faltering." Zyid carefully peered over to look.

The assembled army's core had shattered at the sight of a dragon. Some ran toward the city walls where a few attempted to place ladders on the wall were met with arrows and boiling water from the ramparts. A group was fleeing back through their camp falling over fires and tents.

The muffled yelling of nobles at sergeants trying to get the troops to stay in formation. But they too got caught up in the stampede of men and animals. The few that had stood their ground soon clashed with the mounted warriors, which fully put them to flight. Kasala roared and released another gout of acid before she landed among those fleeing nipping at a few. Zyid jumped down onto shaky legs. She strode through the encampment stepping over the carnage that moments before had been an organized camp.

Those remaining soldiers were being rounded up. Zyid stopped in front of the remains of the largest tent, thrusting his sword into the air. "Victory!" A cheer went up from his warriors. The troops on the wall had gone silent. Their outlines could barely be made out in the dim light. The tension could be felt in the air. Thalon had arrived next to Zyid and Kasala.

"What do we do now?" he hoarsely whispered to him.

"I am honestly surprised that they ran so fast, so round up the prisoners and put them near the gate then we will pull back into the woods. Hopefully, they will come charging out of the town to attack us."

Thalon nodded and ran back off into the darkness. Zyid watched as the prisoners were marched past toward the gate. Kasala had moved to an aggressive stance to ensure they did not lose the fear in their eyes. The prisoners shuffled and were left at the gate.

Zyid could barely make out Thalon's shouts at the gate. "We have broken the siege. We shall be leaving on our way now. We wish you the best." If there was a reply, he could not hear it as he watched Thalon ride back with a few men. He motioned as everyone slowly shuffled back into the woods quenching the campfires as they went, so they could begin to get some rest.

Zyid and Kasala waited till they had all gone then she motioned for him to get back on, but he waved it off and jogged back to camp as she launched herself back into the dark sky.

The early morning found Zyid and Kasala riding toward the gate. A light fog hung in the air. "Do you think they will let us in?"

Zyid shrugged in reply. "I hope so I would like some bread that I do not have to dip in beer to make it edible."

Kasala laughed heartily nearly falling from her saddle. "All the possible things and you just want fresh bread."

As they neared the gate, Zyid called up.

"Greetings!" Time seemed to crawl in the silence before a head poked over the parapet.

"Who goes there?" the figure called down.

"It is us the merchants, Zyid and Kasala," he called back.

"You two sure picked a bad time to come back."

Zyid tilted his head slightly. "Oh! Why is that?"

"We were just under siege then suddenly some crazy people came charging out of the woods! A blasted dragon in tow too. I could hardly believe my eyes. I am still not sure that I do believe what I saw. Terrible and amazing all at once. So what brings you two back here? We all thought it would be much longer before you returned."

We did indeed finish just stopping on our way home. "We have a few more people with us this time. Will we be allowed to buy supplies?"

"Yes, Zyid really wants some fresh bread." Laughter could be heard from the parapet. "I will send a runner to the duchess, and we shall see what she says."

"Fair enough," he replied.

Kasala leaned over in her saddle, nudging him with an elbow. "Seems you will have to wait on your fresh loaf of bread a bit longer yet." He looked at her but gave no reply.

CHAPTER 14

E MMA FOUND HERSELF IN THE SHADOW OF the great statue. The three heroic figures holding their stone banner aloft. She could not help but smile at the memory of Zyid retelling the story of the Dragon War yet another time. An unfamiliar voice brought her out of her thoughts. "It is a very lovely statue. Time seems to have had no effect on it." Emma peered back over her shoulder to see the recent arrival with her two attendants strolling toward her.

She gave a curt bow of her head and returned her gaze to the statue before answering. "Zyid once told me that they placed a spell on it so that it would not be affected by the wind and the rain. But I have no idea if it is true or not."

The woman nodded as she bent down, placing a hand onto its base. "There is indeed a spell of some sort on it though I cannot tell what purpose it serves exactly. It is quite potent whatever it is."

Emma nodded. "So you are a mage then? I would kindly request that you do not go around causing trouble with your magic."

The lady laughed. "I will do no such thing, good Captain. My spells would be very obvious as I can only control and create ice with it after all. But I swear that I will not use it within these walls."

Emma slowly nodded in reply. "So what is it that brings our guests out and about so early in the morning?"

"Truth be told, I just wanted to see everything this place has to show me."

Emma laughed. "Well, it will certainly not take you long to do that then." They both laughed for a moment before silence fell over them.

"This place is very much like that man described it."

Emma looked toward her. "That man?"

"Oh, sorry, I was speaking of Zyid. He often spoke of his home. He seemed to love and hate it in equal measure."

"I can understand why he would be that way."

"What do you mean if I may ask?"

Emma took a deep breath, running a hand through her hair before answering. "Before he left, he only played in the forests and would spend any other time reading in the town hall. The other boys made fun of him for spending time reading instead of helping his family. But his father encouraged him to go find what he wanted to do."

"So what is it he wanted to be?"

Emma thought for a moment. "I am not really sure. His real dream was to make this place a real city to make it prosperous." She paused, rubbing her chin. "So I guess the answer is many things."

"We seem to know two sides of the same man." She ran her hand down the statue. "The Zyid I know was strong and sure of what he wanted and did not let anyone push him around. But yet, I can see that part you mentioned. He is not so different now than he was then it would seem."

Silence came over them as they stared at the statue.

Emma broke the silence first. "Are you here for him then? Seems the only reason you would come here."

She nodded. "I am here to give him a message, that is all." She paused for a moment before continuing. "My father asked me to go so I did." She smiled. "That and my father knew I would enjoy traveling so along I came. That man is like a brother to me and a great personal inspiration. I train daily because of him. And for that I am grateful."

"I see" was all Emma could reply weakly. "I am sure he will return soon, but he is not good at keeping in touch." She laughed. "Well, at least not with me anyway."

"I will wait as long as it takes for that is my duty."

"He is very good at making people wait it seems."

"Also, I have been very remiss in not introducing myself properly. I am Rashida, and it is a pleasure to meet you in person." She gave a bow. "I look forward to getting to know you better."

"I am Emma and the pleasure is all mine." She reached out a hand. She stared at it for a brief moment before a smirk crossed her face as she took the offered hand.

*****

Zyid and Kasala stood once again before the duchess. Her bloodshot eyes gazed back and forth over them both. "I welcome the two of you here once again though I wish it were under better circumstances." Her words came out slow and tired. She snapped her fan shut and leaned forward in her chair, speaking again in nearly a whisper. "First a siege and then a dragon out of the forest. Dark times indeed."

The pair nodded and Zyid replied, "It does not seem you have much to fear of it if it left you be. I mean a dragon seems as if it could very easily destroy one town if it so desired."

She nodded slowly though her expression failed to soften. "But for now, we rebuild and send envoys to our neighbors. Perhaps news of a dragon being about will let calmer heads prevail instead of this constant foolishness."

"I wish you the best in your efforts, but we and our group wish to enter the city to barter. We shall be on our way in the way once that is concluded."

"Yourselves and a group of representatives may enter. You must understand we cannot have so many strangers on the streets so soon. Also, do not be surprised if prices are a tad high."

Zyid shrugged. "At the very least, the high prices should work both ways."

The old woman smiled. "Spoken like a true merchant." With that, they bowed and were ushered back out into the street.

The pair began weaving through the crowd. Sellers out at their stalls. Families crying together for those lost or of great relief. The shadow of the guards and militia still walking the ramparts. The sound of animals being moved toward the city gates. The inn they passed was full to bursting with people raising mugs to the sky. Kasala pulled Zyid out of the path of a cart full of rubble that creaked and groaned as it passed.

"Are you okay?" she asked, a hint of concern in her voice.

He looked around again before answering. "Yes, I just was lost in thought. This was a very minor problem."

Kasala laughed. "Do not tell them that."

"Well, I am just hoping that we can avoid this in our home." He let out a slow deep breath. "But I have a grave feeling that is asking for far too much."

She patted him on the back, and they began walking once again. Thalon was waiting for them with the rest of the company just outside the gate.

Thalon waved them over. "So what did they say? Can we come in at all?"

"Well, not much fresh bread," Kasala called back. Thalon hung his head.

"Well, that is no good. I suppose we just need to pack up and be on our way then." A laugh went through the gathered crowd.

Zyid stepped in front of the group "Well, it is a mess in there, but a small group will go in and trade for what we can. So pick five others and get some lists of things to get and see what you can do. Though I would not expect much. Well not much at a reasonable price that is." The group grumbled and began speaking among themselves. Thalon and the other two walked a slight distance away.

Thalon spoke in a low voice. "So how does it look in there? Do you think they suspect anything?" Zyid stroked his beard for a moment before answering.

"I do not think they are certain, but I would be wary if I were in their shoes." The three nodded in agreement.

Before they could speak, Bellenta interrupted. "Well, we are off. Have fun waiting out here." Thalon smiled as they kissed.

"Have fun, dear, try not to be too hard on our friends." She flashed a coy smile before leading the group and several pack animals into the gate.

"But they probably suspect us but would not want to say it out-right," Zyid said, finishing his thought.

Kasala shrugged. "Not as if it is easy to detect a dragon who really wants to hide. I do have a bit of practice at it after all. So how do we pass the time?" The other two only shrugged in reply.

"Should probably go to the mining guild and show our faces though sure that grubby old man will be overjoyed I am still walking."

"Guess we are off again Thalon our men cannot seem to sit still. Do not let anyone cause trouble now."

Thalon laughed heartily.

"You have already spent too much time with my wife." They all laughed as the pair walked back into the city.

*****

"Good Captain?" Emma heard a voice call. She turned to see Rashida leaning on the gateway leading to the guard's training yard. Looking past her, the two attendants a short distance behind as always. "Could I trouble you and join in your training? I feel that training with a new opponent would be most beneficial." Emma silently motioned for her to enter. "Most fun a new opponent," she said with a smile beaming on her face.

"Well, I cannot very well say no to you now, can I?" Emma wiped her brow. "What of those two?"

She looked back at her attendants who had only moved to the gateway. They took their place standing guard facing back out into the town. "Those two will be fine. They are not much fun away." She waved the air for emphasis. "I am sure they would have said something along the lines of." She made her voice deeper. "Princess, we cannot protect you if we are sparring with you here. Your father would punish us if we failed." She laughed at her own impersonation. "But my father would just make another child if anything happened anyway. But far more importantly, I must keep my skills sharp. After all, I cannot let that man outshine me forever."

Emma took an arrow from a quiver slowly knocking it. "Why is it you call Zyid that man if I may ask?" She took aim and released an arrow as the princess answered.

"It is a habit of mine. I mean him no disrespect. For many years, I only knew him as that boy. Then he grew into that man. I met him in person before that, but my father kept calling him that for almost as long as he was a student." Emma drew her bow slowly again, releasing the air from her lungs before letting her another arrow fly. The arrow whistled through the air before hitting with a dull thud in the sod target.

"So when did you first meet him?" She took aim again.

Rashida pursed her lips. "I believe I first saw him as soon as he arrived at the castle or very soon after. I remember sneaking into the great chamber to see what all the fuss had been about. There he stood with my teacher. He was afraid of my father but seemed to be trying to look tough." She laughed. "I can understand him being afraid of my father."

Emma laughed as she let the arrow fly so it flew into the wall behind the target. "I see he was trying to remake himself." She stopped for a moment before starting to take out another arrow. "He really has changed then." She put the arrow back as if realizing something. "I apologize. You came to spar and I just continued on with my routine."

She waved Emma's comment off. "All in time hearing of this other side of him is quite fun. I must go look for those books he told me all about."

Emma snorted. "Well, I guess he has not completely changed then." She wiped a tear away from her face as she spoke again. "Now...What is it you would like to spar with?"

The pair walked a short way to several barrels of practice weapons. Emma motioned over at them. Rashida looked them over a moment before taking one out, shaking her head, and returning it to the barrel. She then pulled out another turning it over in her hand several times before nodding in approval. "Just a basic sword then? If that is agreeable with you, that is?"

Emma nodded, taking out an identical wooden waster. "Training is about working on what one is weak as just as much as what one you are strong at," she replied softly. Emma motioned her to follow, and they walked around a corner to the sparring yard. Several guards were conducting basic drills and the pair hopped over the fence into an enclosure at the center. They both readied themselves.

"Ready?" She nodded lightly in reply. "Then begin!" For a moment, neither moved. A few moments passed before Emma stepped quickly to the side before lunging in for a strike. Rashida parried, taking a step back and swiping at Emma's exposed torso. Emma was able to roll away from the slash. She could feel the blade cutting through the air it passed so close. They stepped away and assumed their ready stances once again. Rashida took a few strikes at Emma, testing her guard. Emma began circling and tried to strike but found it easily deflected, leaving her wide open. She moved to leap away from a blow she felt would be coming. Just as she started to move, Rashida's palm collided into her chest, taking the wind out of her and throwing her to the ground. Several boos and hisses brewed forth from a growing crowd. Rashida's shadow fell over her as she looked up with a cough. "I suppose this round goes to you then." She took several deep breaths to recover.

Rashida shrugged. "It does indeed seem that way. But you are not unskilled." She smiled and offered a hand to Emma, hoisting her up. Emma dusted herself off. "Shall we go again? You will need to work harder if you want to catch up to that man after all."

Emma rubbed her chest. "Is he really that much better?"

Rashida nodded. "He has even defeated me on more than one occasion. So I would say that he is."

"Is that so?" Emma snorted softly. "And here I thought I could keep up with him." She rested a hand on her hip. "He must be cheating."

Rashida chuckled and shook her head slowly as she readied her sword. "No. He is just someone who has a goal."

Emma readied herself again. They began circling once again. "Do many in your lands use two swords?" Emma asked, striking several quick blows.

"No. He developed his own techniques since he wanted to impress his teacher." She slashed out to force Emma back. "It is not a useful technique for fighting in groups, so it really is not something to teach soldiers. A style for show many would call it." She lunged, taking Emma by surprise and forcing her back. "You must really work on that footwork, dear Captain." Her lips curled into a smile. "This will be fun."

*****

Kasala and Zyid entered the guild headquarters, a faint burning smell wafting through the air. They weaved through the various workmen and clerks to find the guild master at his desk in the back admiring the small hole in the ceiling near his desk. As he turned back to his work, he saw the two approaching. "Ah, you two have returned." He gave a curt nod before continuing. "And by the commotion of extra dwarves in the streets, I presume your venture was successful."

"Indeed it was," Kasala answered with a grin. "My mine is sure to bring in even more money now with their aid."

Zyid lightly slapped the back of her head. "Our mine. I will remind you." He sighed, shaking his head. "But yes, we have extra help and presumably more customers. And with the trouble, you were just having more customers certainly could not hurt."

"No, it could not, but that will take time. In the meantime, it was good. We partnered with you. We are well on our way to recouping our investment with you. We look forward to continuing this profitable venture together."

Zyid gave a shallow bow. "As do I, good sir." The guild master thumbed through a few stacks of paper before handing Zyid a receipt.

"Here is what we have done so far. The amount should be to your liking." The old man smiled as he rested his hands on his desk. Zyid scanned over the document with Kasala peeking over his shoulder. Nodding as he read.

"All seems to be in order. For now, I will just reinvest in our venture. And take out a small amount of silver." The old man nodded, pulling out his paper and quill.

He swiftly wrote out the appropriate letter. "Does this amount seem satisfactory?" Zyid peered down, nodding in satisfaction. The master pulled a lump of wax and seal from the desk and quickly pressed the seal onto the paper and handed it to Zyid. "Well, we look forward to our continued business and hope that next time will be under even better conditions." The pair politely bowed before taking their leave.

"Why take any money out?" Kasala asked as they weaved their way toward the bank.

"Always need some coin on hand. Not everything can be bartered for after all. Could not hurt to throw some more coin Emma's way. I do owe her a big favor for everything she has done. She is very close to abusing her power as it is. Some coin would help smooth some tempers." He laughed. "Though pushing the limits does seem to run in her family, so I am sure she is fine." Zyid smiled as he placed his hands on the back of his head, staring up at the sky as they walked.

"You should probably watch where you are going."

"Probably," he answered absentmindedly.

"So what do we do know? After we exchange our note."

"I guess we just wait until morning then head out. We really need to get back home. We have been gone quite a while."

"You spent most of your life away from it and you still call it home. Why is that anyway? Is it just because you were born there?" He stopped for a moment, stroking his beard before he continued on.

"It just is home. My family is from there. And to me that makes it home enough. Besides, the lands to the east where I spent all those years was never really home. I was welcomed but never loved." He turned his head to look at her a questioning look on his face. "If that makes any sense."

They arrived at the bank, placed the note, and received their goods in short order.

"I am surprised they were not short on coin."

"This place does have a silver mine so it is not that odd, but you are correct perhaps people did not want to hide it in their homes." They scanned the crowds, moving around the square. Zyid heaved a sigh, nodding his head. "Well, time to go rest at our camp then." He shielded his eyes from the midday sun as he scanned the crowds again. "After all, not much to do around here at the moment."

"What, no drinking?" A hint of sadness touched her tone.

"I believe I have drank enough for several lifetimes thanks to being around the king."

Kasala laughed. "And I thought I was bad at holding my drink."

"Well, you are, but they just kept pouring them. What is a man to do when a king eggs you on to drink?" Zyid held his stomach as he spoke. "Never party with dwarves ever again I think should be a new life motto for me."

"Has anyone ever told you you are no fun?"

Zyid nodded. "I believe you have told me several times, but I have been hearing that most of my life." He ran his hand down the great doors of the city gate, stopping once they came out from the gateway. He began counting on his fingers. "My brother, my sister, the town bully." He smiled and began waving a finger down at a shorter version of himself. "You spend all day reading those silly books and playing in the woods. You should be working the farm helping your father."

Kasala burst out laughing. "Ah yes, that does sound about right!" Zyid turned his head, a puzzled expression on his face.

"Oh nothing," she spat out. "That just sounds like something people would say. What did your father think of your antics anyway?" Zyid smiled, staring at the sky for a moment before bending down and speaking in a deep voice.

"Now, Zyid, I want you to go out and find what you want from life. This farm could be yours if you so want, or you can walk away and never return." His cast an arm toward the road. "Son, my dreams are not your burdens. I have gotten all I ever wanted out of life. You three are the gifts of the gods, and all I want is for you to find a purpose that suits you." He paused then snapped his fingers as if remembering something important. "Ah yes and always remember what your mother told you, son." He stood spinning around on the heels of his feet. Kasala cocked her head to one side.

"So are you going to finish, or is that as far as your poor head can remember?"

Zyid glared at her for a moment before continuing. "Mother always said, 'My son, do the noble deed. You have to finish what you started, no matter what.'" Kasala smiled. "What are you smirking about?"

"Oh, nothing at all. It just sounds nice is all."

"Sure, but I guess I will leave it at that. Now let us go do nothing for the rest of the day for that is always fun."

"Do not make fun of a dragon's favorite pastime so lightly," she huffed in return.

*****

Emma fell onto the timbers of the training enclosure exhausted and wheezing for breath. She felt the beginning of many bruises. Her opponent did not seem nearly as tired, but she certainly seemed to have slowed her movements. "Emma, you are very determined. I commend you on that. You set a fine example for those under you. This has been very enjoyable." She offered a hand and hoisted Emma back on her feet. "Shall we go get a drink to finish off our day?"

Emma laughed lightly after starting to catch her breath. "I think I will need many drinks and a long soak in a tub. I have not felt this tired in ages." She rubbed her stomach. "You are very skilled. Have you always been that way?" The pair began down the streets. Emma noted all the new faces mingling with the old. The city was growing ever so slowly as people came to find opportunities in new markets.

Rashida laughed. "Oh, by the gods, no. I was very much unskilled in years past." She chuckled. "But my parents were strict teachers. And I trained from a young age. A delicate life I was not destined to have."

"Do you ever wish things were different?" Emma asked quietly almost to herself.

Rashida furrowed her brow in thought. Several buildings passed before she had her answer. "To be honest, I am not sure. It is hard to miss what you never had. And while my training was grueling certainly, it was never that I felt unloved or that I was missing out on what life had. Life honestly was not bad."

Emma was silent. "Why do you ask? Do you feel overly burdened, Emma? For that seems to be what you are really asking."

"Well, many people do depend on me. But it is not as if I had to take this position. Though I did in a way feel obligated to since my family has been serving as guard captain for as far back as anyone remembers. So I suppose maybe I do now that you have asked." The pair laughed.

"We all have our burdens to carry and demons to face as my father would often say to me." As they neared the inn, they could faintly hear Arlana's sweet voice carrying over the dull murmur of the crowd. Kalgrin's beaming smile greeted them as they entered. He motioned them over to the counter near him. Arlana passed back to the kitchen singing all the way.

"Tough day out there, Captain?" Kalgrin asked with a laugh.

"I suppose one could look at it that way." She gave a hard glance at Rashida.

"Hard certainly, but I believe you have learned much today."

Kalgrin set two tankards down on the counter.

"Well, it seems you could both use one of these so here is one on the house."

"Kalgrin, how do you even stay in business?" Emma asked as she took a mighty swig from her tankard.

"That, my dear, is my little secret," he replied with a coy smile as he wiped a spot of foam off her nose.

"You seem to be enjoying your stay here in our little town," he said, returning to his work.

"I am indeed. It is always most enjoyable to experience new things." She smiled as she spoke. "I wish I could explore it more as this land is full of new sights and sounds. But alas, I will do my duty and report to home once that duty is done."

"We all must do what we must," Kalgrin replied quietly as he scrubbed out a tankard.

"So what do you ladies plan to do with the rest of your day?" Arlana asked, placing two bowls of soup in front of them.

Emma sniffed herself. "Well, I think after food is a bath. Then maybe sleep for a day or two after today. But you must keep sparring with me. A new opponent will do wonders I believe."

Rashida smiled. "I am glad I could be of some assistance to you. But Zyid could teach you just as well, could he not?"

"I suppose he could, but he has barely stood still since he has been back." Emma fixed her gaze on the ceiling. "Even when he first came back, he did not even stop by to say hello. Just came here, moved into a room, and went to read books. It is like he does not care about people at all."

Rashida paused, thinking for a moment. "No. He is just fixated I suppose. He is actually very caring of people. He just chases his goal like a wolf on the hunt."

"So what you are saying is that, he is an animal?" Kalgrin added cheekily.

"In a manner of speaking, yes. Just spend some time with your friend, dear Captain, and you will see."

Emma shrugged, blowing on her spoon full of soup. "He is still a fool, so I suppose that will have to do." She ate her spoonful of soup slowly. The warmth from it warming as it passed to her stomach. "You, Kalgrin, are an amazing cook. I really should eat more of it."

"And that, my dear, is how I stay in business," he said, stabbing a stubby finger at her.

CHAPTER 15

"SO HOW EXACTLY ARE WE GOING TO explain me?" Kasala whispered in Zyid's ear, startling him out of his daze.

He looked over at her for a moment before the question seemed to run across his mind.

"Well…Well, to be honest, I have not quite figured that out yet. But we should probably go have a talk with the mayor and Emma."

She laughed. "Oh, Emma will not be happy with you. She is going to give you quite the browbeating for this one." She continued to laugh despite Zyid's harsh glare.

"But yes, since everyone here already knows, probably best we let them in on the fun."

She wiped a tear from her eye. "I am so looking forward to this."

"Well, at least one of us is," Zyid said with a sigh. "I think I just need to stay in bed for a while."

"You do not seem the type to just sit in bed," she said after a deep breath. "We have much work to do. Like wall building and loads of fun stuff." Zyid gave a half-hearted nod and went back to admiring the view.

The forest had been cleared back a considerable distance from the road and a fence erected along the edge of the road. He could not help but smile at all that had been done.

Passing another small watchtower, a guard called down. "Finally coming home again, huh? You just cannot stay away it seems."

"Just bringing some friends for a visit is all. Buy them a drink and I am sure they will tell you all the best stories," he yelled in return as they trotted by. Zyid could see him shaking his head.

"You know things are going to get a little crazy real fast right?" Thalon chimed in as he rode up.

"Just a little you say?" Zyid laughed. "Oh no things are going to get very interesting I think." He sighed. "It is going to be a long day today, I just know it."

They arrived in the town just before the closing of the gate, sending most of the group on ahead to the mine head to begin setting up their accommodations. Kasala and Zyid rode up to the tavern to find Kalgrin standing on the front porch smoking his pipe. "So you two have finally made it home, huh?" he said with a scowl on his face. "I have been very busy since you left. But"—a smile broke out across his face as he spoke—"it was a lot of fun at the same time." He waved them both inside as they hitched up their horses. "Do not worry. Emma is not here right now. She and her new friend went to go look at the archives."

"New friend?" Kasala asked with a puzzled look on her face.

"Oh, do not worry, young one. It will be very fun, trust me." Zyid just sighed. "He is always against my fun."

"Yes, I am. It usually just makes work for me."

"It may be work but it is still fun. Now let us go sit in the back and have a nice chat about you two." He led them to the table in the farthest corner. "Now tell me everything."

*****

"So you knew about her the whole time."

Kalgrin snorted. "Of course I did, I am a mage." He leaned in speaking in a hushed whisper. "We are kinda good at the whole magic thing after all. I am far more interested in what poor Emma will think when she hears what the two of you have been up to."

"This is not going to be a fun next day or so, is it?" Kalgrin shook his head.

Zyid stood stretching. "Is the tub still out back? I think I could use a soak in it before everything goes crazy."

"Same place as always," Kalgrin called behind him. "So what are you going to do?"

"What else does one do in an inn? Drink and probably fall asleep near the fireplace." She nodded to herself. "Yes, that sounds like a wonderful plan I think." Kalgrin smiled.

"It is nice you are very easy to please." She smiled but said nothing as Kalgrin stood and headed toward the bar.

Zyid headed up the stairs looking down over the mostly empty tables as he walked along the balcony, his room hung off the rear of the inn at the end of a small hallway. He took out his key. The lock came open with a light click. It was just as he had left it. His small bed was in the corner with its threadbare blanket, a towel draped over the end. A small table next to the bed with an empty pitcher on it. His small chest holding his extra clothing.

He smiled at his small existence then grabbed some fresh cloths and his towel and headed back down and outside. A few more people had entered for the evening, and Kasala had moved to the bar and was holding a tankard in one hand and stuffing her face with the other. Kalgrin's face wore a hearty smile. They nodded as he passed. The tub was in its usual place in the stable, and he dragged it out into the yard, filling it with water from the well. He took care to fold his dirty clothes then gently eased himself into the freezing water.

The night was clear with the stars all dancing and twinkling in the sky. If he closed his eyes and focused, he could just barely hear the dull roar from inside. "You could have taken some warm water from the kitchens, you know?" Arlana's familiar voice drifted through the air from behind him. "Or is the cold your way of having the tub to yourself?" She laughed at her own joke. "But welcome back again. It seems as if your trip went well."

"Better than I could have hoped for really." He paused for a moment. "And thank you. I am sure patrolling the roads was not something that was very fun for you two. I hate having to drag everyone into what I am doing."

She laughed again. "It is not a bother, let me assure you. The roads are much quieter now anyway. There are not many weak targets now so they have mostly moved to easier pickings. It is good to get out and away now and again after all. You should know that fairly well by now." The near silence settled for a moment only broken by Zyid's huffs as he tried to find the right words. But Arlana spoke first. "But everyone should be thanking you. In your short time back, you have done more to breathe life into this place in gods know how long."

"Even if I am only doing it for my own reasons?" Arlana heaved a heavy sigh.

"If your idea of selfishness is giving people hope and energy, then you can probably be forgiven for it."

"What if it only causes more pain and suffering down the line?"

Arlana leaned down onto his head. "The whole weight of the world does not rest on your shoulders, Zyid." Her tone was authoritative. "Things will happen regardless. I know you fear what is to come but ask for help when you need it. We are your friends after all."

"I hope that will be enough," he answered flatly.

"That remains to be seen."

*****

Emma's candle cast an eerie glow on the archive walls. As she tread down the well-worn staircase, she ran her free hand low along the walls tracing its familiar pattern. Her footstep softly echoed as she reached the bottom and stepped into the main chamber. Its wall lined with scrolls and books. Only one table with several chairs took some space. Rashida sat at the table thumbing through one of the volumes. "I hate to interrupt you, but I need to lock up for the night." She nodded as she stood, closing the tome.

"It is amazing that records like this survive. The war did not leave many written records." She took up her own candle, holding it up to illuminate more of the room. "Does the captain of the guard always have the key?"

"No, not always, but my father started carrying it after Zyid and I took it and snuck down here to read some of the books. So I suppose I just do it out of habit." Emma could see her smile slightly before it slipped from her face.

"I see. Well, I best be back to the inn then. Time to rest." She started out with Emma close behind. "It is hard to imagine him as a boy who got into trouble. He was always so serious for the few times I met him." Emma giggled.

"He and I got into our fair share of trouble running through the woods and all that. Kalgrin and Arlana often had to bail us out of trouble. Good times…" Emma trailed off.

"It sounds nice," she replied softly. They stepped out into the dimly lit courtyard.

"Will you need any help getting back?"

"Oh no." She waved off. "I will be alright, not as if those two will not be with me." She hooked her thumb at her attendants. Emma bowed her head to them slightly

"Very well then, have a pleasant evening." Emma started to turn but stopped. "Oh yes, and I think Zyid might have returned, but I will have to have a chat with him tomorrow. I am slightly worried about what I have heard." Emma heaved a sigh, waved, and ducked back inside.

"We have indeed confirmed that he has returned," one attendant said in a low gruff voice. "What shall we do, my lady?"

"Only what I was ordered to do, but it can wait until the morning. He will be tested, and I shall deliver my father's message." She smiled as she walked into the night. "It will be fun to recount to my father what he has been up to. He does miss his favorite son after all."

"Of course, my lady." The three settled into silence for their trip to the inn. The trio strolled through the nearly empty streets rays of light shining from the windows of homes and shops. They followed the sound of the crowd emanating from the Trolls Heads.

Upon entering, she found that it was nearly empty. Kalgrin stood as she entered.

"Ah, I see you have returned, young lady. How did you enjoy your time in our lovely library?" He laughed at his own joke.

"It was interesting indeed, good innkeeper. It seems very quiet tonight. It is odd to see."

He laughed again as he dunked a tankard into a barrel of ale. "Oh, everyone just spent all of their money already, so it will be like this the next couple of days." He sat them on the bar top, motioning for her to sit. As she sat, he leaned over, covering his mouth with his hand. "Do those two ever have any fun?" he whispered as he gazed at her attendants.

She shook her head as she whispered back, "Never when we are out of the capitol." Kalgrin nodded, shrugged, and took a swig out of the second tankard.

"Have you heard Zyid has returned?" She sipped her drink before answering.

"I did indeed from your good captain. She seemed very…" She moved her mouth side to side as she struggled with the correct words. "She seemed rather annoyed. She seems to be dreading tomorrow."

Kalgrin let out a hearty laugh. "Most probably, but it will be interesting to say the least." He smiled over his tankard. "If you wanted to talk with him, he already went to sleep. He is quite exhausted from his travels."

"I would expect no less. Travel is always tiring. Best it wait until the morning anyway. I must cross blades with him. Will that be a problem?"

"Not so long as you do it outside the city walls. Then you two kids can test your limits if that is what you are asking." She smiled and gave a curt nod.

"Sleep will be difficult tonight. To do battle with him again will be most enjoyable." A wicked smile crossed her lips.

*****

Zyid awoke to the gentle murmur from the main room. The night shift grabbing a bite of dinner before heading off to sleep. He stood opening the small window beside his bed. The crisp autumn breeze ran through the room. He took a slow deep breath, bracing for the day to come. He wandered down stairs after dressing and put his hair up to find Kasala scarfing down a plate of food at the bar. "Did someone drink too much last night?" She stopped, turning her head to reveal her messy face, which garnered a few laughs.

"I will have you know I did not drink too much. I drank the perfect amount." He cocked his head, a look of disbelief on his face Kalgrin just shrugged.

"Well today should be fun, should it not?" he asked as he settled down next to her. The three laughed before Kalgrin spoke.

"That it will for you, young people. You should eat before you go. I have a feeling it is going to be a long day for you."

Zyid waved the idea away. "No time, sadly. I am sure Emma is already pacing, waiting for me to arrive."

Kalgrin smiled. "I am sure she is, but at least take this." He set down a small loaf of bread. "Arlana got up extra early to bake it so be sure to eat it while it is still warm." He stopped midturn, a finger raised. "Oh, and one more thing. Your friend from the east said she would wait just outside the eastern gate for you when you are done." Zyid stood taking a great bite from the loaf, giving a single wave as he walked out the door. The loaf was the perfect temperature with a slight taste of honey. He savored the taste in his mouth as he strolled through town.

Kasala quickly caught up to him. "Planning on leaving me behind, were you? I am kind of important to this, am I not?"

He swallowed another bite before answering. "That would probably depend on who you asked, but yes I suppose you are correct. I knew you would catch up when you had finished your breakfast."

She snorted at him. "I can hardly believe there are so many people here now. It is so nice to see that I am making some difference."

"Some? I would say more than that, but yes it is nice. This place has been empty for too long. So what is today's plan?"

"Same as always. To get ourselves ready for a war."

"You seem pretty ready as is. And I might be ready so what is there to do."

"True, we are ready but…" He took the final bite. Continuing, his mouth full of bread, "But two is not an army no matter how mighty. I have been sending letters, but it is hard to buy mercenaries when there is no immediate action. That and I do not want to make poor Emma's job more difficult."

She laughed as they passed by the statue and into the courtyard. "I am fairly certain you have already failed miserably at that part."

Emma was just as Kalgrin had guessed, pacing in front of the main steps. Kasala nodded. "Yes, yes, you have definitely failed." Emma turned her head toward them before returning to her pacing for another few steps. She suddenly stopped turning to look again and stormed toward Zyid.

"You!" she roared as she approached. "What in the hell do you have to say for yourself this time? Are you just trying to make my life miserable? First a bunch of miners and now you have a band of dwarven mercenaries following you?" She sighed as she covered her eyes with her hand. "And who by the gods is this?" she asked in an exhausted tone. Zyid opened his mouth to answer but stopped then looked at Kasala then back to Emma.

"Perhaps it is best we take this inside. It is going be a long conversation." He nodded at Kasala and the two began walking at a brisk pace past her.

"Hey! I am not finished with you yet!" she shouted after them.

"Well, good Emma, we do need you in this meeting after all!" Kasala yelled back. She caught back up with them as they entered the building.

"And who are you to talk to me like that?" Kasala laughed but said nothing. "Are you just going to let her come with us?"

Zyid could feel Emma's icy stare on the back of his neck. "While she can be a pain, she is also important. Believe me, she does need to be here. I hope the mayor is ready for this one." Emma huffed but remained silent as they made their way through the building. They weaved past several guards and a few clerks arriving at the mayor's door. Zyid went to knock but he only found empty air as Kasala stormed into the room. Zyid let out a defeated sigh and followed her with Emma close behind. The mayor sat unfazed behind his desk, only pausing from a piece of parchment to scan the new arrivals with his deep green eyes.

"You know you are not permitted to enter these chambers unless invited." The secretary protested in his squeaky voice. The harsh glares from the rest of the room caused him to fall silent. The mayor took several moments to finish his work before placing down his quill and resting his hands on his desk. He slowly looked over the three of them before speaking.

"I heard some interesting rumors this morning as I was riding through the fields this morning. You seem to have been a busy little boy it seems?" Zyid opened his mouth to speak, but the mayor's raised hand stopped him. "You go to the mountain and fight a dragon. Then you open a mine and run off to go get more money and people to help you run it." He paused, heaving a heavy sigh. "And now not only did you bring back some dwarves to grow your enterprise, but you have brought her along with you too." He nodded at Kasala. "All of that is crazy enough, but you made a deal with a dragon?" The words hung heavy in the deafening silence of the room. Emma and the secretary began stepping back.

"You are a dragon?" Her voice came out shaky. "And you brought it into the town? Have you completely lost your mind?"

Kasala simply smiled at her. "Oh, I have been in this town many times, Emma. I have lived here since before this town ever existed. I watched as it was carved out of the wilderness." She stopped, stepping across the room and opening the window behind the mayor. A cool breeze blew her hair around her face. "This is my second home, and it was sad to see it so empty for so long." She turned back to face Emma. "You two children were much more fun when you were getting into trouble. Running through the forest ignoring your chores." She stopped again, a smile crossing her lips. "Always with loyal dog in tow." She closed the window, striding toward Emma and taking on a canine form and sitting in front of her. A look of confusion came over Emma's face as she knelt down to look the dog in the eyes. Kasala cocked her head to one side, a happy grin on her snout.

"It just cannot be, can it? You were that dog? I had a dragon as a pet?" Emma massaged her nose. "Did you know about this?" She looked at Zyid.

He shook his head slowly. "I had a feeling like I knew when I saw her eyes. But no, I had no idea for sure."

The mayor cleared his throat. "If the three of you are done with your trip down memory lane..." He paused, looking over at the secretary who had fallen shaking to the floor. "Pull yourself together, man. We have work to be done yet. Anyway, the two of you had best not raise too much of a stir, though we are probably well past that point. Do not cause me and this place any trouble and pay the taxes due, and we will have no issues. Though many in town might not feel the same way."

Kasala laughed as she changed back into her human form. "They may be worried, but there is not much they could do about it, but I will watch my back."

The mayor nodded and continued, "The papers have been sent to Worstan. I am sure he is eager to speak with you." He stopped and scanned the room Emma was leaning on the wall while the secretary was beginning to pull himself together. "Please, by the gods, do not cause any trouble our poor captain will not be able to take the strain." He smiled and shooed them out of the room. They all bowed and walked out, shutting the door securely behind them. The mayor picked up the next stack of papers and began reading through them.

"Sir, you cannot just let them go about their day like that. Think of all the problems they will cause," the secretary spoke firmly.

The mayor gazed at him without moving his head. "What else should we do? Lock them in our jail cells? It is a stone-walled cell, but I have a feeling it would not hold a dragon and company. Besides, she has always been here. Why would she cause trouble now? This is her home as much or even more than ours."

"Yes, but what if she is lying?" he protested.

"Then she is lying, and we will have to deal with that when the time comes. Zyid is a good man. I think I will trust him on this. Not only that, but Kalgrin and Arlana see no issue with her then it will more than likely be fine." He put down his paper and leaned on his hands. "I remember those two with that dog of theirs in tow. If that does not give you faith, then I do not know what will."

*****

Emma released a deep breath as she pushed past Zyid and Kasala. "You two come with me. We are not done speaking yet." Emma shoved her way through the halls, throwing open the door to her room and slamming the door behind as they all entered. She strode to her small desk, dropping herself into her chair. She looked between the pair for several moments before opening her mouth then closing it again.

Kasala smiled. "My, you are so much the same as before, little Emma." Emma cast a glare at her. Kasala paid it no mind and continued, "Though a lot has changed as well. Zyid is the one dragging you around now instead of you wanting to run around in the forest."

"So we had a dragon as a pet? How is that even possible I mean..." Emma trailed off.

Zyid shrugged. "It would appear we did, Emma. A wild story to tell that is for sure."

"You were just hiding this from me and laughing at me the whole time I bet?"

Zyid frantically waved his hands. "No, I only suspected something, but I did not know for sure either." She bore into him with her eyes as if trying to be sure he was not lying. Satisfied, she cleared her throat and began again. "Well, now I have a dragon wandering about the town. This will just make everyone just that much more skittish. You just have to come home and make everything crazy. Could you have just stayed in the east instead of all this?"

Zyid shrugged. "I could have but I missed home."

Kasala burst out laughing. "I see that nothing has really changed." Calming her laughter, she continued. "I know many will fear me. It is logical after all to be weary of things, but in time, they will treat it as normal and see the many benefits it could bring them. Besides, the dwarves sing my praises." She placed her hands on her hips. "So I have that going for me to start. Or we could just say your hero here beat me and that should rest most of their minds." Emma let her head drop onto the desk with a thud.

"This is just. I just do not know what to think anymore. Just go for now, I guess, and if you both could refrain from causing any trouble for me, I would be very thankful."

Kasala bowed deeply. "I will do my utmost to not stir up trouble." She thumbed and Zyid. "This one I am not so sure about." Emma said nothing as she waved them out of the room.

"I am sorry about all this, Emma. I will try and keep disturbances to a minimum." Zyid bowed as he spoke.

"Sure you will." She sighed. "But thank you I suppose. Now off you go. Let me just sit and let my headache wash over me." Emma listened as her door opened, letting in the dull roar from the hall then shut leaving her in near total silence. She listened to the silence for a few moments, letting the weight of what she had just heard wash over her. She shook her head, lit the candle on her desk, retrieved quill and paper, and began writing furiously.

*****

They stood once again in the shadow of the statue. "So now that is out of the way, what shall we do with the rest of our day?" She rubbed her hands as if rubbing off dirt.

"I thought you would start drinking all day."

She scoffed. "You think very low of me."

He tapped a finger on his chin. "I wonder why?"

"You were much more fun as a child. Are you aware of that?"

He laughed. "I am sure that is true. A lot less weight on my shoulders back then that is for sure. But I have a feeling that meeting was only the start of my troubles for the day." He began walking toward the eastern gate with Kasala trailing behind. The crowd ebbed and flowed as they weaved through. "How long did you stay after I had left?"

"I stayed at your home until your father passed away." She paused, thinking it over. "Probably about five years or so." Zyid stopped suddenly, causing her to slam into him.

He turned his head to face her. "What did he say about me?" Zyid spoke in a low hushed voice almost as if ashamed of the question.

She smiled back at him, running a hand down his cheek. "Your father was always proud of his sons. Even when everyone else talked bad about you both. What terrible sons you were. He would just smile and say, 'I could not be more proud of my boys. They are chasing their goals just like I taught them.' He grew old quickly after you all left. But he died peacefully. I stayed with him till the end, so do not fret." Zyid stood deathly still, a single tear running down his cheek, which she wiped away. He walked out of the gate in a daze, not even hearing his name being called.

"Zyid!" Kalgrin shouted in his face as he shook him by the shoulders. "People are talking to you. You should pay more attention?"

Wide-eyed, he came back to the world. "What? Huh?"

"I brought you your swords. Your friend asked that I bring them outside the gate for you." He hooked a thumb over his shoulder at Rashida who stood flanked by her attendants.

She gave a curt bow, halberd in hand. "It is good to see you again, champion. I hope that you are well this fine day?"

Zyid's gaze narrowed, and he took his swords from Kalgrin, arming himself quickly as he stormed toward her. He stopped a few paces away, dropping himself onto one knee. "It is good to see you as well, Princess. I had thought it would be longer before you would come here."

Rashida laughed. "Why must you be like this, Zyid? You know that you are not required to bow before me. You are not beholden to me or our people. I believe you said as much yourself."

"I did say that very thing but…" He paused, raising to his feet. "I still must show proper respect or my mother could not rest in her grave." She smiled before turning toward Emma who had just arrived.

"Do not fret, Captain. I will keep my word and not cause any trouble in your city. But he and I must do battle now." She turned back to Zyid. "Now it is time to have a test as my father requested. Where shall we have our battle?"

Zyid stroked his beard in thought. "There is a clearing in the woods not far from here that would probably be best. I do not want to destroy any fields. The farmers would never let me live it down if they had to do extra work to prepare for planting in spring." With that, he turned toward the woods and started out with everyone in tow.

CHAPTER 16

THE GROUP REACHED THE CLEARING JUST AS the sun began passing overhead. Zyid swept his hands through the air. "I believe that this spot should serve us well. Nothing to destroy and we can use all our skills as I am sure you wish, Princess? Or more correctly as your father wishes."

She nodded. "Yes, I believe this will do." She motioned to her attendants. "Please clear out some of the debris and then we will commence our battle."

"If I had known I was to take a stroll through the woods, I would have brought some food with me for a picnic." Kalgrin laughed to himself as he plopped down on a fallen tree. "I am looking forward to this. Best make it a good show, son." Zyid gave a flourishing bow to him.

Emma sat down next to Kalgrin. "Why is it that he is so polite to her?" She crossed her arms with a huff.

Zyid shook his head. "I am polite to her because that is what was expected of me. Though she probably enjoyed you treating her more as a regular woman."

"It is tough to put such weight on the young," Kalgrin said as he bit down on his pipe. "But the young also must be the ones to truly change the course of things." He pointed with his pipe. "They seem to have finished clearing up. Now go show us what you can do, boy."

Zyid strode forward into the rough circle they had cleared. Rashida nodded her satisfaction. "This will have to do for our battle. As you said, Zyid, we should cause no one any trouble here."

"Except maybe those watching." He nodded behind her at the small crowd that had formed at the far edge of the clearing. She turned to shout at them.

"If you wish to watch, you are free to, but you should keep a fair distance." A few startled people stepped back, but their spaces were quickly filled. "Now then." Her voice booming. She took hold of her halberd, twirling it into a ready position. "As the challenger, do you have any conditions for the battle?"

He slowly shook his head. "I have none. If this is to be a true test, then we must use all our abilities, do we not?"

She nodded with a smile. "As expected from you. Then we shall do battle until there is blood drawn on the torso."

"Very well then." He drew his swords, setting them into a guard position.

"On your signal" She nodded to her attendants.

His gaze shifted between the combatants for a few moments. The older one raised his hand and brought it swiftly down toward the ground cutting the air. "Begin!"

Neither moved for what seemed an eternity. The air began to chill. Rashida shifted her foot slightly, causing Zyid to begin charging toward her. Closing the distance, he moved one blade to parry hers and the other in a slash toward her side. The first moved her blade aside, but the second found itself slicing through a sheet of ice she had erected. Zyid growled in frustration as he rolled out from below her hammer blow. He barely regained his feet when shards of ice sailed past him. She had closed the distance again and began unleashing a flurry of blows at him, placing him on the back foot.

"Kadan!" He roared, smashing the pummels together. He took hold of one blade using it as a spear to regain some distance from her. Blood ran from his hands as they began to silently circle around one another. They exchanged a flurry of swift thrusts trying to get past one another's guard before she shot forth a pillar of ice toward Zyid. He tucked himself into a roll, regaining his feet as she came diving from atop her wave of ice.

He moved to properly hold his swords, blocking her blade. His feet slid back from the force of the bow, but he flung her roughly to the side. The gathered crowd let out a cheer as she bounced back onto her feet. "You have not slacked in training I see." She nodded before letting loose a barrage of ice shards.

"Nor have you it seems." Zyid ducked and swatted at the ice before charging forward bringing a great overhead blow down toward her. The weapons met with a mighty crash. "Valtalen." Her eyes grew wide as if in slow motion. She saw the forward blade fall and felt the pommel of the second collide with her chest, throwing her onto her back and taking the wind from her chest. He stood over her blade raised, and he plunged it toward her throat.

"Halt!" The command stopped his blade with a jerk. The tip of his blade nearly at her throat. He blinked and then felt the small ting of pain from his chest and the gentle flow of blood.

"I see that I lost sight of the goal, and you have triumph in this contest." He retrieved his fallen blade and sheathed them before reaching down to pull Rashida to her feet.

She smiled, tossing away the shard of ice in her hand before taking hold of his wrist. "That was a very fun battle. I would say you have passed the test." She paused, looking back at the ground "Of course, if this had been a true contest, you surely would have been the victor." She nodded. "I only prevailed because you lost sight of the goal for just one moment and assured my victory."

Zyid nodded as he examined the tear in his tunic. "I did indeed." He laughed. "I am sure some people just lost a lot of money in bets!" He scanned across the crowd. Several were laughing, more than a few looked disappointed. "But, lady, what is your wish for being the winner as is customary?"

"I believe that you are already aware of what is required of you."

He nodded a scowl on his face.

"So when is it I should arrive then?"

"You should arrive in a few weeks as the competition will commence two weeks upon my return. Though you as the champion have some leeway in time of course." Murmurs could be heard from the crowd. "We shall take our leave this evening now that my task is complete." She gave a bow before turning on her heels and marching off toward the town, her attendants falling in behind her.

"It does not seem wise for a king to invite someone who wishes him dead." Another murmur ran through the crowd as she stopped to call behind her. "If you succeed, we will simply follow you." She took a step before stopping again. "And besides, what is one more funeral to you?" The clearing was deathly quiet for a long breath before everyone began to disperse.

Zyid flopped onto the ground before Kalgrin and Emma. "Well, that was an interesting fight indeed." Kalgrin tapped his pipe against the log clearing out the ashes. "Though I believe the last part may have been the most interesting. Do you not agree, Emma?"

She moved to speak, but Kasala cut her off by striding over, placing her hand on Zyid's wound and, with a flash of green light, sealed the small wound. Nodding her satisfaction, she sat next to Zyid with an inquisitive look in her eyes.

"Yes, I am also quite interested to hear what the last part was all about."

Zyid heaved a heavy sigh.

"So why did she say another funeral?" Emma's tone was firm. "And what is it you are the champion of anyway?"

Zyid gazed up at the passing clouds for a brief moment before answering. "Well, why another funeral? Well, I killed her older brother. So if I killed the king, it would be another funeral." Emma's mouth hung open for a moment as she collected herself.

"You killed her brother? And yet she is on friendly terms with you?" Emma furiously crossed her arms. "I am not sure I can understand that." Zyid nodded, still staring at the sky. "How is it you were not executed for killing the king's son?"

"Well..." Zyid sat himself up. "In this case, it was his fault for challenging me to a duel to the death. In the eastern lands, it is an accepted practice. Unfortunately for him, he was quite drunk at the time. But in those lands that does not make it null. A challenge is a challenge."

They all fell silent for a moment before Kalgrin spoke up. "So he challenged you whatever for?"

Zyid rubbed his chin. "If I recall it correctly, my master had sent me to the tavern to retrieve something one rainy night."

*****

Zyid rushed through the rain-soaked street, dodging people and carts while trying his best to dart under vendor stalls to avoid the rain. He skid to a stop, panting for breath to check the parchment he had been given. Scanning the street and spotting his destination, he darted off once more into the night. He stopped before he pushed aside the leather curtain hung in the doorway. The panting youth trudged his way to the counter placing the soaked piece of parchment upon it. The elven barkeep peered down at it, nodding ever so slightly, and turned to head into the back room. Zyid sat himself on one of the stools at the counter sitting ramrod straight as he awaited the man's return. The smoky room was filled with all types—dwarves, elves, humans. Many had the reptilian features that marked them as born with dragon's blood. Time seemed to have slowed, but over the murmur of the crowd, he could hear heavy boot steps. The elf had returned a small wooden box holding several bottles. "This should be everything. Be careful with it on your way back now." Zyid had taken hold of the box when a massive hand slapped him from his stool, sprawling him on the floor accompanied by the sound of breaking glass.

"Little whelp, out of my way." Zyid looked in horror at the sight before him; he turned his head and a look of rage on his face. A giant of a man stood before him. One he recognized as the crown prince. The prince snorted down at him as his attendant reset the stool. "Be gone." He waved a dismissive hand at Zyid. "That woman may think something of you, but you are lower than dirt."

Zyid labored to his feet, clutching the last unbroken bottle and hurling it at the man. The bottle shattered, covering the prince in

160

the drink. The prince looked down at himself and snarled with rage, sending his stool once again tumbling over as he stood. He stormed over to Zyid, his steps wobbly, reaching a massive hand and grabbing the youth by the collar and hoisting him up to eye level. "You little mongrel!" Zyid's head was sent swimming by the smell of his breath. "How dare you strike me!" Zyid found himself hurtled through the curtain landing roughly in the street. Zyid grunted in pain as he landed. The prince's silhouette appeared as he came out from the curtain. "Now be gone!" he spat toward Zyid. Zyid's hand found a large stone and cast it at the man. It missed hitting the doorframe above his head. The prince smiled as he came fully into the street. "Is that how we are going to be, child? Fine then." He words slightly slurred. "Fine!" He hiccupped, thrusting a finger at Zyid's dirty form. "I challenge you to a duel to the death as is our right for a slight against one's honor such as you have committed tonight." Zyid could see the anger in his eyes and bloodlust in his crooked smile. "Do you accept, child?" The words seemed to echo through the mostly empty street.

Zyid pushed himself back to his feet, brushing off his pants and raising his fists in a guard. "I accept your challenge!" He definitely tried to roar back at him.

The prince started to laugh with a slow clap. "Good, good. It will be so much more fun like this to show your master what a waste you were. Do you even have a weapon? Does your master not trust you with a sword outside of training?" He laughed again, throwing his hands wide to the gathering crowd. "Is there anyone who can lend this poor little child a weapon with which to face his end with dignity?" For a moment, the crowd was eerily silent. "No one? Well, is that not—" He was silenced by the rough clanking of a halberd landing between them. "It seems someone cannot let you die without some dignity after all."

He moved forward, kicking the weapon toward Zyid with a splash of water and muck. Zyid took hold of the weapon without shifting his gaze. When the prince's attendant's gaze shifted between the pair, they each nodded in turn. The prince drew his sword as the attendant silently raised his arm, held it aloft for merely a breath then let it drop, cutting the air before them to begin the duel. Zyid lunged forward, bringing his weapon straight down at his opponent's head. The prince deftly parried the strike, bringing his own blade across Zyid's chest, causing him to roll away, blood oozing into his tunic. Zyid's breathing was heavy as he readied his weapon and charged once again, unleashing a flurry of thrusts. "Is this all the talent you have, boy?" He took a step back before charging forward himself, forcing Zyid onto the defensive. "So weak. You are so weak. All I hear day after day is how you are doing. It is so pathetic."

Zyid ducked and rolled under a blow aimed at his head. He recovered, swiping at where the prince had been finding the space empty. Before he could turn around, a sharp blow landed on the back of his head sending him flat on his face. "Get up!" The words seemed to be even more slurred. Zyid slowly rose to his feet, turning to face him once again weapon braced. The world spun around him, and it took several deep breaths to steady himself before launching forward, unleashing a flurry of thrusts to try overcoming the prince's guard, driving him back into one of the market stalls. Zyid roared, swinging a wide blow, cutting down the support poles in a shower of splinters, his ax blade finally connecting with its target.

The drunken brute did not seem to notice his wound. Zyid could see his beaming grin in the dim light. "So you are capable. Come on." The prince lunged forward, swinging wildly with his sword forcing Zyid back and causing him to trip over his feet. Once again flat on his back. He could only watch as the prince slowly strode toward him. Zyid closed his eyes, bracing for the final blow when he heard him call out and a loud crash as he had stepped onto something and fallen drunkenly to the ground. Zyid groaned as he rose to his feet, weakly dragging his weapon with him. The pair locked eyes before Zyid raised his weapon over his head and brought the blade down onto his skull.

"Go to hell" was all he could weakly muster before dropping to his knees, clutching the gaping wound on his chest before falling over into unconsciousness.

*****

162

Zyid took a slow breath as he finished his story. He watched clouds slowly drift over the trees as they all sat in silence for a long while. "Who knew that my boss had such an interesting younger life." Zyid looked behind him to find a pair of boots striding toward him.

"Worstan, it is good to finally see you. Zyid got distracted and did not come visit you yesterday when we returned."

He chuckled as he stopped with his shadow stretching over Zyid. "Oh, the only part I am mad about it not getting to see our resident dragon's beautiful face that much sooner."

She smiled back at him. "Not afraid of me being a dragon, you smooth talker you?"

He shrugged. "Not much point in worrying about it if you had wanted to do something. It is not like you did not have ample opportunities. Would you not agree, master dwarf?"

Kalgrin nodded. "It is very true. Most people will be uneasy at first. But I am sure people will get used to it in time if we push it hard enough. People have lived with dragons in the past, and they can do so again."

Worstan nodded in return. "My thoughts exactly." He peered down at Zyid. "Boss, I know you just got back, but if you could come to the office and do some work, we would be very happy for it."

Zyid nodded slightly. "I will head over soon to look over all the paperwork I am sure has piled up." He rose to his feet, brushing himself off. "Well, I suppose it is time I got something productive done today."

"Not going to see her off?" Emma asked as she stood.

Zyid shook his head. "No. I will be seeing her again soon enough." He turned and made his way back to the road, Worstan and Kasala in tow.

*****

The town was already abuzz with the news of the duel in the woods. Many eyes followed the trio as they walked back to the inn.

Arlana greeted them with a wide smile as they came through the door. "Ah, our glorious victor has returned."

Rashida smiled and gave a slight bow in return. "I may have defeated him this time, but it has not always been the case in the past. He is a great warrior, so do not tease him too harshly for this loss." Laughter went through the patrons. She stepped up to the bar. "But with that, we must be on our way home. So after another wonderful meal for the road and some provisions, we will settle our debt and be on our way."

Arlana frowned. "I am sad to hear you are leaving so soon. You are always welcome to come back." Arlana took out a pen and parchment, looking over it and tallying the numbers before sliding it across to her. "If this seems satisfactory to you, we will prepare it all, and you can be on your way after you are done with your meal."

She scanned it over sliding it to one of her attendants whose reptilian eyes scanned it and nodded ever so slightly. "This will do then." She counted out the coin, dropping a few extra. "The amount plus a gratuity for your wonderful service and good times had here. I am certainly going to miss your cooking."

Arlana ran them through her hands and, satisfied, slid the coins into her apron, smiled, bowed her head, and went into the kitchen. The trio made their way to the table farthest from the door. Rashida sat facing away from the door. They sat in silence for a moment. Eventually, her older guard spoke in a hushed tone.

"Will this satisfy the king, my lady? We have not learned anything about this place?"

She smiled in return. "He will be most pleased as we have done exactly as he has instructed he has no interest in knowing about this place only about that man."

His cloak moved ever so slightly as he nodded in return. The second guard continued. "Still it irks me that he speaks to you in such a manner. It is most disrespectful."

She chuckled under her breath. "That is simply your jealousy speaking. He turned down all you have ever dreamed of in an instant. If you had the strength, you could be in his place. But you are not, if you truly wish to change that only you can make that a reality."

The older guard laughed openly. "You speak truly, lady, but you are both young and one must always strive to be stronger." Rashida nodded in return. The approach of Arlana's humming voice silenced any further discussion.

"A hearty meal for our trio as they head home." She set down a large platter, holding a bowl of stew, loafs of bread, and containers of honey.

"A hearty meal indeed." The older guard commented.

"One must eat heartily for a long journey. Now eat your fill. The stable hands have packed your mounts and tied them out front. They will stay with them until you go to leave, so do not fret about them being taken."

Before they could reply, she was off again to the bar. Another maid brought drinks, and they all once again sat in peace.

"I hope she packed some of this for us to take. I will have to see if anyone at the castle could make it."

The older one sighed. "Sadly, my lady, I do not think that there will be anyone that can."

She shrugged slightly before digging into her meal.

CHAPTER 17

ZYID PEERED OVER HIS STACK OF PAPERS and down the empty hall outside the office door. A single candle could be seen near the main door of the building. Zyid's three candles nearly drowned out its light. He heaved a heavy sigh, sliding his chair back roughly as he moved to lean on the windowsill to put air on his face. He scanned left and right slowly. "What are those two doing? She is probably dragging him all around to show him her handiwork. I almost feel bad for him."

"Feel bad for who exactly?" Zyid recoiled in surprise. Thalon nearly doubled over in laughter. "Sorry, Zyid. Did not mean to scare you there."

Zyid waved it off and resumed his position. "You did startle me there. I was just a bit lost in thought. I almost feel bad for Worstan." He hooked a thumb toward the two shadowy figures. "That is who I was referring to."

"Ah," he replied, nodding his head in the dim light. "I am surprised you are still here. Figured you would be looking forward to resting up now you are home again."

"I could say the same to you. But I do own this place. So I should have some semblance of an idea about it." He paused momentarily.

"But I think I am much better suited to a soldier's life than running a mine."

Thalon laughed again. "I believe I know exactly what you mean. Being a guard is not the greatest profession but it suits me better than being a noble at court."

"You should probably get used to it sooner or later. Bellenta will want to go to all the fancy parties. She seems that type."

He snorted. "If they happen to take place near her forge perhaps. Until then, I do not think I have much to worry about." They both laughed before falling into silence with only the distant grumbling of men and pack animals echoing faintly through the brisk night air. "Zyid, you just need to follow your vision. I am sure you will be fine if you can do that."

"That simple now, is it?"

Thalon tilted his head slightly before nodding. "Yes." Thalon crossed his arms and nodded. "Yes, it is. Well I must be off to my rounds. Do not work yourself to death. You are slightly important after all. That and dwarven heroes do not die reading paperwork."

"I will endeavor to live up to the dwarves' lofty ideas of me."

Thalon waved as he walked off into the darkness. Zyid moved and slumped back into his chair, sliding it roughly back into place to continue reading. A pebble bounced off the papers and sailed past his face before he could get drawn in. He slowly looked up a glare on his face to find Kasala beaming ear to ear. "Still full of energy after walking all through the mines?"

She moved around the desk, leaning onto his shoulders before answering. "Of course I am. I, unlike you, am full of youthful energy."

He nodded slowly in response. "So did you two have fun?"

"Some fun to be sure, but one can only stare at rocks for so long. I am surprised you are not asleep staring at all of this."

"Soon I think I may keel over. But I will have to try not to since that would make a terrible tombstone."

She nodded. "Yes, it would. Anything interesting buried in there?"

He took a sheet from the top of a pile scanning over it. "Yes and no. The veins are producing well enough but getting it out and to market is going to be a problem from what I am reading."

"Is that why you asked the dwarves to finish the road through the mountains?"

Zyid looked up toward her and stroked his beard. "No, it was not. I asked them so that when war comes they could easily send troops. But I suppose that would help with the whole making money thing too."

She laughed, slapping his shoulders. "You are still that little boy with a one-track mind that you are. I am glad you have stayed true to yourself even after what you must have gone through."

"It is frustrating that you know me so well and yet I know nothing about you. At least not like this. You were a good companion as a dog." He could feel her strong glare on the back of his head.

"While that may be true, I do not like the way you said it."

He held up his hands in defeat. "But it is merely the truth. Why did you decide to stay with us kids anyway?" A silence fell over the room. "Kasala?"

She wrapped her arms around his neck, laying her head next to his. "Is it so wrong to not want to be lonely?" Zyid opened his mouth but took a deep breath and said nothing. "I am fairly close to your age. In dragon terms, a few hundred years is very young. I had watched this land for so long. But it is not as if I could pretend to be another child that would stand out. So a dog seemed easy enough. And with that I was allowed to feel alive again."

Zyid tapped her hand. "Sorry I asked."

"No, friends should ask, right? It is so nice to walk freely around." He felt her tilt her head back and forth. "Well, freely more or less. People will always be on edge, but it is not like they could seriously hurt me."

"That and use some of your healing magic and you are sure to win some friends."

"That is a very good point, my friend." Zyid moved her hands and stood.

"I think it is time I went and got some sleep. If I stare at these numbers any longer, I may just die after all."

"And no one would want that now, would they?" The pair laughed as they began the long walk home.

*****

The tavern was nearly empty with Kalgrin behind the bar as Zyid came dragging himself through the door. Zyid slumped onto the stool opposite the dwarf and laid his head on his arms. "No dragon companion tonight?" Kalgrin asked, inspecting the mug he had been cleaning.

"No, she said she was sleeping in the horse stables. She likes to be near the animals." Kalgrin nodded as he took another tankard from the soapy water. "I will not keep you for too long, just the stairs are too much at the moment."

"Take your time, boy. I am not going anywhere. Your princess left very quickly after you two battled. Did not even want to wait on you."

"But she left a message with you I presume." Kalgrin laughed.

"Yes, she did, but she also said you would probably say that." He chuckled as he continued. "She just said she was glad to see this place and was looking forward to your next battle."

"I am certain that she is," Zyid mumbled into his arms. "She will never be satisfied until she can truly defeat me. That makes me change my mind." Zyid slowly rose to his feet. "Sorry to make you wait on me. I shall see myself off to bed. I have a busy time until I am off once again. Maybe someday I can stay home for just a little bit of time."

Kalgrin chuckled with a shake of his head. "You foolish child, home is in your heart and with the people you care about. No matter how many times you go away, you can come back to here. Leaving one's home is never sad as anywhere we choose is home after all." Zyid nodded and plodded his way up the stairs to his room.

CHAPTER 18

T HE TRIO TROTTED SLOWLY TOWARD THE TOWERING city gates. "It is good to be home, is it not, my lady?" She gave no reply for a while as they passed through the gate, the crowds parting as they went.

As they stopped outside the citadel at the center of the city, she finally answered, "It is good to be home, and yet it is such an adventure away from it." She threw off her hood. "But more importantly, we must deliver our report to my father. You two are dismissed."

Taking a deep breath before she entered brushing the door slowly open to find the main room nearly empty. Searching the castle, she found her father on the battlements looking out over the great city. "Father, I have returned from my mission."

He embraced her briefly before turning back to look over the city. "So how was your adventure over in the western lands?"

She moved and leaned on the crenellations next to him. "It was quite fun, I must say. It was very much like he said it would be."

He nodded. "And what of the boy?"

"He is training just as hard if not more, but he is gaining allies as well."

"So his strength grows in many ways then." He nodded absently to himself, speaking again in a hushed tone. "That is very good. He continues to grow."

"Where is Mother?"

"Hmm? Oh, she is out flying along the far eastern mountain range." He swept his arm to the horizon. "Also, how did the duel between you go?"

She dropped her gaze. "I was the victor, but only since he lost himself in the battle for a single moment. His strength continues to grow at an incredible rate."

"As one would expect of one who has both talent and determination. Of course taking in the dragon's blood has only made that more evident. Is there anything else of note?"

She thought for a moment, running her hand along the battlement. "Yes, now that I think about it. The innkeepers, a dwarf and an elf; they seemed somehow off to me." She paused, unable to put her thoughts into words. "They both had…" She paused again searching for the right words. "Odd magic from them."

"A dwarf and an elf you say." He rubbed his chin. "Interesting… How very interesting."

"Other than that, only the dragon was there as you thought. He may have acquired more blood from her as I overheard some dwarves talking that he was injured fighting a spider queen."

"Very good, my daughter. You have done very well in your mission. Now you should go and rest up."

"As you wish, Father." She bowed and took her leave.

The king waited for her to leave before taking a long deep breath. "The future is certainly going to be interesting. I suppose it is time we start preparing for him to arrive."

*****

"So you are just leaving again, are you?" Zyid peered around his horse to find Emma glaring at him.

He finished tying down some supplies before answering. "Yes, Emma. I must be off once again. It would be nice to be home for more time, but sometimes life gives you few options." Emma merely huffed at him and moved to lean on the tavern railing. "Why ask? Are you going to miss me while I am gone?"

"Of course she will not!" Kalgrin's voice boomed as he came outside hands full of supplies. "Trouble when you are not around definitely more trouble with you around." He laughed to himself as Emma turned to hide her face.

"You are probably right, Kalgrin. Will be good to get the dragon out of here for a while. Let people get used to the idea while she is not around." He stopped, taking a glance around. "Where is she anyway" Kalgrin hooked a thumb toward the door.

"Still asleep by the fire." Zyid slowly shook his head

"I should have known. She stayed up after we got back to drink the morning away again."

"That she did." Kalgrin laughed. "But it is alright. She will be fine after a little sleep. Besides, all the dogs enjoy sleeping by her, so I at least get some rest from them."

Zyid smiled. "Keeping those dogs around, huh?"

"Yes, indeed they may be underfoot most of the time, but people like them and spend more time in the tavern so it works out for me in the end." He smiled to himself.

"I never knew you were such a greedy dwarf." Kalgrin shrugged. "Sorry that I have to leave you all again so soon."

"Do not worry, lad. We will do our best. I have a feeling you will not be gone nearly as long this time around."

"I certainly have to agree with that," Zyid mumbled. "Someday maybe I will be able to settle down, but that seems to never get any closer."

Kalgrin slapped him on the back. "Even if you had a quiet world, you would never be able to sit still."

Zyid sighed with a nod. "You are probably right."

"Are we leaving already?" They both turned to see Kasala sleepily making her way down the front stoop rubbing her eyes. "Why must we always leave so early in the morning anyways, always in such a hurry." She let out a loud yawn.

"Not quite ready to leave yet, but soon." She turned to head back in. "We do not have time for you to nap more." She huffed and turned back around, walking to her horse and leaning on its flank.

"You are just trying to leave before Emma comes to scold you again." They all turned to look at her, but she only snorted at them.

"That we are indeed." He untied his horse and mounted it in one smooth motion then waited for Kasala to do the same. She huffed and slowly made her way into the saddle. "Well, Kalgrin, we are off. Hold down the fort for us." He shooed them away and went back to lean on the railing.

They watched them disappear down the road before Emma stood and headed back toward the guard station. "Well, I am sure there will be even more work now, so I will be on my way as well. I will be sure to stop by again later."

Arlana had taken a place next to Kalgrin. "Have they left, my dear?" Kalgrin nodded. "I get the feeling that this is very much the calm before the storm." He nodded once again. "I do not think we can leave this all to them, can we?"

"No, I think not, my dear."

"I suppose I will have to train again. Cannot be holding back everyone when we are needed." Kalgrin nodded, snapping his fingers, keeping a small flame in his hands. She giggled with a smile. "We are going to need more than parlor tricks, my dear."

He laughed and stood up. "You are as blunt as ever to only me, my dear, but yes we will need to step up our game to not let those young ones show us up." He pounded his chest. "Though to be honest, I am fairly certain they have already overtaken us."

"Well, that just means we can trust in the future they will create. Now come in and get to work. We have customers coming soon. And more than likely a frustrated captain to console later today."

*****

Emma slowly opened her eyes. Her room dim from the light drifting in from her under the door. Sitting up, she wiped a tear away from her eye. "He just up and leaves again." She stood and reached out pushing her shutter open. She sighed as the chill evening breeze fluttered through her hair.

She shut the window and removed her armor. Resetting her sword belt in front of her mirror, she headed out. Her trip through the town had been taken at a brisk walk, a beaming smile plastered on her face. She rushed through the door and dropped roughly onto a stool at the bar. Arlana smiled upon seeing her and ducked into the kitchen, returning with a steaming bowl. She set it down gently on the bar before patting Emma's shoulder and disappearing back into the kitchen.

Her smile faded as she picked up her spoon, stirring her soup to mix the bacon and greens that Arlana had carefully placed on top. Emma smiled in spite of herself, taking a large bite of her potato soup, the flavors washing over her tongue, and a warm feeling in her soul. She took a few slow bites before a bump to her leg interrupted her thoughts. She looked down to find one of Kalgrin's dogs running around her stool. It lay down across her feet.

"I see you have a new friend, Emma." She heard Kalgrin laugh from behind her. "I hope you are enjoying your favorite food though I am sure it is not like your mother makes." He threw down the wood he was carrying next to the fireplace and moved behind the counter, leaving the rest of the dogs near the fire.

"It is quite good, Arlana. How I like it after all this time." She blew on another spoonful.

Kalgrin chuckled. "That she does. One of the reasons I married her. A good cook is essential to a successful tavern."

Emma laughed in spite of herself. "Thank you for this. It is taxing that he leaves me so much more work."

"He knows you have things you must do, dear. He is not leaving you with more than he is sure you can handle. Aside from that, the captain cannot be crying in front of her men after all."

She gave a weak smile. "Thank you both so very much for the compliments."

"I only speak the truth, my dear." Kalgrin puffed out his chest.

Arlana's laugh cut through the noise around them. "Sure you do, dear, sure you do."

Kalgrin shrugged. "Well I speak the truth most of the time at least."

"That is at least closer to the truth." She flopped a towel on his head as she joined them at the bar.

"So how long will he be gone this time? Did he mention it to either of you?" They both shook their heads.

Kalgrin took the towel and began wiping down the bar top. "I do not think it will be terribly long this time. He did not seem as if he was preparing for an extended stay."

"Why would he have to go at all? It is almost like he was being forced to. Maybe not forced really, but you get what I mean." She scraped her bowl clean as she finished.

Kalgrin shrugged. "He has not spoken much of his time away from home. Just always talking about preparing for a war." He chuckled. "I think some think he has lost his mind. But I hope he can bring something to stir people to action if he is not just crying wolf." He smiled to himself. "But I am sure he is not. So we must be prepared to do our parts. So be sure to call on us if you need some help, Emma."

"I would prefer not to keep asking you two for help. You have enough problems of your own with all the new people in your tavern."

Arlana set down a fresh bowl, taking the empty one. "Oh my dear, this place has been far busier before we can handle a few miners and dwarfs. So if you are ever in need of our help, be sure to ask."

Emma sighed in defeat. "I would still rather avoid asking. The last thing this town needs is a fire mage running around trying to help."

"I will make sure he does not burn down the town, my dear."

"Maybe I should," he huffed. "Then they would actually have to build this place up properly, a real wall and all." Emma's harsh glare caused him to hold up his hands in defeat. "Well, it seems you are back to your normal self now with good food in your belly, and your harsh tone returned." She looked down at her second empty bowl.

"It certainly fills the stomach but does not ease my burdens."

Arlana set a slice of pie before her. "No food does not have that property sadly. But keeping busy will make loads lighter. If you have extra time, why not help chop some wood out back since Zyid neglected it while he was here?" She smiled and left before she could answer.

Emma sighed and silently nodded, scarfing down her pie before heading out behind the tavern. She took the ax from the stables and surveyed the many piles of logs in various states of splitting. "This is what she calls slacking?" With a small huff, she placed the first log on the stump to begin her work.

She stopped after a while as she spotted several children peeking around the corner with sad expressions on their barely visible faces in the dim light. "And just what are you all doing here?" she boomed at them as she placed another log to be split.

"We heard wood being chopped so we came to attack Zyid, but it is just you. So we will have to find other fun today," one boy answered sadly.

"Oh, I see. Do you bother him every time he is out here?" One of the girls shook her head with enthusiasm. "And why is that?"

"We attack him, and if we win, he will pay us some copper coins," the girl answered, a grin beaming across her face.

Emma stopped, leaving the ax in the stump. "I see. And what would you do if you won some money?" The little girl tilted her head from side to side as if not sure how to answer the question. Then she broke out into a beaming grin.

"I would go and buy lots of sweets!"

Emma could not help but shake her head with a smirk on her face. "You could fight me, I suppose." The children looked at each other. "How do we fight, hmm?" Emma was placing another log to be split but was interrupted by the children running and tackling her down. "Hey now, this is not how one should fight!" Emma struggled to pull herself out from under the pile of children.

"This is how we always try and fight Zyid."

"Ya, he always throws us off though."

Emma and the children fell into a rolling mass. Each time Emma got her feet, they would pile on again dragging her back to the ground. The struggle continued in the dim light until a loud clap rang out and caused all to stop and look.

"Okay, children, I think you have won this round. Come and get your reward." Arlana stood just out of the back door. Producing a small pouch, the children saw it and at once released Emma and rushed to get their rewards. They each received a silver coin, which they took, and ran off into the darkened streets. Emma spent a few moments lying on the ground before starting to get up but deciding against it and flopping back down. Arlana came over staring down at Emma. She swept off the chopping block properly arranging her dress as she sat down.

"Does he really deal with those children on a daily basis?" she said breathlessly.

Arlana smiled, staring off into the distance. "Not every day but most. It was one of the things that he seemed to really enjoy."

"Is that why there is so much chopped wood back here then? I am sure it is a fire hazard."

Arlana gazed around with a smile. "It probably is, but I live with a fire hazard so I am not terribly concerned, my dear. I am glad you had a good day and not only found your smile but you also brought a few other smiles to this place."

"Is that why you sent me out here?"

Arlana gave a shocked look. "Why, whatever do you mean, my dear? I merely offered you something to pass the evening." Emma frowned at her sly tone but said nothing for a long while focusing on the wind and the laughter of the children fading into the distance.

Arlana broke the silence after a while. "Zyid knows how hard it is on the little ones when everyone is struggling. He did not grow up with much as you are aware. So every little bit helps at least as far as he was concerned."

"The more I think I knew him, the less I seem to actually know him at all." Emma got to her feet, taking a log and setting it next to Arlana. "I just remember him being so meek before letting me drag him all over the town and the woods. Was he always like this?" Arlana shrugged but said nothing. "I think I might just stay like this for a while if that is alright."

"Of course, dear. When you are ready, wash up and feel free to have some of the leftover soup before you head to your room. Will be a busy night tonight. The miners have gotten paid, so it should be interesting." Emma groaned loudly but said nothing, focusing instead on the deepening darkness and the dull roar of the streets.

*****

"How much longer do we have to ride today?" Kasala yelled over the constant wind. "I stopped feeling my ass ages ago it seems."

"Soon!" Zyid tersely shouted back.

"That is all I get? Soon. What does that even mean? It is already dark, and I would prefer to not sleep in this howling gale." She waved her hands around to emphasize her point. Silence fell heavily over the pair before he turned off the path into a small alcove in the rocks. She followed revealing a space large enough for many more people, one wall was black from many previous fires, and she could just make out the sound of water dripping into a pool a short way farther into the rock.

"See...soon, just as I said," she huffed at him as he began to build a fire. "We can stay here for the night as the next place to stop is at the very end of this canyon. It should take us another day to reach that."

"Did you come this way often?" She watched him shake his head.

"This is only my...what? Third time in this place. Second time not by myself. At least it is not raining this time. The other times were terrible downpours." She nodded and began looking around the small cave, small piles of bones, and piles of hay littered the edges of the cave. A few former travelers had scrawled their names or short messages on the walls and ceilings.

"What was it like the first time you came this way?"

"Hmm?"

"I said what was it like the first time you stayed here?"

"Cold and wet. And only a little bit terrifying." She heard him stop striking his flint and steel. "It was here that leaving home really sunk in." She heard him chuckle to himself. "My boyish crush had gotten me this far, but it really started dawning on me that things were going to be very different from now on." He resumed trying to light the fire.

"Is it smart to light a fire? Will that not stand out?"

"Sure, people can see the glow." He huffed out between strikes, "But this place is not well traveled, and it will be very cold if we do not have one. The wind never really stops through this place."

"This is why we should have just flown there."

"Yes, because that would not have been cold and windy or anything. Also, I think I have had my fill of flying for one lifetime."

"Oh, so you are afraid of things." She laughed as she flopped onto his shoulder. "Who would have guessed flying was what made you soil your britches."

"It is not so much the flying part." He stopped to blow on the small ember he had started, feeding it some small tinder to grow the flame. "It is the fear of falling, which really has me worried."

"Well, if you do fall, I will do my best to catch you," she whispered softly.

"Hmm…Did you say something?"

"What? No, just the wind I think." She felt him shrug as he placed a few small logs on the fire before moving to dig food out of one of the saddlebags. "So will our journey really take two whole weeks?"

"It probably will not take quite that long, but it can go both sides of that by a few days. In the summer, the longer days let you travel longer, but in winter you cannot travel as fast."

She simply nodded as she stared into the small fire. "So why did you come back after all that time you spent away?" She heard him pause as he was removing the horse's saddles.

He took a long time to answer. "Well, the short answer, I suppose, was I feel I must stop that man. After winning in the tournament, he took me to see his plans. They were written out on a huge map table. I saw what he wanted, and I knew I wanted no part of it." She heard him flop the saddle on the rock. "So that night I packed my few belongings and slipped away and came back home."

"You ran away from an opportunity to fight in his army? That must have taken some courage." He settled down on the other side of the fire, his blanket wrapped tightly around himself as he leaned up against the wall. "To turn away from such gifts must have been hard to do." She watched his lips curl in a small smile before he spoke again.

"No. I think I ran because I was scared."

"If you say so. Did he not send anyone after you?" He shook his head.

"I never encountered anyone on my journey home. Which now that I think about it seems rather odd. Maybe he was not prepared for me to leave so quickly." He waved the thought away. "It matters not now. I have my goals, and I will find a way to reach them no matter what it will take."

"That can be a very dangerous way to think young man."

"I am well aware of that, young dragon. Now we should get some rest. We need to leave as early as possible so as to not keep them waiting too long, lest they start doing something foolish."

"Who, the people of these lands? Or you?" He smiled but said nothing. She watched him stare into the fire for a while before he fell into a deep asleep.

*****

The dim morning light cast long shadows over the city. The breeze carried the mixed smells of the city, part fresh baking bread and partly the stench of waste and rotting food. Far off to the east, the great mountain range could just be seen peeking over the city walls. "Princess?" She turned to see one of her guards peeking around the door. "You are to begin training soon. Do you wish to eat before?"

"No. I would rather just take in the view." She waved him off. "Let the soldiers know I will be along shortly."

"As you wish, my lady." She listened to the door close and inhaled deeply. A smile crossed her lips

"Soon, you should be here, brother. I cannot wait to see the battle you will bring this time. My father is anxious to see you again as well, so be sure to hurry now, brother." Standing, she took her halberd; and after gazing into the distance once again, she began her slow walk to the courtyard down below.

CHAPTER 19

"S O THAT IS WHERE WE ARE GOING, is it?" Zyid nodded. "It looks more like a fortress than a city, so many walls and towers. And that citadel must be massive if we can see it clearly from this distance." The pair had stopped on a small rise, letting them just see over the walls.

"It is very much a fortress and all around it stretch farms in every direction." He swept his arm across the sky. Those villages we went through all are placed to be on the most fertile land or most valuable resources to supply this one city."

"Well at the very least they should have some good food and drink then."

"You are a very focused dragon." He laughed.

"Food and drink are two of the things that make life worth living after all. But I think it is best not to keep our hosts waiting." She spurred her horse down the rise, Zyid in tow.

They merged onto the wide paved road. People stopped as they saw the pair trotted by. The people gossiped and pointed as they rode past a few bowed or inclined their heads. A few of the children whooped and hollered. As the sun reached its peak, they arrived under the gatehouse, its massive wood and iron door wide enough to swallow four carts line abreast. The dark gray stone of the flanking towers gave it a sinister appearance. The lines of people parted before them like water until they stopped at the inspecting guards. The women stared for a brief moment before bowing and motioning them through into the city.

As they passed through, Zyid saw one of the guards quickly mount up and gallop quickly toward the citadel. "So where should we head now?" Zyid pointed at the citadel. "Should we really stay in the very heart of enemy territory?"

"It will not matter too much where we stay if they wanted to kill us. It would be very difficult to get out. This society is very martial, but they do not generally use a trap like that on two people. Besides, the king will want to see me before anything else can be done."

"You understand him rather well it seems," she said with a giggle.

"I think I understand him at the very least. Now let us move. Your talk of food has made me hungry now."

As the pair slowly made their way toward the castle, the streets which had been overflowing with people going about their morning business, began to slowly stop and soon the crowds lined the roadsides and filled the windows above. Zyid shifted his eyes back and forth as they rode. He could hear the hushed whispers of the crowds, but they slowly wound along the streets back and forth, making slow progress to the center of the city.

"One would think getting to the castle would be easy."

"No. It makes more sense to make an enemy go as far around the walls as possible." He motioned to the battlements casting shadows on the buildings below. "Add that to all these buildings making it difficult to reach the wall to batter it down. Hellish to make an attack." She nodded but fell silent.

As they began nearing the gatehouse, soldiers slowly began to replace the crowds of people. Until under the gatehouse in the shadow of its massive tunnel astride a steed as black as he sat the king, his honor guard surrounding him. Resplendent in their black and brass trimmed plate armor. Wielding halberds, they stood silently.

The king smiled as the pair halted before him. For a long moment, all was silent save for the flapping of a banner in the wind.

"It is good that you have come." His voice seemed to fill the whole space. "I had hoped to see you again before we must battle. Will you honor us by taking your place at the festival?"

"I am here only for that," Zyid spoke flatly. Wringing the reigns in his hands, he continued, "I will do this and no more as I am sure you are aware." The silence once more settled over them before the king gave a curt nod, turning his horse and motioning for them to follow.

"Are you sure this is a good idea?" Kasala hissed at him.

"No. I know this is a terrible idea. But if it works, this war will be over before it has begun." As the procession passed through the gate, it slowly swung shut behind them, covering them in a cold darkness, emerging forth once again into the blazing sun. The structure before them dominated the courtyard seeming to stretch to touch the sky itself. Its plain appearance somehow making it all the more menacing. Arrow loops seemed to cover the entire structure, and the only window could be seen at the very top that seemed no larger than a small bird.

The procession stopped at the base of the staircase lined to bursting with soldiers and a few gawking citizenry. The king ascended the stairs deliberately, motioning for the pair to follow as he went. The main doors were swung open gracefully as they reached the top. The hall beyond was as Zyid remembered tapestries hung from the walls, and the small amount of light filtering in through the arrow slits, which lined the gallery.

The two thrones at the far end of the room sitting stately on their raised pedestal. As they passed through the doorway, it closed, leaving the chamber in eerie silence as they strode toward the end of the chamber. The queen and her daughter stood waiting to receive the party. Time felt sluggish, and after what felt like ages, the pair stood at the foot of the thrones with all eyes firmly fixed on them.

"Welcome, Champion. We are honored that you have come." The king threw his hands wide as he spoke. "With your arrival, we can soon begin our great festival."

Zyid inclined his head slightly. "I am honored that you would have me here. I look forward to the events to come." The two men exchanged menacing glares.

"But today let us start with a grand feast to welcome our guests. Let us eat and drink our fill tonight." He laughed, snapping his fingers and seemingly out of nothing tables and chairs appeared. Set by many dedicated servants.

*****

Emma with her group of guards marched toward the Trolls Heads. They had been called about a tavern brawl, and she feared the worst. They found several men battered and bloody laying outside. She motioned some men to deal with them and went inside with all the rest. As she entered, she saw Worstan fending off two men with a surprising amount of skill. She was awestruck for a moment before shouting to the room. "What, by gods, is happening here? Break this up at once." One man turned, allowing Worstan to give him a quick one-two punch to the face, sending the man tumbling over a table. The second saw his friend go down and quickly thought less of his chances and threw up his hands in defeat. Worstan kept his guard up for a moment longer before dropping his fists and letting out a relieved sigh. Emma slouched her way toward him. "Would you care to explain all of this?"

"Oh, I did not expect to see you here, good Captain," he said sheepishly. "Well, you see, conversations got a little heated is all."

"A little heated?" She mockingly retorted as she surveyed the room "Where are Kalgrin and Arlana? And I would appreciate it if you would tell me exactly what happened."

"Well, you see, first some men got to playing some dice all well and good. Then a few drinks later, someone starts winning a bit much. Someone else claims they are cheating. Then next thing I know, everyone decides it is time for a punch-up." She glared back at the old man. "Do not fret. The damages and fines will be paid for. Out of their wages!" Some men groaned from the floor. "Send me the bill and payment will be arranged."

She heaved a heavy sigh, sinking her head in her hands mumbling, "I do not get paid enough for this."

Kalgrin's familiar laugh cut through the murmur. "I leave to get more firewood and a brawl breaks out. And no one invited me!" He continued laughing as he weaved through the mess of chairs tables and people strewn about the room.

"What would you like us to do with them, Master Kalgrin?"

He turned as if only now noticing the guards. "Oh, I will get it settled with Worstan. Just take them outside and we can get the payments sorted out. Looks like it was all miners in the fighting so no townspeople to annoy. What is a tavern if it does not have a few brawls now and again." Emma heaved another heavy sigh and motioned for her men to go. She picked up a stool, plopping down onto it.

"Are you quite sure that this is alright? And, Worstan, where did you learn to fight? You told me you were just a miner."

The old man laughed. "I am just a miner, but part of being a miner is knowing how to throw a good punch. You will not last long otherwise. People go crazy in confined spaces day in and day out. If they do not blow off steam, this is what happens." He motioned around the room to make his point. She shook her head before standing and heading out the door with just a wave. Worstan turned to Kalgrin. "I did not think she would leave so easily. Are you sure that everything will be alright?"

Kalgrin grinned as he returned behind the bar and began cleaning mugs. "This place has seen far worse." He laughed as he stared at the ceiling. Worstan followed his gaze to find a huge gouge out of a roof beam. He began to ask but Kalgrin answered cut him off. "That is from the first brawl that happened here. When the town was fairly new and all the races mingled here more freely. A man, a dwarf, and an elf had a bit too much to drink." He closed his eyes as he spoke. "A discussion turned into an argument, and an argument turned into a fight and flying tables and chairs. At first, they fought each other, then others tried to break it up. Then more soldiers appeared. The fight raged long into the night. At some point, the three had forgotten why they were fighting and slumped asleep back to back." He exhaled deeply and returned to cleaning.

"What happened after that?" Worstan asked anxiously.

"Well, they went their separate ways." He paused for a moment. "Or so I was told. I was not here for that fight. But the former owner told me about it."

"This tavern has a lot of history it seems." He peered around the room taking note of all the dents and scratches that peeked through the paint on the walls. "Any other good stories?"

"I think you two have had enough excitement for one night." Arlana strolled through the front door.

Worstan sighed. "I do believe you are right, good lady." He stood and bowed. "Be sure to send me a bill for damages, and I will arrange for it to be paid in full." Kalgrin nodded as Worstan left. Arlana stood under the gouged beam staring at it for a long while before smiling and beginning to clean up the mess.

*****

Kasala awoke as the sunlight landed on her face through the tiny windows of the room. Rubbing her eyes as she peered around the empty room. Quickly dressing, she strolled out into the hall. Finding it empty, she began wondering searching for Zyid. Having found her way out into the courtyard, she found Rashida training by herself. Kasala sat on the steps quietly for a while. A small smile crossed her face as she watched. The halberd blade whirled, slicing straw dummies asunder, shards of ice flew embedding themselves into archery targets. Kasala could not help but clap as she finished. "You and Zyid are very alike I see," she said laughing.

Rashida gave a curt nod. "I suppose we are in some ways. Though perhaps it is more fair to say I am more like him."

"Oh?" Kasala leaned forward, chin resting on her hands to press her question.

The princess walked over, taking a seat and resting her weapon on her shoulder. "When first he came here with his master, I thought very little of him. A boy with no training and puppy eyes for his master. What could I think of him but a failure."

Kasala laughed at her mental picture. "Yes, that does sound very much like him indeed." She wiped a tear from her eye and motioned for her to continue.

"I saw him only a few times over the next few years. Nothing about him ever seemed to really change. Becoming more fit but with that same look in his eyes." She paused, closing her eyes as if trying to picture it clearly. "It was that stormy night he had killed my brother."

"He told me about that fight."

The princess nodded. "When he stood before my father, I finally saw that he was different than before. He stood unflinchingly at my father's gaze. But what my father said to him is what really opened my eyes." She let out a long breath before continuing. "I see that you have finally matched your effort to that talent of yours."

"Zyid did not tell me how he got out of that whole thing. It really does not make any sense to me."

"No. I suppose it would seem odd to an outsider. But in these lands if both parties agree, then a duel may be to the death. My brother made an unwise decision that night." She took a deep breath. "And for that he paid with his life."

"What did your brother have against Zyid anyway? The whole thing seems a little strange to me."

The princess huffed before replying. "The answer to that is unfortunately simple. He was jealous of Zyid. He took that which he coveted. Zyid's master was our first teacher, and my brother resented that she took someone else as her pupil. He was always a fool and in a way that was the final straw. He was blinded and did not see that Zyid was someone who was both hardworking and talented. Something my brother did not think to realize."

"So he killed his son, but the king has to let him go." They gave a small nod. "Do you hate Zyid?"

She shook her head. "No. I do not hold it against him. My brother was always a fool." She took to her feet. If you are searching for Zyid, the roof would be the best place to look. He always liked the view from atop the battlements." Kasala stood, brushing herself off, giving a thankful nod and strolling back into the castle.

As Rashida had predicted, she found him staring over the battlements of the castle. She started toward him in a rush but slowed as she got closer. Stopping just behind him before resting in the next crenel next to him. "I talked to the princess about you killing her brother."

"I thought that might come up again. You are a curious one after all." She looked over at him, but his gaze was fixed far off on the horizon. She followed it to see a faint glimpse of mountains far off to the east.

"It is just such an odd thing. And the way everyone talks about it." She watched his shadow move as he slowly nodded yes. "But still you killed her brother and the king's son. It is crazy he did not execute you."

"It would have been a certainty in any other kingdom. But here things work differently. But..." He paused before continuing. "Even so, I had to do all I could to keep my knees from buckling under the pressure of his gaze. He just stared as the events were recounted. When that was finished, he simply smiled, saying, "I see that you have finally matched your effort to that talent of yours." Silence flooded over them for a long while. He continued again after letting out a deep breath. "And with that said, he dismissed me back to my master. She was waiting outside the castle, and we went back up into the mountains to continue my training."

Another long silence came over them.

"So that festival or whatever starts tomorrow, does it not?"

"Well, it is already going on right now. Lots of people travel to the capital to trade goods. But the battle tournament starts tomorrow, yes."

"Is it really that big of an event?"

He nodded. "Yes, it is. With winter setting in soon, it will be the last time most people can easily travel to trade. So it is time to stock up for the winter months to come. Add to that people testing out their skills for prizes and that makes it a very big deal."

"What kinds of skill tests?"

"Magic, archery, the basic skills of war. But the main event is the group battle. Everyone goes into the arena and they fight until there is one left. Then the last person challenges the champion the next day."

"And you are the champion I am to suppose?"

He nodded. "So what is it you do in the meantime?"

"I have the honor of sitting on a chair in the center of the arena on a raised stone dais. It is quite boring from what I have seen in years past."

"More importantly, what is our plan for all of this?"

"I was hoping that I could find something I could steal to show everyone that these people are planning to make war soon, but I have not been able to find anything as of yet. So beyond that I am not entirely sure what I am going to do. If I can defeat the king in one on one combat, I might be able to stop this whole mess. But that was only a last resort."

"So the last resort was stopping the war before it starts? Call me crazy but that seems like it should be the first resort." He laughed, slapping the battlements as he tried to stop himself. "And what about that idea is so funny?"

"If I could have killed him before." He stopped to take some deep breaths. "Before we would not be in this mess to begin with. The last time we battled, he defeated me soundly." She could see him slump his head down. "I thought with my new power I could do it after I learned what his plans were. But it was not to be. I remember how easily he defeated me. Then the next day I left determined to find a way to stop him."

CHAPTER 20

E MMA DRUMMED HER FINGERS ON THE BAR top, her fierce gaze shifting from her lieutenant to a pile of partially burned parchment. "If you could tell me one more time exactly what happened, I would be very grateful." The man winced from her tone but began again.

"Well, ma'am, some woodcutters told us they had spotted some suspicious people in the woods. I took a few men from my patrol to investigate." He looked around to find the men in question seeing them nod in agreement before he continued. "We found a fairly large camp with about ten or so people milling about. Suspicious types to say the least, Captain. I sent those two to get more men and stayed in hiding to observe the camp. As I was waiting, a hooded figure came into the camp. They began talking to one of the men I think he was the leader. Produced those papers." He pointed at the small pile. "They talked briefly then the hooded figure walked off and the man threw the papers onto a table. It seemed like ages until they arrived and to my surprise our fair maiden Arlana was with them."

A small cheer went up through the guards. "I was just starting to make a plan when she just strolls into the camp like she owns the place." The men laughed but he continued. "And she in the most deadpan tone is all. What is your business in these woods?" He looked out to see them nodding, ensuring he was telling it correctly. "Then these men just start laughing and cheering at her like you made a bad choice, elf girl. By the gods, I have never seen her smile like that, and I hope to never be on the receiving end of it. The first man comes at her and gods knows where she got it from, but it was as if a sword appeared in her hands, and the first guy falls back chest gushing blood. Of course his friends did not take too kindly to this and came at her, but the men and I joined in. Though to be honest, we almost seemed to be in the way." He scratched his head bashfully.

"Oh, you boys were a great help. Keep up the good work."

"So how did all of the documents get burned then?"

"Well, we may have been a bit overzealous in the fight. Some people got knocked into tents and such was quite the mess really. By the time I realized it, most of it had burned. But I tried to save what I could."

Emma stopped drumming, her fingers pounding a fist onto the bar. "You all are the biggest fools and need to be more careful." She exhaled a weary sigh. "But you all did well. But I do not need you taking unnecessary risks. Several men are at the healers in bad shape. We can only hope they pull through. But for now, we celebrate our small victories." She raised a mug. "To you all and especially to Arlana."

"Here, here," they cheered in unison. As the guards began drinking again, Emma resumed drumming her fingers on the bar top in silence for a while. "Guren, you need to be more careful in the future." She sighed as she stared at the documents. "You all got off easy this time, but if there is one large group in the woods…"

The man nodded. "Yes, Captain, then there are certainly others."

"We will need to have bigger patrols, and maybe it is about time we tried to improve the city's defense as well. Finish your drink and go and get some rest. We will talk more in the morning." He nodded, finished his drink, and strolled out the door; the others soon followed.

The silence of the room was only broken by the crackle of the fire for a while before Arlana seated herself next to Emma. "You should not be so hard on them, dear."

"Yes, I should. They would have been in serious trouble had you not been there." She let her head rest on her mug. "What did you really do?"

"It was as Gurlan said. Those brigands were very foolish to keep coming after me. They thought they could take one elf." She laughed. "As the first one came, I used the wind to bring my sword to me, slashing open his chest." She slashed with her hand, mimicking the motion. Two of his friends rushed at me rather upset about their friend. I parried the first one's blade removing the second man's head. The first lost a leg as I swept my blade around, setting into a guard position."

"My dear, you should not play with your opponents," Kalgrin called from the kitchen.

"You are just upset you were not there, which is for the best since you would have burned the whole forest down." Kalgrin said nothing and ducked back into the kitchen. "After your men started rushing in, one of the brigands thought to use a bow, and it was quite a good shot. But someone called him out and his stunned look on his face as his arrow seemed to just drop out of the air." She smiled to herself. "It seems in the fighting these documents got into the fire a bit, but they are interesting nonetheless." She looked over Emma's shoulder as she tried to arrange them. "Something about payments maybe?"

"Maybe, but it sure means one thing." She furrowed her brow. "Well, two things I suppose. I need more men, and we should maybe look into getting the walls of the city built up. If there are too many more groups like this nearby, we are in some serious trouble."

The mayor shifted his gaze between the documents laid before him on his desk. "So what you are telling me is that more brigands are gathering, and they seem to be organizing?" Emma and the lieutenant nodded. "Could you make out anything about the person who originally had these documents?"

Gurlan shook his head. "No, sir, I saw none of their features though I swear they looked right at me for just a second as they were leaving. They walked out of the fire light, and *poof*, gone almost as if into thin air." The mayor continued nodding as he picked up Emma's paper.

"I am not sure if we could manage any of these. While we are taking in more revenue, I am not sure we could afford any of it all the same."

"Well, if we do not do something, then we might not have a place to call home at all!" She slammed her fist on his desk.

"Our best bet may be to find where they are gathering and strike before they can gather too much strength." He sighed, looking at the parchment again. "But we are missing those parts. We may just have to start scouring the countryside to find them."

"I certainly do not have the manpower for that," Emma scoffed. "But if anyone has seen anything odd, it would be the hunters and such out there we might be able to enlist them. Gurlan, please make it so and offer them a cash bounty for their help. Gods know they will never do anything out of the goodness of their hearts." He saluted and saw himself out. "We should start preparing supplies here at the guardhouse since it at least has a small palisade around it."

"Yes, that would probably be wise if we can find any way to improve our defenses. We should look into it as well. I already have my assistant looking into our treasury. Building a wall would be very expensive, but it would be best to do it if we can. I will also send out some letters looking for proposals. Let us hope that something can be done before it is too late."

"I hope Zyid gets back here soon. We really need his help on this matter."

The mayor set the stack of parchment to one side, taking out a fresh page. "Let us hope he will not be needed."

CHAPTER 21

"**O**UR CHAMPION LOOKS VERY BORED SITTING OUT there, does he not, my dear?"

The king chuckled, a wide smile on his face. "He does indeed, my dear. But that is to be expected as he is only here to do battle with me." The king surveyed the arena. The raised seating was full to bursting, and people jostled at the arena's edge to gain a view of their favorite contenders. His gaze settled on Kasala for just a moment before he once again focused on the melee down below.

"Your Majesty? What is the point of all of this?" The young dragon had turned a steely gaze toward him.

The king laughed as he looked upon Kasala with a bored expression. "The point of it all? If you mean of this? The battle before you." He swept his hand across the arena. "This is to find those that are worthy of more training to be the leaders for my armies. But if you mean this..." She followed his gaze onto Zyid. "Well, if one does not have strong opponents, then what is the point of battle?" Kasala opened her mouth to respond but just furrowed her brow and sat down instead. The king rested his head on one hand before continuing in nearly a whisper. "In time you will see."

Zyid's gaze darted back and forth between the many small battles being fought. A small skirmish to his right between two dwarves and three human fighters. Two mages clashed in a storm of spells fire, ice, and lightning thrown with reckless abandon. As the sun reached its zenith, a break was called in the fighting.

Healers continued their work as some competitors collapsed onto the ground in exhaustion. One stood before Zyid, weapon raised toward him in silent challenge. After what seemed like ages, they lowered their weapon and wordlessly marched away.

With the field cleared, the remaining competitors returned and on the king's signal the battle was resumed. The competition was much reduced, allowing Zyid to fully analyze the fighters. A few familiar faces were among those remaining. Spells and blades clashed across the sand. Zyid focused his gaze on a fully human warrior as they were currently fending off a dwarven pair. The dwarves rained blows down, but their opponent deftly parried and deflected with their armor. As the pair slumped, having exhausted themselves, their foe dispatched them with swift brutal blows to the head rendering them quite still. Zyid winced internally at the sight. He watched as he scanned the arena looking for another opponent. Their gaze fell upon a battle between an elven spell sword and what seemed to be a giant of a man in full plate. They watched for a moment as a flaming blade classed with a mighty hammer.

The spell sword opened the distance, unleashing a huge gout of flames engulfing the giant in the flames. The spell had taken its toll on her. Zyid saw her grimace with the effort of remaining upright. The crowd had fallen silent waiting for the flames to die out. As the flames began to die, they revealed the giant standing his armor blackened from the flames. He strode forward, his feet crunching the sand now turned to glass underfoot. His shadow engulfed the elf; he rested his hammer on his shoulder. The crowd roared as she raised her hands in defeat. With her defeated, the pair continued to survey the arena.

Zyid noted that their armor was similar, and as they approached and clasped hands did he realize they were fighting together. Those few who remained also realized this and came charging at the two with reckless abandon.

Back to back, the pair fended off all comers. The smaller one could block and hold an opponent in place allowing the giant's hammer to reap a fearsome toll. As the sun hung low in the sky, only the pair remained standing on the arena's sand. The crowd began chanting a song of victory as they moved to take a place under the king.

As the king stood to speak, the crowd fell to silence. "This day's combat has come to an end!" The crowd roared. A runner had whispered to the king. He gave a nod before continuing. "It seems our victors wish to challenge the champion as a team. Long has it been since this has been requested." The crowd cheered again. "So long as the champion accepts these terms then they will face off against him in combat tomorrow!" The crowd roared in excitement again yelling and banging their feet on the ground. "What say you, Champion?"

Zyid stood turning to face the king. "I give no objection with this and will gladly accept their challenge!" The crowd's roar grew deafening. Kasala glared down at Zyid.

The king let the crowd expend their energy before responding. "Then tomorrow at midday these brothers will try to unseat our champion. Will they be triumphant and attain great glory? Or will our champion keep his crown and gain greater glory still?" The crowd drowned out all other noise as Zyid felt the pair glare at him before striding out of the arena.

Turning, he found Kasala stomping toward him fuming. "What is wrong with you? You should not have taken those two on together. That is obviously what they wanted."

"I am aware of that." He stepped down from his station and began strolling out of the arena.

"If you knew that, then why play into their hands?" She heaved a sigh, waving a hand in front of him to stop him answering. "No, no, let me guess. You feel that if you cannot beat them, then you will never be able to defeat him." She threw an accusing finger toward the royal seats. "You have not changed even one bit after all these years, have you? A silly child and now just a silly man." She closed her eyes and took a deep breath. "So what is it you plan to do until the contest?"

"I will do as I have done before train rest and probably sit with a tome of some sort."

She sighed again as they strolled off. "It seems you really have not changed at all."

*****

Zyid checked the buckles of his sword belt one more time as Kasala cinched his brigandine closed. "So they just let you borrow some armor? Why did you not take some plate?"

He shook his head as he moved his arms. "None of the plate armor is fitted for me, so it would be overly restricting. One of these days I should probably get some made for me."

"You do not look very intimidating in this getup, you know?" She chuckled for a moment at him as he glared back. "Are you ready to face them? Are you certain you can win?"

He nodded. "I am ready, and no, I am not worried. But it is never advisable to underestimate an opponent. They did not work together yesterday so as not to give me any insight into how they fight. That will make this battle more difficult." He plucked his bassinet off the small table as trumpets blared from the arena.

"Give those two hell out there."

He nodded as he shoved his helmet on. "I will defeat them." He began to walk away but stopped and looked back, stabbing a finger at her. "And no matter what happens, you must not intervene." She gave a confused look back but nodded and headed up toward her seat. With that, he stepped out into the burning daylight.

He could feel the pair's burning gaze from where they stood near the arena's center. They were armored as before, but the smaller one carried a large two-handed sword; its flamberge blade plunged into the arena sand.

The crowd roared as he entered but fell silent at the king's raised hand. All eyes turned toward him as he began to speak. "Today on this glorious day we witness once again a battle to decide the stron-

gest. Many came to test their mettle but only these three remain."
He opened his arms toward the three warriors. "But only one may be
crowned the victor of this battle. Our reigning champion has chosen
to take the challengers on together." The crowd roared again. "Many
years has it been since we have seen this. More glory to him if he
should emerge victorious. But enough of this! At my signal, begin!"
The pair readied their weapons as Zyid drew his swords, ensuring he
had them properly set in his hands. He watched in his peripheral as
the king dropped his hand. "Begin!"

The crowd roared and for a moment nothing happened. The
pair slowly slid slightly apart then darted at and around Zyid, moving into a pincer maneuver. Zyid began running toward the giant,
lunging under his hammer swing and thrust toward a gap in his
armor. His strike sliding off the plate, Zyid moved behind to find
the second opponent waiting for him unleashing a flurry of strikes,
pushing Zyid back under the onslaught. As the first leaped back, the
giant's hammer filled the void. Zyid blocked and tumbled with the
force of the blow rolling him clear of the pair.

Kasala struggled to keep from wincing as the three combatants
once again clashed. The pair kept up the pressure, never allowing
Zyid to rest. He was fending them off, but she felt a feeling of doubt
welling up inside of her.

"I see that my best student has continued to improve himself."
She turned to see the owner of the voice, finding a tall woman standing next to the king. She seemed unremarkable aside from her odd
yellow eyes and a large scar marring the side of her face.

"He has indeed, Milinde. You taught him well after all." She
nodded as she focused on the battle below. "He can become even
more powerful, but this battle will be a good test if he can reach it."
The woman nodded as her gaze shifted back and forth following the
fight, resting only for a moment on her. The gaze felt cold and uncar-
ing somehow as she quickly shifted back to the battle. A roar from
the crowd caused her to look back to the arena floor, finding Zyid
slowly rising from the ground, a grimace of pain on his face.

"It was quite foolish of you to allow us to fight you as a pair.
Victory would have been within your grasp. But soon we will retake

the champions title that should never have left in your hands." Zyid stayed silent, spitting out a wad of blood.

The smaller of the pair continued, "I had thought you would be more of a challenge, but it seems I was mistaken." The giant ran forward to strike Zyid, swinging the hammer in wide sweeping arcs. Zyid ran under the strikes and sprinted toward the other one unleashing a flurry of strikes at his opponent before sweeping his legs, which he jumped to avoid. Zyid planted his hands and kicked his opponent's chin, flinging him back onto the sand. The giant had recovered closing and swinging just as Zyid recovered his footing. The hammer smashed into the sand once more as Zyid brought his blade onto its shaft, severing its head. Unfazed, the giant began thrusting wildly, forcing Zyid back. The pair stood together, throwing off their helmets before releasing a storm of lightning bolts from their mouths, engulfing Zyid in a storm of sand and electricity.

*****

Emma watched as great timbers were carted through the gate. "Hard to believe we are able to get this started."

"It is not so surprising. People are very skittish and farmers doubly so." Worstan mused as he leaned on a stick, "This is the best you can do at the moment sadly, but a wooden wall is better than no wall. But definitely not like the ones back home."

"Oh? Do tell." She crossed her arms as she gazed at him.

"Well for one, they will not be falling down so that is a good start." He snorted and continued. "But the lack of stone will certainly be noticeable as well." He held up a finger. "But more people see a nice wall, more people will come, and a town relies on its taxes and trade. And in a few years, you will be rebuilding your nice wooden palisade into a solid stone wall. Then you are really a city."

"Hoping to stay in my city, are you? I am not sure there is room for more people like you, enough fools around here as it is."

Holding a hand to his chest, Worstan winced.

"You wound me, Captain. I would never." He laughed. "But this place might not be too bad to settle down for some time. Until the taxes get too high and then I will be off again."

"Always thinking ahead, I see."

He shrugged. "Miners have to go where the work is. And that is why more are coming every day."

"That is true enough I suppose. Soon I will need an army to manage this place."

Worstan laughed. "Well, with that kind of protection, people would definitely come."

"And that is what worries me."

*****

Kasala attempted to jump from her chair, but a firm grip on her shoulders held her in place. She twisted her head in anger upon her face. She found the master staring at her a grin beaming on her face. "Stay your rage, dragon child. This will not be the end of that one." She pointed back to the arena. "Now watch and see." Turning her gaze, she found the lightning storm dying as they slumped to their knees from the effort. The dying storm revealed Zyid on his knees, swords plunged into the ground for stability. As he stood, a thin trail of smoke emanated from his clothes as the last flickers of electricity ran around and through him. The heat had turned the sand to glass, scorching his exposed skin. Rising slowly to his feet, he grimaced through the pain of the burns as he took up his swords again.

"You see, young one. The power he was granted was more than just physical. He also gained some resistance to magic." Kasala glared at her once again, and she released her grip. The women quickly turned and gave a curt bow to the king and quickly strode away, flashing another grin at Kasala as she left. Turning back, she saw the three all on their feet but only just. Zyid's swords begin to glow as he brought them together, forming his great blade. The pair launched themselves at Zyid. He charged to meet them, a swirling melee developing as they all poured out the last of their strength. The giant collapsed to the ground first, kicking up a cloud of sand as he began bleeding on the sand.

"It seems that we cannot win this battle after all." The second man wobbled as he spoke his breathing labored. "But I will fight until the end." Charging, Zyid met his blade with his. Zyid reared his head back and crashed it into his opponent, throwing him to the ground. He stood over the man and drove a blade down with all his strength. The armor held for a moment before cracking, allowing the blade to work its way through. The blade stopped as it pierced into the skin below.

An eerie silence fell over the arena before the king motioned for the match to be ended. The match over, Zyid slumped to his knees, pain evident on his face. The crowd began cheering wildly as healers rushed to the combatants. Over the crowd, Kasala heard laughing behind her as the king stood, making his way to the viewing box's edge and hopping down into the arena. Striding over to Zyid, he removed the blade and threw it to Zyid. "We have a victor!" The crowd had begun to chant. He threw up his hands and the crowd quickly fell silent. "And as is our custom, he may have his victory toast." He motioned over an attendant carrying a large ornate goblet. Bowing, he held it aloft and the king gingerly plucked it from his hands and raised it into the air. He lowered it down toward Zyid. "Drink your fill, Champion. If you think you can handle it." He grinned down as Zyid struggled to his feet.

Steadying himself, he walked forward gently, taking the goblet. Peering into it, he saw the sickly black liquid he knew so well. Closing his eyes and taking a deep breath, he quickly forced the liquid down his throat. The king began laughing once again as he watched Zyid struggle and fall to his knees. "Very bold of you to drink it all." He plucked the goblet off the ground, returning it to the attendant and shooing him away. "Now I wonder what will come of this?" The king began walking around Zyid. "I knew you would win this battle. Will this be enough power for you to finally defeat me?" Zyid glared back angrily, clutching at his swords. "Perhaps you will try now? That would be just like you after all."

Zyid launched himself toward the king, blades whirling. "Valtalen!" A sword separated, flying forward at the king. Batting the blade, he found Zyid slashing upward.

"I see you are already faster. Good, good." He smiled as he caught the blade firmly under his arm. "But you are far more injured than you think you are, child." Zyid's blood hissed on his clothes. "In your current state, there is no contest. I look forward to fighting you once you are fully recovered." A mighty headbutt caused Zyid to fall limply to the ground.

*****

"Father, it is good to see you enjoying this nice weather for once instead of hiding inside all day." The old man looked up, smiling at the sound of Emma's voice.

"I cannot spend every day staring at the fire after all. And it is nice to listen to all the new sounds that now drift across our town. It is nice of you to take time out of the day to visit us." Emma pulled a stool over to sit next to her father.

"Well, Father, I have come looking for some advice." The old man nodded, motioning for her to continue. "I am sure you have heard that there is a large camp of brigands somewhere in this area." She stopped and scanned around before continuing in a hushed tone. "We have not been able to find any large camp. Only a couple small ones and that is very worrying to me. I was hoping you might have some ideas." He closed his eyes and began stroking his chin as his other hand moved in the air mentally following a path.

"Yes, I have heard of this matter. Some of the guards have been speaking about it within earshot. Still gossiping as always it seems." He smiled to himself as his hand continued weaving through the air. "If you have to, find those guards who can see best at night and have them scour the woods to find the fires of any camps. But failing that, you should look farther afield. I would guess that the men have not truly gone far off the roads. They do have a healthy fear of the deeper forests after all."

"I have had the men looking in the night, but perhaps you are right about them not venturing too deep into the forest. Thank you, Father. I will think more on this." She moved to stand but he grabbed her shoulder.

"I just remembered somewhere that might be worth investigating."

"Where is it, Father?" He could hear the excitement in her voice.

"Near the western entrance to the valley there is a plateau that you cannot see from the road running through the valley. But it is large and defensible. If people wished to stage for an attack that may just be the place to do it from. If you go, be very careful. I would bet that any path leading to it will be under watch."

"It seems I may have to ask for Kalgrin's help once again."

"Yes, indeed that dwarf sure knows his way around, and he may know more about it he has lived here for quite a while." She nodded and nearly jumped to her feet. She took a step but turned around and hugged her father.

"Thank you, Father. I will try and visit again soon and not just for advice this time." He patted her on the back.

"Do not worry, my dear. You are not a bother. As I told you as you were growing up, learning to rely on others is not a weakness, it is a strength. Now get going you have much work to do." She nodded and marched toward the Trolls Heads.

CHAPTER 22

"YOU SHOULD STILL BE RESTING IN BED. That battle took quite a toll on you." Kasala let out a sigh and leaned over the battlements. "So how do you feel now that you have time to absorb your new blood?" He finished his swing and replaced his blade in the scabbard, flexing his hand as he turned it over.

"I am not sure. I see that my skin is tougher and slightly more scalelike."

"Your eyes are more dragon-like as well. Do you feel any mana inside you?" He shook his head. "It seems your transformations were physical then. I suppose that for you it is best."

"I suppose so. Magic has never been something I have had the ability to do."

She laughed. "My mother spoke to me while I was still in my egg about warriors who had bonded with dragons. Sometimes great warriors would gain mighty magics. And many a mage was saddened by gaining no more magical power at all." She stopped for a moment. "She also warned me that there is always a risk when taking dragon's blood. Do not take it lightly. It may still be the death of you."

He nodded. "We shall see. Soon we must leave before the winter sets in. We should make ready to leave tomorrow night, I think.

Hopefully we may find a way to convince people back home of danger."

"What happens if we do not find anything?" He started to answer but stopped and for a moment a look of defeat flashed across his face. "So we will figure it out as we go then."

"I am afraid that is most likely the case."

"Zyid, I believe that has always been your plan." He spun drawing and readying his blade. "Stay your blade. I did not come to do battle." The princess held up her hands, showing they were empty. Flicking his blade, he sheathed it and moved to stare over the battlements.

"What is it that brings you to visit with us?" Kasala let out with a snarl.

"I am merely here to deliver a message from my father. He knows you would be leaving soon. He commands you to meet him at the mountain training ground."

"We are under no such—" Zyid held up a hand, cutting her short.

"I knew he would do this." The princess gave a deep bow silently returning to the bowels of the castle. Kasala stuck her tongue out at the door.

"If he thinks we will be meeting him there, he is sadly mistaken. Right?" She leaned around to stare at his face. "You are not seriously considering doing this, are you? You know he just wants to test you again, and this time he may kill you."

"I must go. If I defeat him, then the war will be over before it can begin."

She slammed her fist on the stonework. "This is just like you! You go along with anything people tell you. We should run! If he kills you up there, what will happen to everyone else? I thought you wanted to protect your home?"

He heaved a heavy sigh. "I will protect my home, but—"

"No buts! You dying is not an option. You cannot die out here."

"It is not as simple as leaving. We will be escorted to see him now."

"As if they could stop the two of us." He stood up waving a finger in her face.

"Do you think the queen is the only dragon that calls these lands home? And even if that were not the case, we cannot kill everyone in this city!" He paused, taking a deep breath. "So it is either go there willingly or be dragged to see him. Which would you prefer? Now we must go prepare to set off and get some sleep. I prefer to see him early in the morning."

*****

The moon shone brightly in the clear night as the pair checked over their equipment one last time. They nodded at one another, throwing themselves into the saddle as quietly as possible. They wound slowly back through the deserted streets. The horse's hooves reverberating off the walls and buildings.

They soon found themselves staring at the massive gate looming over them in the dark. They waited in silence broken only by the horses neighing. Kasala began to speak but was cut off as a smaller door opened allowing them to pass through. They dismounted and led their horses through and the door swiftly closed behind them.

"Who are they?" Zyid followed her finger and found a group sitting around a small fire. The group stood filling the air with metallic noises as buckles and plates moved across one another.

"They are our escort," he answered dryly. The group silently mounted their horses and lined up next to the road. Zyid spurred his horse forward, and the group silently took up position around them as they approached.

"How long will it take us to reach this place?"

"We should arrive shortly after dawn I would hope."

"Was he concerned we would try to flee?"

"He is just showing he is one step ahead of us is all. He knew I would go to face him." Kasala started to speak again but struggled to find the words and so remained silently as they trotted along the road.

*****

"Why are they not following us to the summit?" She peered over her shoulder, seeing their escort stop and dismount and the base of the path. "How much farther do we have to go?"

"Not far. Just a short way now." He pointed up in the dim morning light. They rode in silence through the early morning fog. Rounding the final bend, the path opened into a large clearing. The edges hidden in the mist. A small light drew her gaze as they continued. As they drew closer to the light, she saw that it was a small fire next to a large mountain lake. It stretched as far as she could see in the mist. She was jolted from her daze as her horse suddenly halted. "We are here." Zyid's boots made a squishing sound as he landed on the soggy ground. Tied up his horse and walked up to the fire. The king sat staring into the mist over the fire, a knowing grin on his face.

"It is good to see you, son. It is good that you have come. It would certainly be a shame if we did not battle to test the limits of your newly acquired power."

"It is not as if we were given a choice in the matter."

He snickered as he shifted his gaze to Kasala. "Ah, but that is simply not true, young dragon. We always have a choice. Just as we must accept the consequences and that is the true limit to what we do." Kasala began to speak again, but Zyid held up an arm to stop her. The king stood surveying the valley. "This is a most fitting place for our battle. This is as much home as any other, is it not?" He gave a sideways glance at the pair before continuing. "Once the mist has been burned off, we will ready ourselves." He motioned for them to sit. Zyid wordlessly complied. Kasala moved behind him, finally noticing the pot suspended over the fire. Taking a bowl, the king filled it and handed it to Zyid.

Kasala's gaze drifted between the pair as they finished their meal and silently stared into the distance. The fog slowly retreated showing the valley in all its splendor.

The king slowly stood brushing himself off. Taking up his sword and shield, he marched a short distance away to a patch of dead grass and mud. Zyid followed drawing his blades and handing his scabbards and belt to her as he passed. They readied themselves for a few fleeting moments. The world seemed to fall nearly silent except for the wind blowing across the lake.

The king closed his eyes, taking a deep breath. "Begin." Zyid launched forward, blades flashing in the early morning light. The king deftly fended off Zyid's blows and countering as he saw opportunities. "Good. You are faster already I see. How about your strength?" Zyid blocked the heavy downward blow with one blade, sweeping the king back with his second blade. A laughing grin grew on his face. "This is what I was hoping for."

The sound of clashing blades filled the valley. Stepping in to attack, the king shoved Zyid with his shield, shoving him to the ground. He tried to slash at him on the ground, but Zyid sprung to his feet parrying the blow and giving a counter thrust, which narrowly cut the king's face. They separated once again; the king running his thumb down the cut on his cheek. He began laughing again. "Now this is a feeling I have not felt in so long. Now come on show me more of that spirit from before. Show me how you defeated your master."

"Kadan." Zyid gently brought the hilts together before twirling his blade to reset his grip. He leveled his weapon seemingly satisfied with it.

The king motioned for him to come again. "That is my boy. Now come show me what you can do."

"I am not your son." Zyid charged forward. "And I am not going to be his replacement."

"So you say, but what you want is of no importance. You will play the part merely for being as you are." He met his charge, bringing down a heavy blow. Mud flew from the ground with the force of the blow. Zyid brought a blow of his own, biting deep into the king's shield. The king flung him over his shoulder, retrieving his blade and striking once again.

The sun moved slowly overhead as the pair broke apart again. Both men dripped with sweat and breathing heavily. The ground sizzled as blood dripped down from both combatants. "You have tapped into more power than I would have thought. If we continue on like this."

"Stalemate."

The king nodded. "Indeed, so I think it is time to see if you can find your wings." He closed his eyes, taking a deep breath as his wings quickly sprouted on his back. The leathery wings outstretched, casting a menacing shadow on the ground. With a mighty beat, he hovered just above the ground. "If you can unlock the last stage of your power, then you will have the ability to truly stand against me." Soaring into the sky, he became nothing more than a dot in the sky.

"How am I supposed to find my wings?" Zyid felt a hand fall onto his shoulder as he stared up to the sky.

"Long ago when I was very young I asked a very similar thing to someone I knew." Kasala squinted as she stared upward. "He told me that you had to look and focus inside of yourself to find them. It will be as if finding something you always knew you had to tap into the magic."

"That is not very helpful. Valtalen!"

"Well, you just give that a try while you use my wings to fight him for now." Kasala stepped around him, shifting into her massive dragon form. The ground shook as she released a mighty roar followed with a blast of her rancid green breath. Zyid took a hesitant step before leaping aboard her back.

"Forgive me for this." Zyid thrust a blade into her back as she howled and looked at him over her back. "I need a firm place to fight from. You can yell at me later for it." She huffed at him before launching into the air with a mighty beat of her wings. They soon hovered eye to eye with the king.

"This is not quite what I had in mind but—" Kasala lashed out with her powerful jaws. He deftly avoided her strikes, skimming down her flanks to fight Zyid. Zyid blocked his blows, clashing their blades together suddenly finding himself dangling briefly as she rolled around swatting the king away with her tail. Zyid landed heavily as she rolled back over. She peeked back as he woozily got to his feet. The king's laughter made her snap out and unleash her breath at where he had been.

"Oh, now this is fun. Best find your wings quickly, boy. She cannot keep this up for long." She brought her gaping maw toward him once again, getting a slice down her neck for her effort. She howled with pain as her blood oozed out. A flap of his wings took him once again hovering just above the pair. Zyid squinted up into the sun. Taking a deep breath and closing his eyes, the world around him seemed to drift away. The rhythmic beating of wings went silent. The chill of the wind passed off his skin. Soon he felt as if he was standing inside himself. He felt a warmth there reaching out a hand. A great warmth came over him. His eyes shot open. The world seemed more clear and the sun seemed less bright above him.

Zyid clearly saw the grimace of the king staring down at him. "Now you see that was not as difficult as you would have thought." Zyid removed his second blade, rolling them in his hands. The king motioned for him to come at him. Zyid's face twisted in anger as he launched himself into the air for the first time.

*****

Kalgrin wiped the sweat from his brow as he peered back down into the darkness. Hugging the stoneface, he shimmed for a short distance, crouching down as the face ended. He listened intently through the gnarl of trees and vines. Satisfied, he began to pick his way through as silently as he could. Once done, he moved swiftly in the dark toward a growing chatter of voices and the glow of many fires.

There in the plateau's center stood what seemed a sea of tents in the dim light. Peering from the shadows, he saw the many figures shifting about and many more slumbering in their tents or next to fires. The men around the fire drank deeply from their tankards. "The boss did great with bringing us here."

"Easiest job we ever had. Sit and drink and wait for something to happen."

"Wish we had known about this place before we could set up a small kingdom up here." The two laughed drunkenly. He saw the man slowly look around peering deeply into the darkness around him and spoke in a hushed tone. "But between us, I hope we move out soon. I do not trust things will stay quiet in this place for long. Too much bad blood round here." The other man nodded as he took another swig.

"But until something does happen, best to enjoy the good times."

"You have that right, brother." Kalgrin heard footsteps and darted back the way he came. Waiting for the man to pass, he began slinking the opposite direction. Dodging another stumbling drunk, Kalgrin found the large pillar he had been looking for. Parting the overgrown vines, he ran his hand along the damp, rough-hewn steps leading to its top, stepping in and listening intently. Satisfied, he heard nothing. He gingerly stepped his way toward the peak.

Laying on the cold rock and peering just over the edge, the full extent was laid bare before his eyes. "Hey, have you ever seen this before?" Kalgrin nearly jumped at the voice.

"What are you on about?" Kalgrin rolled over slightly to back down at the dim torch light below him. "No, I have not seen it, and who gives a damn about it."

"We should check it out." The light began to brighten as the man stepped forward.

"No, we do not. If we are late on our rounds again, we are gonna get a beating for sure. Besides, probably just some spot people sneak away to get some private time up here." He heard the man heave a dejected sigh and darkness once again fell over the space. He released a nervous breath before he rolled back over. Taking out a scrap of parchment and a piece of charcoal, he began scribbling out a rough diagram. As he was finishing, a blast of cold air rushed across his back. Rolling over once again, he found a pair of feet. For a brief moment beyond them he saw through a portal. As it closed, he looked up into the hood of the figure before him. Even with his dark sight, he could only see their eyes peering back at him. He hesitated for a moment before pulling his dagger from his belt. He heard the figure huff waving his dagger away with one hand. "I see you are as spirited as I was led to believe." The figure spoke barely above a whisper. "Take these to its rightful owner when he returns. He will need them I presume." She held out two scabbards wrapped in its belt. Keeping his dagger at the ready, he slowly raised himself up, gingerly taking them from her hands. Seemingly satisfied with herself, she cast her gaze to what she saw below. "The battle to come will be very interesting, do you not think?" Before he could say anything, she stepped off the edge. He listened but did not hear her land below.

"I think that was my signal to leave," he mumbled to himself under his breath, shoving away his dagger and parchment. He clutched the scabbards close his chest and began slinking back the way he had come.

*****

Zyid slowly opened his eyes. He was greeted with the deep darkness of the night. Kasala's talons wrapped tightly around him. So clenched he felt each beat of her great wings. He could feel the burning from his chest. "What happened?" he yelled into the wind. The wind was his only reply for a while before he heard her voice in his mind.

"So you are finally awake? That is good." The words reverberated in his head long after they had been ended. "I am sorry for speaking into your mind directly. I am not adept at it, so just bear with it for now." They flew in silence for a while longer, Zyid turning his head to see the barest hint of the ground below them in the dark. "I am sure you want to ask what happened. Well, you leapt into the air. Then well...here let me see if I can show you. Close your eyes and we will see if I am capable of this."

He did and for what felt like ages he saw nothing but the darkness. Slowly a sliver of light came in and a picture began forming. Soon he was watching as if from Kasala's eyes. He saw himself leaping into the air with a mighty flap of his wings.

The pair clashed, the king moving up under the impact. He saw his mouth move but could not make out what had been said. As he finished speaking, Zyid watched himself begin to fall away from the standoff. With a shove of his shield, Zyid fell, and as he fell downward, the king made a deep precise cut across his chest, unleashing a great spray of blood. Kasala dove after him, gently plucking him from the air with a black claw. Lifting her gaze back up, she furiously beat her wings toward the man. As she closed in, she unleashed a mighty roar and a blast of her breath. He rolled out of the line of attack as she flew past, flipping herself back to make another pass. She lashed out with her claws. He dodged the first then the second strike. He moved forward to attack, dodging her counters and cutting a chunk from one of her claws.

She tried to bite him once more, but he stopped her with his shield. Throwing her off again, he swiped at the air to force her back. He was speaking once again, but Zyid could not hear the words. He saw him laughing again as Kasala roared at him again before turning to fly off licking her wound. The memory ended abruptly, leaving his ears ringing and head pounding. "I apologize for that not being fully clear. My mother was far more talented at directing memories and thoughts to others. You can see as well as that because of your dragon blood. Without it, most cannot make sense of it." They continued flying in silence for a long while before she spoke again. "We can talk more about everything he said once we arrive at home. There is no point in stopping since we left all of our supplies behind." Her words faded as Zyid slipped back into sleep.

CHAPTER 23

K ALGRIN LOOKED UP FROM HIS MAP, WINCING as Arlana tiptoed through the model laid out before him. She gently moved the log back. "Are you quite finished with this yet, dear? Two days seems just a bit excessive."

He shrugged. "Better to do it right the first time. This is going to be important after all."

She continued walking through it eyeing it intently. "Many lives are going to be shaped by this place again I see." He nodded as if focused on something far away. She took up a twig as she stared down near the center. "You missed something." He frowned as she squatted down to draw in the dirt with it. Looking down, he watched her draw a small square and labeled it cave before tossing her twig aside. "Now it is done."

"So it is, so it is. Guess I should get our dear Emma. She has been very impatient."

She giggled. "Yes, I think she would be. Though something tells me she will be here soon to ask you quite sternly if it is done." They were interrupted as a great shadow flew across the ground. Looking up, she saw a familiar dragon lowering herself to the ground in front of the tavern. Rushing around front, they saw her gently put a figure on the ground before flopping onto the ground, kicking up a great cloud of dust and sending a tremor through the ground. "That is Zyid!" Rushing to his side, she looked him over. She stopped and stared at the wound on his chest. "He is alive, thank the gods. I will take him inside and tend to him. You help her."

Kalgrin nodded as he stroked Kasala's head. "You look worse for wear, young one." She groaned lazily, opening one eye at him. "You must have flown a long way to be like this. Should be an interesting story."

He patted her nose, turning toward Emma's voice as she shoved her way through the gathering crowd. "Make way, make way!" Forcing the last person aside, she steadied herself with a deep breath, leading her guards toward the pair. "What in the name of all the gods is going on here?"

"As you can see, good Captain, our fair friends have returned to us from the east. Though it seems in a less than ideal manner."

"I see." She looked intently about. "Where is Zyid?"

"Arlana has taken him inside to tend to him. Now if you would be so kind as to have your men fetch some water and meat from inside. Our friend is quite exhausted from her flight."

She gave the dwarf a sideways glance before sending her men as he had requested. "So what exactly happened?"

He shook his head. "I do not know yet. She is too exhausted to change forms yet. With some food and water, we should soon know of the tale." She rested her hands on her hips for a moment thinking it over before motioning her men into action. Kalgrin plopped down and continued petting Kasala's head.

"Will Zyid be okay?" He looked to see several small heads peeking from behind Emma's legs.

"The dragon lady did not hurt him, did she?" the small girl asked. Kalgrin started to answer but Emma's hand landed gently on her head.

"No, child. They are friends, and she has simply brought him safely home to us. I am sure she did her best." The little girl smiled sheepishly before the children darted off to begin running circles around Kasala.

"Good to see even the guard captain has a soft side to her." Kalgrin laughed as he followed the children.

"Blame it on the politics I have had to deal with."

"Well, if that is the case, then so be it. Still a good thing if you ask me. Much more honest of you." He held up a hand as she gave him a sharp glare.

"Did you finish with the model you were taking so much time with?"

The men returned as he started to answer, and he stood and walked toward her as Kasala noisily lapped at the water. "I have finished it. Come with me and I will go over it with you." With that, he marched off.

"You all stay here and keep everyone calm." With that, she quickly followed after him.

*****

"Is everything in order?"

"Yes, my king. All is ready. They should be attacking soon."

"Good." A sad smile flashed across his face. "Do you think this will be enough to move anyone?"

"So long as some of the new dwarven forces are involved, word of it will soon reach their king. The human cities will as always find ways to ignore it I would assume."

"You are most likely correct." He heaved a heavy sigh. "Time passes and so little changes it seems. If it does not affect them directly, then it is to be ignored."

"It is the way of people, my lord."

"It is indeed. Well, they will not be able to ignore the worrying of their merchants, so they should come around sooner or later. If all is in order, then you may go to ensure all proceeds as intended. Do be careful out there. Many dangerous opponents in this battle."

"As you wish, my king." With a curt bow, Milinde stepped back before opening her portal. She stepped through with a crack behind her as it snapped shut.

"Will this be enough?" The queen's hand entwined with his.

"My dear, I do not know, but this is the path we have chosen and we must stay the course."

The queen stood next to him on the main castle steps. "A storm is coming."

He nodded. "We must do what we can to prepare for it and enjoy the calm before it for it will wait for no one."

"We shall see who has the strength soon enough. That boy carries a heavier burden than he knows."

"If he did not wish to carry it, he would not. He made that choice the moment he left this place for his home."

They both smiled at the memory. "Hopefully, that will be enough then."

*****

"Does everyone understand the plan?" Emma scanned the gathered crowd in the evening light.

"Did we really need such an in-depth plan for this?" someone chimed in.

"Yes! And what is even more important is to know the general layout of the battlefield. This is going to be a tough battle; the enemy is well positioned and with a fair number of men. But if we do not take the fight to them, they will certainly bring it to us." She threw her arms out wide. "And defending this place would be near impossible."

"But, Captain, we would get to impress all the ladies!" another voice shouted to a few chuckles.

"As if you lot could impress any ladies." The men roared in laughter. "Now if that is all, inform your men and begin moving out. We will attack as soon as we are in position." She watched them disperse into the dim even light.

Worstan's voice cut through the silence. "I am sorry I cannot offer any help in this matter, dear Captain." She turned as Worstan stood from his bow. "But sending the guilds assets directly into a battle is not something I can do without losing my position sadly."

She shook her head. "I understand. It is just the way of things."

"Though I have asked a few of the guards and miners who are off duty to wander around town this evening doing their best to look like guards."

She smiled despite yourself. "Just what I need is your drunken lot wandering the streets pretending to be official guards." They both laughed. "I very much appreciate having them meet at the guard headquarters so they can go on patrol with the men I leave behind."

"As you wish, my lady." Removing his hat, he gave a deep flourishing bow again. She waved him off as he stood smiling to himself and strode off into the evening light.

She turned to Kalgrin and Arlana. "Are you two really okay with this? Leaving your tavern unattended for the night?"

"It will be fine, dear." Arlana waved away the words. "It is good to get out now and again."

"Besides, Worstan and Bellenta will be watching over it once they finish their tasks for the day." Emma nodded absentmindedly. Kalgrin laid a hand down on her shoulder. "You are not going to be alone in this fight. It will be bloody, but we will win."

"I am worried how much we will lose."

"My dear, we cannot dwell on that. Keep your mind clear and sharp and that will save more lives than worrying about what might happen. Besides, you have us and even some of the dwarven warriors agreed to come. They will be a tremendous help."

"That we will. We dwarves enjoy a good fight. Besides that, if his majesty's trade is interrupted, he will be most displeased. And better to take the fight to them before they grow stronger." Thalon stepped forward examining the model in greater detail. "My troops are already on their way." He crouched down over the model. "Once we are through the choke point, the worst of it should be over." Standing and brushing himself off, he turned to them. "With all our strength, we will be victorious. Kasala and Zyid will be sad they have missed this battle though."

The group walked around the front of the tavern checking their equipment one last time before mounting their steeds and bringing up the rear of the column.

*****

The night was dark and the forest below deathly quiet as the two made their ascent. "I remember this being a much easier climb the last time we did this," Arlana called back behind her.

"And how long ago was the last time we did this?"

"Quite a while now that I think about it. My, how the years have gone by."

"Indeed they have," he hissed back. "Fortunately, we should be near the top and the real work can begin."

She gave no answer as they neared the top. Slowing her pace, she stopped near the edge, listening intently for movement in the dark. After hearing nothing, she raised herself up slowly peering over the edge. Finding it deserted, she crawled her way onto the ledge. Hugging the wall, she waited as Kalgrin slowly finished his climb, taking a spot behind her. Listening intently once again, she gave him a nod, which he returned. Creeping out from their hiding spot, they began making their way toward the makeshift gate only to find their path blocked by the hooded women and a large group of the brigands.

"I see we meet again, master dwarf. I had hoped you would join us again so soon."

"I cannot say that I share your sentiment." Kalgrin removed his hammer from his back, tossing aside the simple leather strap he had been holding on. "It seems we will have to do battle much earlier than I had thought."

"Fear not, my dear." Arlana smiled as she unsheathed her blade. "For this just means we will be a better distraction."

He rested his hand lightly on her shoulder. "No. You must go. I will keep this one entertained. Be sure to open the gate as fast as possible." She nodded and took a step back before spinning on her heels and dashing off into the darkness behind them. The hooded woman motioned and the men left in pursuit of Arlana. A near silence fell over then with only the light crackle of nearby fires casting a dim light over them. Removing her cloak and tossing it aside, the women readied her halberd.

"Did he receive what I gave you?"

"Aye, he has them though he was not up and about to know about them just yet."

"I see." An almost sad expression flashed on her face for a moment. "So he was more hurt than I thought. But that is to be expected."

"Why are you doing this?" Kalgrin reset his grip, slowly shuffling to the side.

"This is simply what I was told to do. This battle must be bloody, and for that I must delay you. With your power, you could easily open the gate and then it would be over all too soon."

"That is not really a reason you know."

She shrugged. "What you think of it does not matter. My king wishes it and so shall it be."

She ran forward, slicing as she came into range. Kalgrin rolled away, spitting out a gout of flame as he recovered. Leaping away from the flames, she quickly jumped back in unleashing a flurry of thrusts.

"You are just as he said you were." On the backfoot, he bashed her weapon out the way and brought down an overhead strike, which shook the ground, leaving a depression in the dirt.

"You are very nimble." She slowly circled around him. "But you cannot dodge me forever."

"That remains to be seen, Lord."

*****

The Trolls Heads, lit only by the dying fire, cast long shadows of the pair seated at the bar. "Pour me some more of that, Worstan. Need to keep my mind occupied."

"Best to not dwell on it I suppose." He filled her glass, placing the bottle back on the bar. "Come the morning, this place will be full to bursting with celebrating people."

"Aye, that it will." She smirked. For a moment. "Celebrating both life and death."

"Aye." Worstan nodded in agreement as he sipped from his cup. He turned peering where Kasala was curled up sleeping with all the dogs around her near the fire. "Not only that, but we will have to hear what those two got up to. Odd to see her so quiet."

"Just enjoy it while it lasts."

"Ya, I—Oh, Zyid, you should not be up and about yet."

"Where is everyone?" Zyid let out between heavy breaths as he leaned on the railing.

"They went out to deal with some brigands."

"I have to go." Zyid moved toward the door, stumbling into Worstan's arms.

"Only place you are going, my boy, is back to bed. You are in no condition to do anything."

Zyid shook him off. "I have to go. She is there. I have to go." He removed Worstan's hand, moving once again noisily toward the door.

"What is all the noise about?" Kasala asked sleepily as she rubbed her eyes.

"Zyid is talking nonsense about going to this fight. Is all. Now you should go back to bed. Emma will never let it go if you go out in that condition."

Zyid ignored them and walked out the door. Kasala stood patting Worstan's shoulder as she passed and followed him outside as well. "You really should get more rest. I healed you with my magic, but you need more time."

"I am well aware of that. But she is there. I have to go." He adjusted his belt.

"And you know this how?" He tapped his scabbard.

She held up her hands. "Okay, fine, but we do not know where they are."

"Just fly west. They are on a plateau. You should be able to see it from the sky." They turned to see Bellenta smiling, her cup in hand, standing in the doorway. "Now get going you two before I change my mind." She shooed them away. Kasala heaved a defeated sigh, returning to her true form and gently taking Zyid in a front talon before leaping into the night sky.

"We are going to be in trouble when everyone gets back you know."

"Better that than not having those two help."

"I suppose you are quite right. Now come back inside. You are letting in the chill.

CHAPTER 24

Kasala tore through the sky, beating her wings at a fever pitch. "Why are you doing this again?" Her voice was much clearer in his mind as he scanned the ground below.

"She is the only person I know of that can teleport without a large ritual." He patted his scabbard. "That is the only way these got here before we did."

"I see."

"There, I see it!" Focusing her gaze, she saw the plateau. She circled high above it. A few times the figures so much as ants below them. There was a large flash of orange below. "There she is. Let me go and I will face her."

"You must be careful. You are not in good shape." She felt him pat her claw. "I will go and open that door then it seems it is giving them some trouble."

"So it would seem. I should be off then." With that, she released her grip, and he plunged into the darkness below.

*****

"Heave-ho!" Thalon shouted. The tree they were using as a battering ram slammed against the gate. Sounds of creaking wood filled the air. "By the gods, this door is tougher than I thought. Again!"

"If we cannot break through soon, we may have to fall back!" Emma shouted over the din of battle.

"I had hoped those two would have come, but they seem to have run into their own problems. We will have to break through on our own." An arrow whizzed by. "But yes, soon would be best." The ground shook. "What was—" A roar cut through the darkness as the air was filled with screams and flying splinters of wood.

As the dust settled, they looked through the open doorway, finding Kasala's massive form. She let out a mighty roar. The assembled dwarfs raised a mighty cheer before pouring through the opening.

"Is Zyid with you?" Emma shouted, standing below her. She cast her gaze back into the camp. Emma took a deep breath and ran off into the darkness.

"After her, boys. Cannot have the captain showing us up!" The rest poured through the gate with a great cheer.

*****

"You are doing quite the job of holding me up, young lady." Kalgrin spit, a tiny flame escaping his mouth.

"I told you it would not be so easy." Resetting the grip on his hammer, he readied himself to strike again. A small vibration crossed the ground, causing him to look around her slightly. "It seems that dragon finally arrived."

"So it would seem."

"Master!" Like a bolt of lightning, Zyid came screaming toward the ground. Leaping out of his path, he landed heavily, kicking up a great cloud of dust and unleashing a flurry of slashes.

They locked blades. "Good to see you, my student, and you have gotten wings. How marvelous." Throwing off his blades, she opened up the distance.

"You should go, Kalgrin. This is my fight now." Kalgrin nodded before ducking off toward the growing battle.

Zyid flicked his wings but did not get them to start beating. "You have wings but cannot fly. What a shame that is, my student. But once you do that." He watched a smile move across her face.

"I defeated you once, and I will do so again. Kadan!" Charging forward blades whirling, he subjected her weapon to near continuous blows. With a loud snap, the shaft shattered. The weapon's head flying off into the darkness. Rolling back, she regained her feet, sword in hand. Zyid overextended, letting her inside his guard. She struck her fist into his chest. Gasping for breath, he made a wild swing at her, but she was already out of range.

"You are already a lot stronger than you were before." She shook blood off her fist. "But you will need to learn to fully control it or it will do you little good." Spitting out a wad of blood, he took a deep breath, closing his eyes to focus on his wings.

Tuning out everything but the beat of his heart, he felt its rhythm. Slowly, he moved the wings to its constant beat. Her chuckle caused him to open his eyes. He narrowed his gaze and launched himself forward again.

*****

"So this is the little cave, is it?" Emma and Thalon stood at its mouth peering into the shallow cave. "I see one person standing around a table." She squinted as if doubting what she saw.

"It looks like we should try and take him alive, probably a leader in this group." She nodded in agreement as she slowly made her way forward.

"Watch my back, will you? And make sure the others are not slacking off!" A few curious men shuffled away. The man stared intently down at the table before him with a crude map resting on it.

"So you have already made it this far. I had hoped my forces would resist better than that." He looked up, staring Emma down in the dim light. "But my last runner mentioned a dragon, so I suppose that was impossible."

"If you know that, you have lost. You should surrender."

The man coldly laughed. "I think not, woman. The only thing that would await me is a noose. I have no interest in hanging."

"That is not—"

"That is the only thing you will do! Your petty town has no place to hold people like me." Gripping the edge of the table, the man flung it toward Emma, putting her off balance. As the table crashed onto the floor near her, the man ran into her, throwing her to the ground. Her sword flew from her hand as she fell. The man yelled, "I will not go quietly into this night, woman." Stabbing downward, she struggled to hold him at bay.

"I too will not die easily." Placing a foot on his chest, she pushed with all her might throwing him off. Circling in the near pitch-black, he stabbed at her several times. Emma stumbled over the table's wreckage. Seeing an opening, the man threw his dagger, lodging the blade deep in Emma's leg. With a grunt of pain, she fell to the ground.

"It seems you are not going to leave this place alive, woman." He heard him lightly kick her blade before plucking it from the ground. "Killed with one's own blade. How tragic." The man laughed once again as he stepped over her. Grabbing her by the neck, he took aim and thrusted her sword with all his might. She felt the blade piece a ring of mail and slide to a stop in the arming doublet underneath. He grunted in frustration as he removed the blade and readied it once again. As the blade flew toward her piercing the same spot, it went through, and she felt blood wetting her clothes. The man tried to pull back the blade, but she held it fast with her left hand.

"I think it is you who will not be leaving here alive." With a mighty effort, she removed the blade from her leg and in a single motion thrust it into the man's exposed neck. With a gurgle, he fell forward dead, a stream of blood flowing from his wound.

"Emma, are you alright in there?"

"I have been better." She rolled the man's corpse off and slowly worked to her feet. Propping herself against the wall, she looked out to see Thalon approaching. "I thought you were watching my back?" She tried to laugh but covered her mouth to keep from retching as her adrenaline wore off.

"I was coming to help but…" He turned and pointed at a bolt protruding from his shoulder. "But I had a small run-in with my own trouble."

"That does look rather—" Turning, he could hear her emptying the contents of her stomach.

"That is it, lass. Let it all out. First time you killed someone, is it?" She stopped for a moment before puking once again. "Best to let it out in here where the men will not see."

"Does it ever get easier?" she asked, laboring for breath.

"Sadly, it does get easier." He went over to her, giving her his good shoulder to rest on as they left the cave together. "And that is a damn shame. But we need to finish this up and find Zyid and see he is not in too big a mess."

She wiped her mouth. "I am sure he already is."

*****

"It seems this battle is coming to its end." One of the brigands came close as he ran, and she swiftly removed his head from his shoulders, his body falling after a few more steps.

"So it would seem, master," Zyid spoke through labored breath. "Is everything going as you intend it to?" He tightened the grip on his swords. "Why must you do this?"

"All shall be clear in time, little one." More people streamed into their clearing as the pair began their deadly dance once again. The roar grew and the ground grew slick with mud and blood. The barely visible blades cut down anything that strayed too close. Zyid leaped back and, with a mighty beat of his wings, thrust himself into the air. The fighting seemed to stop as all below stared up in disbelief or horror. He only hovered in place a heartbeat then came swooping down at the ground, splitting his swords as she blocked the first, the second came from underneath cleaving through the arm holding her blade. The wet thump and clatter sounded deafening in the chaos. Zyid landed roughly wobbling back to his feet.

"It is over, master. I have defeated you once again. Stop this battle." He held his blade at her, but she leaped away clutching the bloody stump.

"You know as well as I do this is only the beginning. I look forward to one final duel with you." A portal snapped open behind her and she stepped through, and it closed with a crack and cold wind.

The remaining brigades threw down their weapons. Zyid fell to his knees exhausted. Feeling his consciousness slipping, he heard Emma starting a rousing cheer.

ROBERT LOGSDON WAS BORN AND RAISED IN northeastern Ohio where he has returned after his time in the US Marine Corps. Husband to his wife of twelve years and newly minted father, Robert is an avid reader of both fiction and nonfiction, lover of table-top gaming, as well as computer games—mostly favoring the science fiction and fantasy genres.

www.ingramcontent.com/pod-product-compliance
Lightning Source LLC
Chambersburg PA
CBHW021545270125
20902CB00024B/279